I0682070

International Crossfire

Books by Stephen L. Thompson

The Crossfire Series

Colorado Crossfire
International Crossfire
Israeli Crossfire
Believer's Crossfire
Spirit Crossfire
Faith Crossfire
Chinese Crossfire
Texas Crossfire
Dark Crossfire
Island Crossfire
Jagged Crossfire
Violent Crossfire
Russian Crossfire
Nuclear Crossfire
End Times Crossfire
Revelation Crossfire
Gates of Hell Crossfire
Assassin's Crossfire
Albatross Crossfire
Global Crossfire
Far East Crossfire

The SFO Series
Station Force One - Onset

International Crossfire

Battling Enemies Foreign and Domestic

Stephen L. Thompson

International Crossfire

In their valiant attempts to help the homeless, Jack and Laura Malone become actively involved with not only disappearing kids, but a violent remnant from their battles in Denver, Colorado. Joining up again with Mark Connelly, they find an ally and enlist her in their quest.

The team crosses swords with a Billionaire who plans to remove the U.S. from its role as an international defender of Israel by sending the entire country into a civil war.

Stephen L. Thompson

International Crossfire

Copyright © 2012 Stephen L. Thompson
All rights reserved. This book may not be duplicated or
reproduced in any form or manner whatsoever, except as
allowed by the U.S. Copyright Act of 1989, as amended,
without the prior and express written permission of the
publisher.

Published by
Stephen L. Thompson
Facebook.com/CrossfireNovelSeries

Unless otherwise noted, Scripture quotations are taken from
the HOLY BIBLE, NEW INTERNATIONAL VERSION®.
Copyright© 1973, 1978, 1984 by International Bible Society.
Used by permission of Zondervan Publishing House. All rights
reserved.

ISBN 978-0-9850758-6-6

Electronically Published in the United States of America

Foreword

To my Christian readers –
The Crossfire series of action/adventure stories include depictions of violence which are unusual in Christian literature. It would be nice if there were no conflict or violence in our world. But we live in a time when evil is increasing instead of diminishing, when some men seem to be controlled by selfishness, madness, or evil forces. When the enemies of decent mankind are bent on subjugation of other men and women, righteous men and women must stand against evil. The yoke of oppression is not lifted by prayer alone. God is our shepherd and we are his sheep. As long as there are wolves about, God will use some of us as sheep dogs to defend the rest of us. These stories are about people like that and the forces they fight against. The stories describe violence because it occurs in the real world and it is active in the lives of all people whether they recognize it or not.

To my non-Christian readers –
The Crossfire series include depictions of spiritual warfare and spiritual activity with which the non-Christian may not be familiar. These stories describe the realms and activities of both God and Satan because they are real and active in the lives of all people whether they recognize it or not.

Steve Thompson

NOTE: All characters, incidents, and venues described in this book are entirely the product of the author's imagination and remain the property of the author. This book and all text are the copyrighted property of the author and may not be copied or reproduced in any form without express written permission by the author.

CHAPTER ONE

The razor-sharp knife blade sliced the air a half inch from her face as a second blade slashed toward her stomach. Evading the blade at her face by leaning backward slightly, Laura Malone simultaneously slashed downward with her own blade. This deflected the second blade and she felt hardly any resistance as her knife sliced deeply into the arm muscle of the man who was trying to cut her guts out.

The 'clang-ting-snick' of the blades rang out in the quiet of the noonday hour. Laura's memory of her husband's comment during her training that "she really had to stay focused during a knife-fight" rang in her mind as loud as the sound of the clashing blades did in her ears. She figured that Jack would be proud of her. She had never been so focused in her entire life! Backed into a corner of sun-heated, bright-yellow adobe brick walls, she had five men in front of her in a loose half-circle and each man was frantically trying to kill her.

Laura took hope in the fact that even though each of the native men was armed with a vicious-looking knife, they were leery of attacking her. She figured that the one reason, albeit a minor one, for the leeriness was that she had already left number seven heaving up his guts and number six trying to hold his arm together so that he didn't bleed to death.

Laura held the large curved blade in her right hand as Jack had shown her, with the point held down below her fist. This was the best technique from which to defend and to slash. Originally, each of the natives had sneered at her as she held the knife. But either they weren't very experienced or something else was bothering them.

She could see the confusion on the face of each man as he tried to attack her. Actually she had cut their numbers down by two already. Number six was the man with the major damage to his arm. The seventh man had unintentionally provided Laura with the knife she held. He was presently lying on the ground near the building, clutching his groin and vomiting.

As she waited for the next attack Laura remembered what Jack had told her. That she was an exceptionally beautiful woman with blonde hair and green eyes set in an

American beauty face. Just the fact that she stood six foot tall, would make her stand out in many cultures. That could be a problem in countries where men fancied themselves as a cut above women.

She had been minding her own business, enjoying the sun and breeze, when the group of men had stopped on the street near where she had been standing and started talking to each other and pointing at her. She didn't understand their language and was not pleased with their attention.

She had started to walk back to the store where her husband, Jack, was buying them some snorkeling gear when one of the men quickly ran ahead of her and cut her off. As she attempted to get past him, he grabbed at her and got hold of her jacket. The vicious look on his face and the knife he was pulling out of his belt was ample evidence that he wasn't just a poor native asking for a handout. So, she'd used the front snap kick that Jack had been teaching her. The move was so quick and unexpected that the man took the damaging kick before he knew he was vulnerable. That was when he dropped his knife at her feet and folded up on the street and started throwing up. The other men quickly cut Laura off from the store and surrounded her. She prayed for the Lord to protect her, picked up the knife, backed into the corner to keep them from getting behind her. She then took a defensive stance.

Even so, two of the men tried to attack her at the same time. The first cut at her face and she leaned her face back away from the blade. The Bolang knife had just missed. The second one arrogantly stepped up and attempted to slash her across the stomach at the same time. He suddenly found out that reality doesn't always match imagination. As he attempted the cross-body slash, Laura blocked his knife with hers. This caught the second man by surprise and Laura was able to let her blade ride on through the meat of his arm. Arterial blood jetted out of the major cut and he dropped the knife from numbed fingers and staggered away from her, clutching his wounded arm and moaning in pain.

As her memories caught up to the present she realized that she should be deathly afraid but she actually felt an exhilaration and self-confidence that she had never known before when she had felt threatened. She knew then that God's Holy Spirit was with her. Now, she thought, with God in her corner who did she have to fear? She grinned with a rush of feeling flowing through her and over her. None of the attackers understood her expression when she should be scared to death.

The door to the store opened up as Jack Malone came out of the building with his packages. He had hoped that he and his wife had left all the fighting and violence behind when they left Colorado for a three-week cruise on a private boat in the South Seas. Obviously, he was wrong. At six-foot four, he really towered over most of the natives in these islands. His gray-green eyes turned icy cold as he stepped out of the store and took in the situation. With almost twenty years of martial arts and the last few weeks of personal combat combined, together with Jack's experiences allowed him to analyze a combat situation and pick out the attack points and the weaknesses. This group had committed one of the most basic mistakes. All the attention was on his wife crouched alone in the corner of the building against the walls. No one was watching outward.

A solid intensity took control of Jack's emotions as an adrenaline surge powered up his muscles. Leaving his purchases on a chair, Jack simply walked over to the group and did a front snap kick between the legs of the nearest man. He knew that a snap kick to the groin from the back can sometimes be much more devastating than the same kick from the front due to the upward circle of the foot on the end of the leg. This kick was accompanied by a loud and pitiful wail. The native lost all interest in the fight and collapsed to the ground. Needless to say, this effort immediately drew all of the attention to Jack and away from Laura, as he had hoped it would.

Still moving, not giving the semi-circle of men time to regroup, Jack turned to the closest attacker on his right while swinging both of his hands to his left. Jack's left hand deflected the thrusting knife the attacker had in his right hand. Jack's right hand went back, over his own left shoulder and snapped back, the knife-edge chopping the man across the front of his throat. This man dropped his knife, grabbed his throat and fell over backward. While he tried to get enough air to his lungs through his damaged throat he passed out. Now, as Jack turned back to the group, he faced only three armed men and knew he already had the battle won.

The man to Jack's immediate left executed a clumsy, spinning back-heel-kick with his right leg. Jack squatted quickly and blocked the leg upward with his right arm so that the leg went above him. Jack came up from the squatting position hard, driving off of his left leg. Using body torque to apply sufficient power, he drove a full-power knuckle strike with his left fist to the groin area of this attacker while he lifted the smaller man into the air. Again, the high-pitched scream. Jack let go and the native became limp on the way to the ground.

Three down, two to go. The last man on the right stepped between Laura and Jack in a karate stance with his arms in front of him and his elbows bent. He displayed his knife in one hand and held up one fist. Jack didn't know if this was a new fighting stance or if the man was simply confused as to which to use.

It didn't really matter. Jack turned to his left and side-kicked the man in the face. The years of training and daily exercise made this kick very powerful and extremely quick. Jack knew he was fast enough to kick the man in the face directly between the knife and the fist and still not get cut. The kick alone would have put him out of the fight, but Laura had emulated Jack's first strike and snap-kicked the guy between the legs from the back as he faced Jack. This particular man never felt the groin kick because he was already unconscious. He fell straight down and flopped over twice before laying still.

As the battered man fell, the last man stepped behind Laura, grabbed her right hand with his right hand, which immobilized her knife, and threw his left arm around her throat. His knife was in this hand. Laura reacted quickly by reaching up with her free left hand and grabbing the little finger on her attacker's knife hand. Pulling sharply back and to her left, she broke the finger joint with an audible 'crack'! This caused the man to scream and drop his knife. Jack saw his chance, stepped up and drove a full-power left-hand front punch past Laura's right ear directly into the face of the attacker. The powerful punch made him completely forget about his finger. The man let go of Laura and found unconsciousness at the same time. As he was toppling over, another native came running up and slid to a halt several feet from the two Americans, who were the only other people left standing at this point.

Jack and Laura faced off against the new man. The man's face had a wild, angry look and he pointed his finger at them and shouted something neither of them could understand. This took some doing because between Jack and Laura they spoke four different languages and understood most of a fifth. Unfortunately, whatever this guy was speaking did not resemble any of the five in the slightest. The wild man reached behind his back and brought out a long bolo knife with an eighteen-inch blade. He raised the blade over his head and prepared to charge the couple. Jack stepped in front of Laura and took a relaxed pose. He had done this particular defense a thousand times in class.

His confidence shook the attacker, who wavered for a few seconds and then broke and ran. Laura reached down and picked up a rock and pegged it at the man's back as he ran. She was just letting off some of her anger and frustration. She knew she couldn't throw straight enough to hit the man. As Jack watched it was evident that the rock didn't know about Laura's throwing capabilities and flew true to hit the man directly in the back of the head. He dropped his knife and executed an almost professional front somersault but lost all of his points on the landing by plopping down hard on his back with his arms and legs going everywhere. He slid to a halt ten feet from where the rock had caught up with him.

By now there were a dozen or so people running up to the area of the fight. One of these was the shop owner who had just sold Jack his purchases. He came over as Jack walked over and knelt down next to the latest attacker. Jack pulled the man's head up from the ground and shook him. The man moaned and opened his eyes. He tried to get loose but Jack had his hands crossed in a 'Y' position and applied a cross choke using the front of the native's rough shirt for leverage. This convinced the man that breaking free wouldn't work. He moaned again and put his hand to the back of his head. When it came away with a handful of blood and loose hair his color paled and sweat broke out on his face. He looked fearfully from Jack to the storeowner. He rattled off ten seconds of high-speed chatter and then shut up.

The store owner looked at Jack and translated the conversation. "He said that you'd better let him go. He also said that the blonde, witch-woman is wearing an evil amulet and they were acting properly to punish her. And, he said that you and the woman attacked his friends without any reason and he's going to bring charges, against her, her big friend with the sword behind her, and you, blah, blah, blah."

Jack looked at the defiant man and tightened up on his chokehold. The man's eyes got really large and then rolled up into his head. Jack eased the hold after the man was sufficiently unconscious. Jack let go, dropping the limp man on the ground, and stood up. He took out a one hundred-dollar bill in American currency and handed it to the storekeeper. "Here, please tend to their wounds and then place these gentlemen in a shady spot until they wake up. This is for your efforts."

The storekeeper nodded and quickly pocketed the small fortune.

One of the on-lookers was a Catholic priest who worked at the church in town. After listening to the accounts of the other witnesses he approached Jack and the storekeeper. As they both turned to look at him, he said, "I'm Father Taylor." He pointed to the man with the cut arm. "He needs medical attention right away. Let me take him to the doctor." Jack and the storekeeper agreed and helped the wounded man to a barrel he could sit on. It was obvious that he was losing a lot of blood.

The priest and another man bound up the wounded man's arm. While they were doing this the priest looked at Jack and Laura and tried to explain the actions of the islanders.

Washing the blood from his hands with water from a pitcher next to a shed, the priest nodded to the men who had attacked the Malones. "I would like to ask you to forgive them for their ignorance. I have been able to teach some of the people here about the Lord but many stick to the old ways. This group has given me no little amount of trouble about my teachings." He smiled a small smile. "I guess that is to be expected. They've worshipped animalistic gods since before their recorded history. The cross angers them because they feel its power over their gods. That's the reason that they were so upset. More crosses for them to bear, no pun intended."

Jack nodded and asked the priest, "Father Taylor, is there anything we can do to help you in your efforts."

Father Taylor just smiled again. "Just pray that God gives me the strength to accomplish His will among these people." He shook hands with Jack and Laura and helped the wounded man toward town.

The store keeper and another man then started dragging the rest of the unconscious men over to a small storage shed and piling them inside. After the storekeeper put a padlock on the door, he came back over to Jack. "How long 'fore they wake up?"

Jack looked at his watch. The sun was high in the sky. He estimated times and said, "After that nap you were talking about taking, you know, whenever you feel like getting up." The storekeeper smiled, stretched, and yawned. "Oh, I think I sleep very late this afternoon. You have a good trip."

Jack walked back over to Laura and put his finger under the golden cross she wore around her neck on a small gold chain. He looked at her with concern and thought about how much he really loved her. Then he smiled, "You really shouldn't wear these provocative religious icons in a strange land you know."

Laura had wound down somewhat by this time. She hadn't reached the stage where she would start shaking when she realized how close she had been to serious injury or even death. She looked down at the small gold cross and back at Jack with a gleam of anger in her eyes. "I'll wear this whenever and wherever I want to!" With the large bloody knife in her hand she looked mean enough to do it too. She saw his glance, stared at the cruel thing in her hand and then gave the knife to Jack. He turned and casually threw the knife twenty feet into the side of the storage shed where it buried itself eight inches into the stout lumber. Jack's training made him very good with knives.

He put his arm around Laura and kissed her on the cheek. Smiling he said, "You were doing really well considering the odds." He was concerned and it showed on his face, "I thank the Lord you didn't get hurt back there." Thinking back on the complaint that the native had made he looked at Laura and raised an eyebrow, "Who's this big guy with a sword standing behind you? I didn't see anyone but the six of you when I came out of the store."

She shook her head, dismissing the other person as an excuse the native could use to say why they didn't beat her, "Christ protects the weak and the foolish and I think I fell into both of those categories, it was Him deflecting those knives more than me." Then the anger built up in her again. She turned and looked at Jack. "They didn't give me a choice! I was too busy to be scared and I was trying to remember everything you've taught me." She reflected for a few seconds, playing the event over in her mind. "I'm glad you think I was doing well because from my viewpoint I thought I was barely holding my own. But if I hadn't been learning and practicing I wouldn't have had a chance."

Jack silently thanked the Lord for her safety. "You convinced them not to attack you all at once and that was a major point in your favor." He smiled to himself, "You really did look strong out there. I hope I didn't intrude and spoil your fun, did I?"

Laura stopped, turned to him with a serious look on her face, held up both hands and said "That's okay! Anytime you see me in a knife fight, you're more than welcome to jump in." She looked at the slit in her blouse where it hugged her hip. She thought, "That was really close!" Jack ran his finger across the cut and smiled. He kissed her again and went over and collected his packages. He waved back to the storekeeper as they headed back to their boat. By the time the men got out of that shed he and Laura would be miles away from here. He thought, "Anyway, those guys weren't going to look for trouble for a while."

Laura too, was thinking about the injuries four of the attackers had sustained, and she frowned. At Jack's raised eyebrow, she said, "I'll bet there is a real run on ice packs around this place this afternoon!"

Jack just smiled and shook his head as they walked through the pleasant sub-tropical heat to the boat quay.

CHAPTER TWO

To Jack, the pulse of the sea was peaceful and smooth and the sky was a cobalt blue wherever he looked. Gentle swells rolled as far as the eye could see. The salty breeze took the bite out of the noonday sun and pushed and pulled at his hair. He closed his eyes and listened. Except for the quiet hiss made by the movement of the boat through the water and the ruffling of the mainsail in the breeze there was only silence. He felt as if he was alone on the face of the planet right then. He could sense the presence of the Holy Spirit and he felt filled with peace again. For a man that three weeks ago didn't think about God let alone know Him, Jack was humbled by the presence. He knew that he knew that the Father had him and Laura in his hands and he couldn't think of a better place to be

Sitting in the shade of the cabin he felt the warm breeze coming over the edge of the teak deck collide with his body and slide around him to go on its way through the world. Oh yes, the "world." Jack knew his fate was no longer bound to this world. Even his thoughts about his actions in the world were cast in an entirely new light after the events of the preceding month.

He could feel the weight of the Bible he had been reading resting on his legs. His mind threw images that were present for only a second, of the hectic two weeks that took him from a staunch non-believer to a fervent Christian. His conversion was not any real record as he had read several times in the scriptures, especially the conversion of Saul, who became the Apostle Paul. Bam! Christ appeared to Saul personally. But Jack, while he hadn't actually seen Jesus, the Lord had drawn close to him and he had heard His voice and seen His mighty works. Works of the Lord on the demonic agents of that foul existence, known as Satan. Being in a room with both at the same time would make any person an absolute believer in Jesus Christ and the battle being waged with the prince of darkness.

Jack knew that the only battle between God and the devil was for souls like his. Jesus had completely beaten Satan at the cross. At that point in time Satan had made the most colossal mistake in his ages-old life. He had murdered an innocent, sinless man. Since then, Satan could only lead people away from God and uses his lies to make himself seem powerful. All the nuclear weapons in the world combined with everything Satan could do against Christ would only seem like a kitchen match trying to stand up to the thermonuclear fire of the sun.

Jack concentrated on the peace and contentment he now enjoyed as his body luxuriated in the cool mist and hot sun. He was not nearly as concerned with the world as he had been before his explosive exposure to the reality of God and His world. He knew he was saved and the thought of death no longer bothered him. In fact, he was eagerly looking forward to the time when he would meet Jesus.

He knew, of course, that God had definite plans for his time here on earth and he was learning to live the statement "Not my will God, but Yours." Not simply to preserve a place in heaven for himself, but to try to return some of the love and daily care he got from the Lord. His heart ached to give back to the Lord some portion of the love that he felt for Jesus who had sacrificed his life for all of mankind.

It concerned him that he had to fight and hurt people when God loved everyone. His prayers had shown him that his "walk" would include combat with those who would hurt God's people or the weak and innocent. He felt that God had appointed him as a sheepdog to do God's will in defending the sheep. But, Jesus was the shepherd and Jack was determined to only use his abilities when the Lord told him to do it. He knew he wasn't a self-appointed warrior. He needed God's permission to do things that weren't done in love. He was fairly certain that his life was headed toward more peace anyway.

Not that everything was peace and light. He still got prideful, angry, and occasionally irritated as the last of their attackers found out. These slips were ones he really regretted and asked for forgiveness every time they happened. He was learning that he still had to put up with the world and its problems. It was true that a Christian walking in God's word could expect the worst the world could throw at him.

The sudden jolt in the motion of the boat was so unexpected that it snared Jack's thoughts immediately. "There's one of those bad things now," he thought. He put the Bible in the locker next to him and closed the latch. He rose and walked quickly to the stern of the sailing vessel. He felt comfortable dressed in casual Dockers and a Polo shirt with no socks under his canvas deck shoes.

Arriving at the stern he scanned the water behind the boat. He quickly picked out the long, low, waterlogged shape of a piece of wood, probably a tree trunk at some time. What it was doing out here was a mystery. He headed over to the helm and spoke to a large, weather-beaten man with a darkly tanned and lined face who went by the title of Captain Smalley. "Beautiful day, isn't it Captain?" The man had merely nodded his head. Jack knew that Captain Smalley was a man of extremely few words. Jack inquired of him "What damage do you think that log did to the boat?"

The captain shook his head as he watched his instrumentation and turned the wheel slightly saying, "Probably none." When Jack asked him why, he thought about for a few seconds and tersely replied, "We hit it a glancing blow on its long axis, partially rode up on it, and then pushed it away so it missed the sailboard and the rudder. I doubt that it even left a mark on the hull."

Relieved, Jack headed back to the main cabin steps and descended to the cabin below. He admired for the hundredth time the burnished teak and walnut finishing and the tasteful fabrics and colors that had been used to decorate the interior of the cabin. It seemed to add a touch of class and home to the sailboat.

Seeing Laura curled up in a ball on one of the bunks made him remember how much he loved her and how they had recently learned to value the time that they had together.

Laura yawned and stretched like a beautiful large cat. The illusion continued as she blinked several times and fixed her gaze on him. The love in her eyes wasn't that of a carnivore, thank goodness. She smiled and asked him, "What's up?"

Jack sat down next to her and took her hand in his. "I was just sitting up on deck thinking about us and what we should do in the near future."

Jack watched as Laura tipped her head to one side and blinked. She said, "I know. You want to do more exercises, right?" They had returned to their daily routine of exercises to stay in shape. Laura had also started taking Jui Jitsu lessons from Jack. She felt that she needed to be more capable of taking care of herself in the future. Between the morning exercises and the self-defense they were working out between two to three hours a day.

Jack said that he was concerned about something other than exercise. As she wondered about what he was thinking about, she said, "Maybe we need to pray about it together." Jack thought about it and agreed. He got down on his knees and Laura slid out of the bunk and joined him on the floor. They both bowed their heads and Jack started the prayer. "Most wonderful and caring heavenly Father, in the name of Jesus..."

As they prayed they weren't aware that the background noises faded away and heaviness settled on their shoulders and arms. It was a pleasant heaviness and it progressed until they were completely immersed in the feeling. Jack felt a wonderful feeling of freedom and vast spaces opening up around him. Laura told him later that she had felt a comfortable embrace and a promise of future happiness.

As they continued to pray silently they felt a wonderfully loving presence that seemed to be made up of equal parts of true love, unlimited hope, tremendous excitement, and yet, oddly, complete contentment. All they wanted to do was to remain there in total awe and satisfaction.

An unknown time later they came back to the reality of the ship around them and a knocking at the door. Jack got up and opened the door. One of the crew was there to announce dinner in the main cabin.

After freshening up, they went down the short corridor to the main cabin and joined the Captain and the mate at the table. Dinner was good hearty food without much fuss or presentation. After dinner they went up on deck to watch the sun set. They were more than a little surprised to find it completely dark already. Jack looked at his watch and then looked at his wife with a raised eyebrow. It was after nine p.m. local time.

They stayed on deck for a while and then retired to their cabin. After they entered, Laura turned to Jack. "How long were we praying?"

Jack subtracted the thirty minutes that dinner took and the forty minutes they were on deck and guessed. "About four and a half hours, give or take thirty minutes."

Laura sat down on the bunk wide-eyed. "I didn't realize the time went by..."

Jack nodded in agreement. "I think that could be one definition of 'resting in the Spirit', where you invite the Holy Spirit to join you and He does. I am really impressed." It was obvious that he was very impressed because he didn't try to analyze it or figure it out, he just accepted it.

Jack looked at his wife with a serious look. "While I was... was...doing whatever I was doing, I got some direction." He looked somewhat embarrassed because he really didn't know what to name the information he felt he had gotten. "I guess it was a direction. I know it was a lot more than just an idea or a suggestion. It wasn't in words or even completed thoughts. It was more like a concept."

He sat down and collected his thoughts. "I think they call this a 'ministry' or a mission. I believe that we are to use our assets and our talents to help the 'downtrodden' of our society. Therefore, I need to use my services and my capabilities, such as the company, to help the less fortunate. While I was feeling so good and getting this 'ministry' direction, I suddenly remembered the LifeCape project that I told you about several months ago. Do you remember the one I'm talking about?"

Laura nodded, which combined with the swaying of the boat made her head describe squiggly circles. "The full-length cape with a hood, keeps the wearer between sixty and seventy degrees, regardless of the outside temperature? I liked the fact that you only had to turn it inside out to get cooling instead of heating."

"Well", Jack continued, "I think we can probably use that for this 'ministry'. When I thought of that I got a definite feeling that God was pleased with the idea."

Laura looked at her husband with a loving concern. "Jack, you know that a person is not saved by their works but by the Grace of God which He freely gives when you become a Christian? You can't earn your way into heaven."

Jack nodded, "That's true, you can be a wonderful person and treat everyone right and do nothing but service for others and still not go to heaven." He picked up her Bible and flipped to Ephesians 2:8-9 *"For it is by grace you have been saved, through faith -- and this not from yourselves, it is the gift of God -- not by works, so that no one can boast."*

"But" he continued, "To be saved, you need to have Jesus as your personal savior as it states in John 14:6 "Jesus answered, *I am the way and the truth and the life. No one comes to the Father except through me.*" and, He commanded all his disciples to help those less fortunate, love both their neighbors and enemies, and do as He had done while He was in the world."

Jack shut the Bible and sat down next to Laura. "I believe a Christian believer can do whatever they are capable of in the way of works and still go to heaven. I also believe that your life should be a gift to Jesus in a small repayment for what he did for us."

He got up and went across the cabin. He sat down at the desk and pulled out some paper and a pen. Jotting down numbers and formulae he slowly let the thoughts he had been thinking for the last few days form into a pattern of business and efforts.

Jack smiled, "Another Bible verse caught my attention after we sailed a few days ago. It was Proverbs 28:29. It goes like this, *"He who gives to the poor will lack nothing, but he who closes his eyes to them receives many curses."* I began to think about how blessed we have been by the Lord with material things in this world. The thing that staggered me was the thought that none of these things are ours. Literally, God has given them to us to use for whatever we will. But, He watches and sees what we do with what he has given to us.

Continuing to smile Jack stated that the Bible also says that we should dedicate our lives to the glory of God and helping others. In John 13:34 Jesus said, *"A new command I give you: Love one another. As I have loved you, so you must love one another. By this all men will know that you are my disciples, if you love one another."*

Jack was enthusiastic as he talked about and quoted the passages from the Bible, a book he had never studied in his adult life until four weeks ago. He spoke as one who has actually seen the truth. Jack was sure most people come to know about the Lord through hearing of the word. Jack had come to know the Lord, personally. His experiences had given him a conviction that was undeniable because it was real.

He continued, "I just put down some numbers and I think that we can not only make it work, but that we can make sufficient quantities to distribute to homeless people without cost."

Laura thought for a few seconds. "You would give these away without a charge? Could the company absorb that kind of cost without bankrupting it?"

Jack realized Laura was in her element here in financial matters. "Yes, I think that we could make the free version of the LifeCape and a commercial version that we could sell to the public and possibly the military. The income from the sales should break even with the cost of the free effort."

Jack, now that he had an idea to work with and time he could spend without expecting to be killed at any moment was excited and wanted to get started immediately to scope out the project and the possibilities. He got up and went to the telephone on the bulkhead, picked it up and immediately got a dial tone. Ten years ago this would have been an odd thing since they were sailing in the middle of the South Seas. But Jack knew the small dish antenna on the mast was kept locked into the communications satellite by a microprocessor and that the signal was bounced down to an earth station in the United States at the speed of light. He placed a call to Bob Wexler, his partner and plant manager. It was six hours later in Denver and across the International Date Line. This made it around four a.m. in the Rocky Mountains.

Getting Bob's phone mailbox at the company, Jack outlined his concept and told Bob to work up some preliminary production figures for such a device.

He described what he had in mind in more detail to Laura and they discussed the pros and cons of the project in terms of what God would want and what would be practical in the world. It was about two a.m. when they finished.

Jack waited and worked on his figures for a few hours. He then placed a call to his father in Dallas, Texas where Steve and his wife Donna lived. It would have been nine a.m. "Hi dad!" he said "I hope you still have your theory, conceptual drawings, and cost figures on the LifeCape project." Jack went on to describe what he had in mind for the project.

Steve Malone listened to his son's concept and endorsed it wholeheartedly. "I think that is a wonderful idea Jack, Jack was glad that he could have their help. "I would really like it if you and Uncle Larry wanted to get behind this thing and give us the support you guys are so good at."

They agreed to meet in Denver on Wednesday of the next week.

CHAPTER THREE

Returning to Denver's International Airport Tuesday afternoon, Jack and Laura picked up their car from long-term storage and returned to the house they had decided to call home. Jack liked the house because it was designed by one of the leading architects in the country and outfitted by one of the best interior designers. The house had been designed and built to showcase his father's NovaStar home defense system.

Jack liked the NovaStar system which was another of Steve Malone's unique concepts. It was an active defense system that automatically caught intruders rather than simply sounding an alarm or calling the police.

When their own home had been destroyed by an enemy attempting to wrest a Christian treasure from him, Jack and others had used this house as a place of safe haven. As it turned out, it functioned excellently in protecting them from a professional hit team sent to kill them.

Jack smiled remembering when they had been cleared of wrong-doing by the Colorado Bureau of Investigation. They had contacted several friends who, in turn, contacted the stores that normally furnished household goods and clothing for Jack and Laura. The results of these contacts were evident by the time the couple returned from their three week cruise in the South Pacific.

Jack had just wanted them to get serviceable, generic items like clothing, house wares, mundane electronics, and replacement computer gear. This would allow them to live comfortably until they could pick out specific items they wanted themselves. Fortunately, Jack's organizational skills included the concept of clothing inventories for both of them, insurance video tapes and software backups stored away from their home. Bob Wexler and Jack's father were able to replace a great deal of the original items that were lost through the use of the videos and the lists and the insurance company's money.

Jack sighed. Of course, valued sentimental items such as Laura's wedding gown and many old pictures were lost forever. But their insurance company was also able cover that part of the loss and that helped to restore the Malone's property to a semblance of normalcy.

As the young couple settled in and started to reorganize their lives that Tuesday evening, Laura saw a blinking light on the telephone answering machine. There were several calls but the first one made her sit down and assume a worried attitude. A few minutes later she found Jack in the den working on the computer, attempting to restore a great deal of archived data.

His back was to her as she entered, so he wasn't able to see her expression when she interrupted him. "Jack, I don't think that we are completely out of the woods on that Don Miland mess."

He turned around at that and asked, "Why? I know Don Miland is not going to bother us again. I saw him as dead as can be."

Laura shook her head, "Well then, who do you think left us a message saying, "Malone, you are dead, hear me, dead!"?"

Jack shook his head in confusion. "When was that recorded? Could it of been before we had our last meeting with Don Miland?"

Laura looked at the piece of paper in her hand. "No, it was recorded just after the time we left for the trip."

Jack thought for a few minutes. "Okay, get me the tape out of the machine. I think there are some more in the drawer below the phone. I'll send the tape to the CBI and see if they can tell us who made it. I can only think of three people that were working for Don Miland that could have made that call, Hugo, Carlo, or possibly Whitey. If it is one of them, the CBI will have audio tapes of their voices recorded during their investigation of Don Miland. They should be able to give us a name by tomorrow and then they can start looking for whoever it is."

That said, Jack got up and hugged Laura. Remembering the power behind Don Miland, Jack told Laura, "Remember, our big guy is bigger than their big guy." Laura smiled at that. It was true that God is much bigger and more powerful than the devil.

That afternoon they went to the martial arts school and spent several hours working on Laura's self-defense techniques. She was a quick learner and had absorbed a great deal of technique from Jack. She would be a purple belt if there had been a formal training going on. She had to admit that the Jui Jitsu was an extremely violent and rude way to treat other people's bodies, but, if it was a choice of her body or theirs, it certainly was effective.

That evening they got to bed early and Laura, being tired from the workouts that day, fell asleep quickly. As she floated in a deep sleep she began to dream a vivid dream. She saw a small baby grinning and playing, lying on its back and watching its fingers and toes. The baby wasn't aware of her presence and after a while it fell asleep. Then the dream changed to a young boy who was walking through a field near woods. Somehow she knew that this was the boy the baby had become. He was walking alone and something in the woods was of special interest to him. She couldn't see what was in the woods, but it wasn't threatening to her.

The boy watched for a while and then went away. After a bit it was starting to get dark. Her view moved forward into the trees and she beheld a young man and woman locked in an embrace and kissing each other. She thought that this is how young boys find out about love and romance.

Then she was at a drive-in theater and it was like she was in the back seat of a car and the young boy had become a young man. He was trying to put the moves on the girl with him in the front seat. The girl was willing to kiss but that was the extent of it as far as she was concerned. Rebuffed, the young man took the girl home and drove to another street and parked. Walking back to her house he went around to the back of her house and peeked in her window while she got ready for bed. Laura noticed a red mist next to his head. After the lights went out he left.

Laura couldn't identify the young man. It wasn't Jack or any other man she knew. She wondered what this dream meant. Slipping back into deep sleep she again found the young man as an adult or college age youth and he was on the beach with a different young woman. The situation was the same as before in the car at the drive-in. The red mist was there above his left shoulder but seemed more solid. This time the man not only insisted, he forced himself on her when she tried to resist physically.

Some indeterminate amount of time later, the woman was sitting on the beach staring out to sea and hugging her knees and crying. The young man was standing there smirking. He picked up his shirt and started to button it up. Laura noticed that the red mist was not near his head anymore, it was inside him and pulsing slowly. She didn't know why she could see the mist when it was inside of him but she did. The man laughed at the woman and when she wouldn't come with him, he left her on the beach.

The next scene drifted up to Laura was one of her running and running to escape the man as he ran after her. She noticed that he had an evil leer on his face. As he closed in on her she tried to remember what self-defense techniques to use and she couldn't think of anything! The man got closer and closer and...she woke up.

Shaking her head she looked at her husband sleeping next to her. She had a mind to poke him awake and let him suffer too! The thing that stopped her was that she was looking in the dimness of their bedroom at the dresser mirror across the room and she thought she saw that same red mist next to her head. This scared her and she cried out "Oh, Jesus what is it?" When she said the name "Jesus" the mist disappeared suddenly and Jack stirred and rolled over in the bed not fully waking up.

Laura slipped out of bed and put on a robe. She went downstairs to the kitchen and put on some tea. The dream disturbed her, a lot. She got out a tablet and a pen and wrote down everything she could remember of the dream. Sitting back with the cup of tea, she thought about the dream and decided to pray about it. As she clasped her hands and bowed her head she praised God for all the good things he did in their lives and tried to show Him the love for Him she had in her heart.

After she reached a place of peace within herself, she asked what the dream meant. After asking, she became as perfectly still both physically and mentally as she could to see if she would get an answer. For several minutes she just rested in her love for the Lord and let her mind wander. She suddenly saw, in her mind's eye, the man she had seen before and he was completely engulfed in red mists. Next to him was a large man who had on normal clothes but was wearing a tarnished crown. The startling thing was that both of their faces matched and their sneering smiles were the same. Boom! That was all! Laura sat straight upright in her chair and started writing again. Then she felt really sleepy. Cleaning up the kitchen she went back to bed and slept the rest of the night without any dreams she could remember.

CHAPTER FOUR

On Tuesday Jack met with his father Steve, and his uncle, Larry Malone. The meeting was held in Jack's home rather than Jack's office to avoid the many interruptions and side tracks which would slow down the conception process.

The interior design of the Malone's new home had been done by someone combining class and taste. Everything from the furniture and fixtures to the tile and toilet paper was excellent quality and pleasing to the senses. The smallest details were done with excellence. A great deal of attention had been paid to the scent of each area. There was a fruity/grainy smell in the kitchen and a floral bouquet to the bathrooms. A pleasant fresh air smell throughout the house was maintained by discrete ion-generators in all of the rooms.

The acoustic and the visual senses had been catered to also. The automatic light controls used a mixture of neon, hi-intensity spots and fluorescent lighting to make a soothing visual environment no matter which way you looked. The sound levels were controlled mostly by the drapes, furniture and wall surfaces. Where sound control was more important and usually harder do, for instance in the den where the 54" wide-screen digital television was, active sound cancellation was used to keep the audio in the den. A microprocessor took the audio from the TV and inverted it and used speakers outside the doors to the next rooms to generate an exact negative sound pattern adjusted for the time delay due to the distance from the TV. When the sound from the TV and the cancellation sound came together, there was no sound. It worked very well.

Bob Wexler joined the three men and brought a set of documents with financial details and possible manufacturing layouts. After working on the LifeCape basic design and requirements, they turned their attention to how to manufacture it in quantity and best cost savings.

While the men were wrestling with the LifeCape project, Laura called the Minister of the Christian Church who had led them to Christ and baptized them. She recalled the violence surrounding that baptism and smiled at the thought of the seventy plus year old Minister who went through a great adventure with them.

The phone rang several times and Alan Throman answered the phone himself. After a few pleasantries Laura explained about her concerns about the dream and possible revelation the night before. Alan listened to her and asked her to come to his church and then describe the dream in the most detail she could. After she arrived and she was finished describing the dreams, he thought for a few minutes and prayed about her dream. Eventually he started to explain what he felt about both the dream and the interpretation. "Laura, you remember I told you that dreams are not usually as literal as they are symbolic? They tend to give you information that is clouded and unclear. Many people in the world feel that everyone in a dream is really one part of you yourself. I, on the other hand, feel that God uses dreams to give us warnings, rewards, and guidance."

The minister's calm, rational discussion eased Laura's concerns. He continued, "The dream you had seems to be someone you might meet soon. The sequence you went through seems to indicate this person will have an abnormal childhood and is sexually frustrated until he is big enough to make people do things his way. In many cases this condition is caused by sexual abuse when they are very young. I believe that the red mist is a representation of one of Satan's demons. The mist represents the demon whispering in the man's ear and telling him that it is okay to make her have sex with him because she really wants to anyway, regardless of what she is saying. You see, Satan uses lust as a beachhead or toehold sin. Once a person gives in and goes along with a little 'breaking of the rules', then the devil has a legal right to enter that person's life and corrupt them more."

Laura asked, "What do you mean a legal right?"

Alan answered in an expressive way to make his point. "You have rights, you know, in the spiritual world as well as in society here in the physical world. You have the right to belong to God or not, just as you choose. God wants everyone to worship Him and Adore Him because he is the creator of the universe and all good comes from Him. But if he made everyone do that, then it is a hollow victory. No, God allows us free will to make our own choices. The demonic world knows this and plays upon fallen man's desires to make them sin. It isn't a free field if the person is a Christian. Satan has to get permission to torment one of God's people. Read Job in the Bible and you see that Satan had to ask God for permission to torture Job."

"Now, Job was one of God's chosen people and many people today believe that Christians are protected from Satan's works. I, for one, don't believe that. I think the mist you saw represented a demon of lust. It kept telling the young man that it was his right to take what he wanted because she dresses the way she does or talks the way she does, or whatever the liar can use to make the man sin."

The minister paused for effect. "Now I think it was very significant that you saw the mist near his head before he raped the girl against her will and that afterward it was inside him. That is the acceptance of the sin and means that this man has now built a stronghold for the demon to reside within him. He will find it easier to sin that way again. As he adds on more and more sins the demon and his kind find it easier and easier to convince the victim that he is totally alienated from God. Or the devil uses the guilt that the accumulated sins generate to convince the victim that it would be better for the sinner if God did not exist at all."

The minister continued, "In every decision a person makes on this earth, they have the chance to turn to God. Christians can confess and repent of their sins and to ask for forgiveness. No matter what they've done. Of course, this implies true repentance for their sins, a rejection of their former sinful actions, and a God-supported effort to avoid them in the future. Otherwise, it is a false repentance and is useless. You tend to see much false repentance when someone commits a crime and is caught or when their punishment arrives."

Laura agreed with that and summed up the conversation so far. "You're saying that the baby, child, and young man are the development of someone who I don't know yet, and I'm possibly going to meet soon and who is a threat? And this is a warning from God?"

"Yes, basically I think that is what your dream means, and I think when you asked God for an explanation you were given an image of that person who will really represent evil. The other man is one who has fallen from authority. At least, that is what I think the tarnished crown represents." The minister finished up, and told her to call him again if she was being bothered by the dreams, or in her case, more than likely, the reality. He then walked her to the church door and bid her good-bye.

The minister stopped on his way out and smiled. "That red mist you saw near you at the end of your dream was the enemy trying to influence you. When you spoke the name of the Savior it was driven off and fled from the name of Jesus." He waved and walked away.

The afternoon flew by and before they knew it was time to eat supper. Laura had enlisted the aid of a catering service and the dinner was tasty and filling. Steve Malone was particularly fond of roast beef and potatoes and declared the meal a success. Everyone agreed and resumed the planning.

Later that evening, after the preliminary planning and cost estimation was out of the way, Jack brought up a subject that had been bothering him for a while. "Dad, Uncle Larry." He sat down next to them on the couch. "I have a concern that I think we need to talk about with this project. Up until now I have always had a feel for the target audience preferences and typical uses they will put our products to. This time I'm working in the blind. I think I need to do some market research with the homeless before we go off and design the LifeCape and possibly make it a great product that nobody really will want to use."

Several suggestions were made to gather input through other means, but Jack wouldn't hear of it. "This project is a "ministry" of Laura's and mine for the Lord. I really feel I need to experience what conditions and social structures the LifeCape will be used in to have a real feel for the needs."

Laura had come into the room and was listening to the discussion. When Jack was finished she added, "It's the only way and anyway, we'll be careful while WE are on the street."

The emphasis on the 'we' wasn't lost on anyone, especially Jack. He considered arguing with her about her participation but knew it was supposed to be 'their' ministry, not just his. Anyway, she was a very capable person in her own right and had her mind made up. Therefore, he graciously bowed to the inevitable and just nodded his agreement.

So it was decided that Bob, Steve, and Larry would meet at the Technological Alternatives company plant the next morning to start the design process and Jack and Laura would do market research on the streets.

CHAPTER FIVE

Adapting to what they imagined the environment would be like, Laura and Jack dressed down for the occasion. They went to a church outlet store and purchased old and oversized clothing and worn shoes. They had to search to find things that were still serviceable yet looked appropriate for the street.

Jack hadn't shaved for two days and had blond stubble on his face. Laura tied her hair down harshly and put on an old hat. They wore no jewelry and carried only the necessary keys and cash. Parking near downtown on the west side, they slowly walked toward an area that was frequented by the homeless.

Jack thought over the plans they had made to blend in and not disturb the homeless people on the street. Their desire was not to fool the real homeless but to give them a feeling of ease and not seem so different. The first thing they wanted to do is to see what the world looked like from the disadvantaged position of a person without an income or a place to live. On their walk they prayed that what they were doing was God's idea of what they should be doing and for safety while doing it.

The first thing they noticed was the total lack of interest or notice they got from the 'normal' people. No one would even look at them in fear that they might have to give something to these 'poor' people.

Of course, not everyone ignored them. The police watched them and then there were the aggressive types. Many kids from preteens to high-school age and young men in their twenties harassed them and occasionally tried to strong arm them. Jack was able to dissuade them without making a great scene although he had to break one wrist and introduce one young man to the side of a building to convince him to leave them alone. Jack was pretty sure when the hoodlum woke up he wouldn't bother them anymore.

Jack found a grassy area about two blocks long and empty back to the alley area. There, several homeless people were sitting or begging for handouts. They went to the furthest area from the street and sat down on the ground and studied the people and the interactions with the 'normal' people. This mid-spring day the sun was weak and the ground cold. The wind picked through their thin clothing until Laura began to shiver. Jack took the surplus Army coat he'd bought and put it around Laura's shoulders to keep her warmer. She smiled her thanks at him and put her head on his shoulder. She said quietly to him, "You know I would live with you even if we were in this condition. I truly love you, Jack." Jack squeezed her tighter, "Me too sweetheart. I thank God that we have the means to help others. But, if this was what the Lord wanted us to do, we would do it and I would love you just as much or maybe a little more than I do now." That last got Jack a solid dig in the ribs.

They begin to notice that there was a great deal of caring people in Denver who went out of their way to share some money or food with the people with their hands out.

Jack was glad that sitting there with their heads down and not bothering anyone else allowed them to blend into the area. Knowing that they wouldn't be able to eat in most restaurants the way they looked, Laura had made a couple of sandwiches for lunch and had them in her coat pockets along with a can of soda pop. They were getting ready to eat when Jack nudged her and pointed at a woman who was sitting in the grass halfway to the street. She was an older lady of indeterminate age with watery blue eyes. She was picking through the grass and every now and then she would find a small something and put it in her mouth and eat it. She obviously had no food and apparently no way to get any. Jack looked at his wife and gave back his sandwich. They got up and slowly walked over to the older woman. She didn't seem to be aware of their presence until they were fairly close to her. When she did notice how close they were, she pulled away and raised her left arm as if to ward off a blow.

As Jack stood somewhat away from the woman, Laura squatted down in front of her and just looked at her for a minute with a very serious look on her face. The older woman lowered her arm but just averted her eyes so that she didn't have to look at Laura. Laura took the two sandwiches wrapped in wax paper and offered them to the woman.

For a minute it looked like she wasn't going to accept the food. Laura did not try to force the sandwiches on her but just sat there and waited. When she wasn't hurt or yelled at for several minutes, the woman reached out and gently took the top sandwich. She had some trouble unwrapping it because she obviously had arthritis in both of her hands. She smelled the chicken and then rather gracefully wolfed it down without much delay. When she was done, she looked at the other sandwich but did not reach for it.

Slowly her watery eyes came up to meet Laura's. Jack could tell that it almost broke Laura's heart to see the wretched condition the old lady was in. Laura looked away and looked at Jack. He knew she saw the tears running down his face. He felt a pull on his jacket sleeve.

Jack looked down at the old woman. She had reached out and pulled on his sleeve. She smiled and nodded at them in thanks for the food. Laura again offered her the other sandwich but she slowly shook her head from side to side. She raised her arm and looking to her left she pointed toward a bunch of boards stacked together near the corner of the lot. She then patted Laura's hand and smiled.

Jack watched as Laura stood up and slowly walked away from the old lady. The tears just ran down her face and she couldn't talk.

They neared the pile of boards and Jack noticed that there was a space underneath that held two small children with big eyes. Both were younger than six years old and they looked thoroughly frightened of the two strangers. They too, didn't say a word but watched every move the man and woman made.

Laura again squatted down and offered the boy and girl (maybe) the other sandwich. Again there was fear, delay, and finally acceptance. While they were eating the food, Laura took out the soda and opened it. She offered it to them and this time they eagerly took it and shared it between themselves. Once again there were timid smiles and nods.

Jack held Laura's hand as they slowly walked back the way they had come to the grassy area and headed back toward their car in silence. They passed an older man whose blank eyes never showed that he knew they were there. A block later they saw a man lying in the garbage in an alley with an empty bottle in a brown paper bag in his hand. It was obviously his answer to the grinding life without hope or a future.

By the time they reached their car Jack had determined they had to do something more than just the LifeCape to help just these few people they had met.

Lost in their thoughts they headed back to their home, which suddenly seemed extremely lavish and wasteful. They considered many options and Laura finally asked Jack. "What do you think about a food service? One sponsored by TA and staffed by volunteers? We could buy a building down there and hand out free food and drinks and maybe, even over the counter medicine!"

Jack had a little more experience with people having managed his company for four years and seen all the red tape and problems involved in offering a "free" anything. But the idea had merit. So he temporized by saying, "I think we need advice before we do anything, but, you are right, we are going to do something to make a difference for these people!"

That evening as they went to bed Laura hugged Jack close to her and fell asleep thinking about the homeless people and their plight. An hour after she fell asleep she had a dream she was walking by a park with a number of homeless people in it. It was a pretty Denver day and everyone was having a good time regardless of their poverty. She was watching a young family when darkness fell over the scene and everyone huddled into themselves like it had gotten cold. She looked up and there was a heavy overcast of dark gray clouds. How it got here so fast she didn't know. Then her attention was drawn to the same young man she had seen in her earlier dream. His face was grim and drawn. He was looking directly at her and walking toward her. She found she couldn't move. All she could do was watch as he came toward her through the park.

Then she noticed that the homeless people were dropping over dead as his shadow touched them as if he was death itself. She cried out for Jesus and was jolted awake with Jack holding her and asking her if she was all right.

She nodded and tried to find her voice. She untangled herself from his arms and got out of bed. Finding her notebook she wrote diligently about everything she could remember. Closing her notebook she got down on her knees and prayed that God would explain these dreams and their meaning to her. She felt peace and safety in the answer. Not necessarily the answer she was looking for, but it would do for now.

She got up and sat down on the bed next to Jack. He had been watching her intently. She told him about her first dream and Alan Throman's interpretation of it. Then she covered the latest dream. "I don't know what it means, Jack." She looked irked. "If Alan is right then this person is going to run into me, or us, soon. He is a threat and obviously God is telling us he is lethal.

CHAPTER SIX

To Jack, the size of the problem became painfully obvious the next day when they went downtown and met with Denver's Social Services personnel.

Jack knew that while the number of homeless is never exact, it can be estimated, and the estimate was staggering in the overall worldwide numbers. By itself, sheer numbers can be overcome with the right resources. Unfortunately, that is just the head count and not the problem. John Vance, the assistant director of the department took the time to outline the actual problems involved with offering a service to the homeless.

In Jack's eyes the assistant director was somewhat overweight or too short for the amount of weight he carried. He sweated even in the air conditioning. His last few remaining hairs fought a losing battle to cover any of his head while his glasses were determined to fall off of his face and crash onto the floor. But his heart was in the right place and he was very interested in anybody that would attempt to help the homeless in Denver. His voice was sometimes sad and somewhat squeaky at other times.

He indicated thirty locations on a city map of Denver as places where the homeless tended to congregate. Denver's weather did not lend itself to living outdoors like, say, Houston, Texas would. For that reason there were less per capita homeless in the mile-high city. But they were there. He fixed Jack with a stare. "You understand don't you, that most of these people are not out there because they have no choice? Eighty to ninety percent of the street people want to be "free" and put up with the harsh weather, sadists, and the bullies to keep their freedom. Of course we could classify most of them as mentally handicapped because they want to live like that!" He paused and drank some water. "I personally think that life just got too much for most of them and this is a simpler form of existence." He reflected on that thought. "I wonder, occasionally, if God ever meant for humanity to become so complicated."

"You have your drug and alcohol addicts, your lesser mentally-handicapped, your social misfits, and your career street people. They don't want help! They will accept shelter

31

and food but don't want strings. They'll go to the missions and listen to the gospel and the Good News of Jesus Christ and go right back out to the streets and forget everything they heard. They got a meal or a bed for the night. But they are too damaged by life to find a job for more than a short time, and they don't want to be found by or to find a family. The majorities of them are very content and stay that way until they die, or are killed."

"Roughly, twenty percent are out there because they don't have a choice. This group is made up of people who are trying to find work and can't, are too old to find employment, or who can't hold a job regardless of the training. This includes people incapable of work who have no hope after they've lost everything. The real sorrow is that there are whole families that are locked into living there because of financial reasons and they are bringing up another generation of homeless people." He walked over and looked out of the window. Talking without turning around he said, "We have all the services you are talking about, free rooms, free food, and free medical and dental care. We just can't get them to take it." He turned around and sat down across the desk from them. "Their problems are complex and, in many cases, unsolvable. They are caught in a misery from which only God can save them. And sadly, they usually aren't the praying kind."

As they left the building with lists of the places where the free services were offered, Jack decided to check them out.

Early that evening Jack sat in their living room and reviewed their day. They had found many of the services available as indicated. They had talked to social workers at many of the places and got the same story or another version of it. One piece of sad news they heard on the television was that one of the mission houses they had visited had been destroyed by fire later in the day and everyone in the place had been killed by the fast-spreading fire. Jack and Laura prayed for the lost lives and realized that God had protected them from the disaster. They had tried to talk to street people but they either weren't interested in talking, or all they were interested in was a handout.

Laura looked at Jack with a resigned smile. "What do we do when the people we think are in such bad shape aren't interested in our help and think that we are the ones that are trapped by our money and society?"

Jack answered, "Take it to God and let him decide what we need to do." So they prayed long into the night. But by the next morning they still didn't have an answer.

Jack called Alan Throman to see if he could get more insight on how the Lord tells you what you should do. Alan was glad to explain that the Lord will talk to you through the Bible, other people, your dreams, in visions, and through your circumstances. He explained to Jack that most of the time people did not get a "word" straight from God or an angel unless they were involved in doing God's will. They rely on the Lord to lead them and guide their steps. Until you are completely submitted to Jesus your agenda will keep shouting louder than God's quiet, still voice. Many times the Holy Spirit will highlight what God wants you to see or understand. For example, he said, "You might be wondering where to tithe or you feel the Lord wants you to bless someone with some extra money you have, but you don't know who. Then when you're walking down the street and a person or a sign is so prominent that it makes you think of a certain person. You will know that is the person God wants you to bless."

Jack replied, "I don't think that I've had that kind of revelation yet."

Alan replied, "Funny that you say that. I got a call from a highly anointed prophet of God this morning and he wants to see you and Laura today if you can make it. He'll come here to my church whenever you two can come down."

Jack asked what it was about but Alan didn't know. So Jack asked his wife and they made a 10 a.m. appointment with the Minister.

When they arrived at the church Alan introduced them to Jim Ballard. Jim asked if they had a few minutes. They went into the sanctuary and sat at one of the tables at the back. Jim Ballard was a tall man with a trim figure for a man of fifty-six. He still had a full head of brown hair and wire-rim glasses over his brown eyes. He was dressed like an executive on his weekend, in a casual Polo shirt over slacks. Jack noticed that he didn't have any rings, a watch, or any other ornamentation.

Jim talked solidly but quietly. "Let me tell you something about myself first. I was the Pastor of a large congregation in

Atlanta, Georgia until three years ago. I left that position when I felt the Lord calling me into a new season in my life. I lost my wife in a car accident about five years ago and we never had any children. So, I kept praying that the Lord would use my availability."

Jim sipped on some water and continued. "The Lord blessed me with the office of prophet and evangelist. He continues to draw me closer to Him as I continue to obey and do His work. One of the things He has given me to do is to confer the Baptism of the Holy Spirit on people He selects. Two days ago I was praying in the morning and God gave me all three of your names. I have known Alan for twenty years. So I called him and he told me of the burden that the Lord has placed on you both."

Jack looked at Laura. "I feel that the Lord has given us an obligation and a duty, but I don't see it as a burden."

Jim laughed, "That's a good attitude. Many times I find that the Lord's burdens are His way of moving us to a higher level of intimacy with him and a more profound service in His will. Anyway, the Lord Jesus has placed a burden on my heart to pray a prayer for you both to be filled with the Holy Spirit."

Jim continued, "Throughout the New Testament and especially in Acts you will find that the disciples baptized followers of the "way" in the Holy Spirit by the laying on of hands. I want to pray for that baptism for you both.

Laura asked him, "I thought we had the Holy Spirit living inside us when we became born again."

Jim nodded, "That's true you do. In addition to that infilling this prayer of baptism will allow God to move you up another level. the fruits of the Spirit which are love, joy, peace, patience, kindness, goodness, gentleness, faithfulness, and self-control." Both Jack and Laura agreed to the baptism. Jim prayed for that baptism and placed his fingers on each one of their foreheads. As he prayed, Jack felt the union of the Holy Spirit in a new and exciting way. He felt that he could feel the God's closeness more clearly. Jim finished praying and then fell backward. Alan was there and caught him and laid him on the floor.

Alan smiled. "Well, Jim will be blessed by that. Normally the people he baptizes fall under the power of the Holy Spirit. It looks like with you two, it was his turn to have more power than he could handle."

They talked for about fifteen minutes and Jim got up and joined them. He was smiling broadly. "I've just had the most refreshing time since I took on this new business for the Lord. You two are highly blessed of the Lord. I will watch your progress with interest. He said goodbye to them and left.

Later that day, Jack heard from the Lord in a vision.

It turned out to be self-confirming. Laura always wrote down any of her dreams or other messages she may have gotten from the Lord. When Jack told her about his vision, she listened and then showed him her notes. The words were different but the meaning was exactly the same.

Jack looked in the Bible and found two quotations in Proverbs, first 22:2 *"Rich and poor have this in common: The Lord is the Maker of them all."* and then 22:9 *"A generous man will himself be blessed, for he shares his food with the poor."* These bible passages were symbolic of the message they had each received. *"Go to the poor and offer them what you can. You are not accountable if they don't take it. But, you are accountable if you don't offer it."*

Jack discussed what they could do and how to do it with Laura. They needed to do it so that the people who needed it would take it without guilt or worry about conditions or requirements. Jack found a concept when he told Laura, "It shouldn't look like it comes from us. It should look like it comes from God. Let them give thanks to the Lord for what they receive."

Laura agreed, "But how are we going to do that?"

Jack thought about that for a while. "How about it appearing like the manna did for the Israelites in the desert? We could find a way to fund a regular supply of food and drink and have it appear every day at a certain location. Then when the word spreads, the ones that want it will show up and those that don't won't."

Laura laughed, "But we can't just make food appear like God did! I like the idea but I've got to see how you do this one!"

Jack nodded in agreement accepting the challenge. Going into the study he sat at the desk and with a prayer for wisdom he brainstormed the concept of a God-like delivery of food and drink for Denver's homeless.

Not having divine powers of transmutation or materialization he knew he would have to use some type of slight-of-hand. "Hmm?" He didn't want to be phony or try to fool anybody. Just provide food and drink without a human sponsor that could want something. "Hmm?"

In his mind Jack was carrying on a conversation with the Holy Spirit. Well, at least he was talking to God's Spirit knowing that He was listening. "Now, if I can only come up with anything that would work over the long haul." Suddenly an idea formed in his mind – a complete concept on how to make the whole thing happen. This was a whole new way of communication from the Lord that was finally clear now that he had been baptized in the Holy Spirit. He started writing furiously so as to not forget anything. When he was done he looked back over his notes and smiled. Then he realized he hadn't forgotten a word of the concept.

He called Laura into the den and explained the concept to her. She thought it was brilliant. She hugged him and said, "You're good, really good!"

Jack smiled and shook his head. "Not me sweetheart. This idea was the Spirit's plan. I just asked him for a concept and wrote down what he told me. All the glory and honor is His. Let me make some calls and see if we can't make this work."

Laura smiled, "If this is God's idea through the Holy Spirit, of course it will work." Jack picked up the telephone and started calling.

CHAPTER SEVEN

Two weeks later, Jack and Laura were again dressed to match their target audience and at the same grassy lot. Watching for the old lady or the kids they remained sitting in the shade for almost three hours. The old lady shuffled into the area carrying a grocery sack. She scanned the people there and recognized Laura. She slowly made her way over to them and sat down heavily on the grass near them. They let her make the first move.

She smiled at Laura and then at Jack and rummaged in her sack. She pulled out a small, thin blue blanket and offered it to Laura. Laura took it and smiled. Then she took it and placed it back into the old lady's hands and held her hands for a second. Looking at her with a friendly look, Laura asked her, "Where are the kids?" and she pointed at the empty space under the boards in the corner.

The old lady was confused by Laura's returning her gift to her and the question. She slowly turned and looked at the boards and then just sat there for a few minutes. Then, putting the blanket back into her sack she slowly got up and started to move off. After a few steps she stopped and looked back at them. She raised one rail-thin arm and waved at them to follow her.

They went down two blocks and to the back of an abandoned warehouse. She pointed at the small hole broken into the boarded up building and said the first words they had heard her utter, "The kids are in there."

Nodding his understanding, Jack asked her if she was hungry enough to get some free food with them. She stepped back a step and looked scared. Neither Jack nor Laura made a move to stop her, regardless of how much they felt they should. They turned and headed over one street to a small, single-story, stand-alone, eight-sided building in the middle of an Island area of the large sidewalk. The building had once been a fish market that sold their products in all directions and had about eight hundred square feet of floor area. The steel shutters were raised all the way around. The old lady watched them and followed them at a distance.

The building had a central core of serving tables facing in all directions and surrounded by tables and chairs set in order out to the walls. Once there, Laura walked in among the tables and counters and picked up a bowl and a plate. She helped herself to some soup and some of the steaming vegetables in the covered containers. She took some of the roast beef that was already sliced and some bread. Picking up a plastic knife, fork, and spoon, she got a napkin and sat down at one of the empty tables near the wall and that overlooked the street.

Jack had remained on the street while Laura was picking out her food. He felt a presence and saw the old lady out of the corner of his eye as she came close to him and also watched Laura.

After a few minutes, Jack went in and also picked up some food and an iced tea and joined Laura at the table. Not a word was spoken and there was absolutely no one in the market or behind the counters. In fact, there was no room for anyone behind the counters because they butted up against each other at the back. Jack and Laura paid attention to each other and ignored the old lady. Before too long she ventured into the market and finally got a plate with some food on it. Not very much because she was sure she'd have to pay for it some way. She came over to the table next to the Malones and sat down. She slowly ate the food and looked back at the counters with longing.

Jack gave Laura a quick look and she got up and went back for seconds. The old lady did also.

After they had finished eating they had disposed of their plates and plastic ware and were just sitting there in the shade, two more shabbily dressed men saw them and came in. They too helped themselves to the food and sat down and ate it. A younger man came in and took a heaping plate of meat and ran out of the place with it in his hands. No one stopped him.

Jack moved back onto the street. Laura and the old lady followed suit. As they began to walk back to the grassy area the old lady waved for them to come over to her. She looked at them with something like gratitude and said, "My name is Betty, who are you?"

Jack made the first name introductions for them both and said that they would see her here tomorrow. She nodded and went the other direction.

The next day the word had gotten out and there was a large crowd when the shutters rolled up automatically and allowed entrance. Still skeptical and unsure, the people formed into the accustomed lines and started helping themselves to the free food. When a serving container was empty, there was another one under it that was full. Everyone ate their fill and by the time the shutters began to slowly close, most everyone was already gone.

Things went well for three days and then the expected problem began. Three toughs got there early and began to push people around and demand some payment before they would let the people eat.

This lasted about ten minutes and then a tall white man in a brilliantly white, flowing robe walked into the crowd and up to the three toughs. He announced in a loud voice, "The Lord has heard the people that want to eat. The food and drink in this place are a free gift. By what right do thee stop people from partaking and why do thee attempt to take money for something thou hast had nothing to do with?"

The lead tough replied, "Because I want to, that's why!" and he pushed at the white-robed man. As his fingers touched the robe an electric arcing sound was heard and the attacker stiffened and then fell back to the ground. The tall man in the white robe looked at the other two men. They turned and ran away from the fallen body of their companion. The tall man smiled at the crowd and motioned for them to help themselves to the food and drink.

The crowd surged into the marketplace and began to help themselves. When they looked back they could not find the tall white-robed man or the fallen victim. There was joviality that day in the marketplace and it was many days before the tall man in the white robes had to make another appearance.

Jack and Laura were happy to see the two little children they had fed the sandwich to before, eating with a younger woman. Betty was there every day. The marketplace would not solve their problems nor make them happy, but it would serve to support them without cost and thereby possibly giving them some hope. Jack and Laura were accepted by many of the homeless now and were able to get many suggestions and descriptions of conditions for the LifeCape project which they offered as a possibility.

Watching the scene several days later on one of the hidden cameras, Larry Malone shook his head and turned back to Jack. "All right, tell me how you make this work."

Jack smiled, "It's sort of a reverse of Jesus' feeding of the five thousand with five loaves and two small fish. We take thousands of people and feed a few hundred. I created a committee of local social services people, local restaurant owners, food supply houses, and a group of religious orders. The members of the committee agreed to supply and deliver the food they don't use, or would normally have to throw out, to one of the religious orders in an operations building two blocks from here. There is a connecting underground garage that is no longer in use below both the marketplace and the operations building.

I bought this place and the underground parking garage and quietly had the renovations installed around the clock. We put hydraulic lifts in for the food and supplies and three secret entrances. When the shutters are down we can come in here for cleaning, maintenance, or whatever. Everything is ready to go twice a day. Early in the morning is prepared by the night crew and the afternoon meal by the day shift. The swing shift cleans and maintains. The committee all contribute to the maintenance costs and staffing."

Jack smiled again, "The food is prepared by the cooks and put into containers which are raised into position in the marketplace just before the metal shutters go up. My company and a conglomeration of other businesses in Denver have agreed to support the operation financially and purchase anything that is not donated. This way, the whole city feeds a few hundred with the excess food they would normally not eat anyway."

Larry nodded, "What about the tall guy in the white robes?"

Jack grinned, "That's Marvin Drexell, a fifth-degree black belt from the Martial Arts school on Bryant Street. He and his staff have agreed to provide protection for the marketplace in cooperation with the police. They watch these same video feeds when the market is open and if needed, they provide a friendly form of persuasion to keep things running smoothly."

Steve Malone pointed at a DVD on the table. "What did he do to that first joker?"

Laura laughed. "That was Jack's idea. His 'robe' has a metallic coating, that's why it shines so brightly, which carries the charge from two stun guns. Touch the robe while you are grounded and the lights go out. Marvin doesn't have the problem because he's grounded to the system and can't short it to ground." She smiled. "Marvin picked up the first guy and just walked across the sidewalk to an entrance to the support building. It looked like he had vanished to the people inside the market. He turned the guy over to the Denver police, who, as it turned out, were looking for him anyway for a parole violation. He won't be back for several years even with good behavior. Isn't it neat the way things work out when you labor for the Lord?"

Steve nodded, "Right, lots of happy coincidences occur don't they? I see the cross over the food counter and inlaid in the tiles of the tables. Is that all you do to evangelize these people?"

Jack nodded. "Yes, that was what I understood was needed and no more. By the way, did you know that there is no word in ancient Hebrew for coincidence?"

The food station was working well, but in their conversations with the street people, Jack and Laura had turned up another problem that had far more serious consequences than just hunger.

CHAPTER EIGHT

Jack shook his head as he read the report. Children were missing, not only the children of the homeless but the unattached street children in even greater numbers. The increasing loss of people on the street had at first gone unnoticed, just missing faces and occasionally a missing acquaintance. But the fact that it was just children rang a collective bell among the homeless that still cared what happened to innocents.

While they spent time with Betty and Jack and Jill, as the two kids they had first befriended were named, the Malones heard many oblique comments to gangs and to some shadowy organization that was hunting and taking kids off the streets, not only in Denver but other cities too. No one had a sure piece of information that could be verified. According to Betty, the one man that knew what was happening, disappeared about three months ago and hadn't been seen since.

Jack talked to the police but didn't get much help. The police are overworked as it is and couldn't get too excited about some street kids not being around. They doubted that it was foul play, more likely it was just wanderlust and they were all right somewhere else.

Needing to determine what was happening, Jack began to make friends with as many of the kids as he could in one area. The idea paid off when one of the girls told him, very casually, that her friend had been grabbed by a gang of boys to be used as a prostitute. She was sad for her friend but was proud that she had avoided getting caught. Jack was able to find out that the gang's name was the "Bangers", which did not bode well for the kidnapped girl.

Finding the headquarters of the Bangers wasn't as hard as Jack thought it would be. Mainly, no one wanted to be around a group of dangerous, violent, anti-social kids, and just because they knew where the gang hung out didn't mean they wanted to socialize with them. They had taken over the whole first floor of an abandoned warehouse on the near west side of the city.

Watching the place in the afternoon did not prove worthwhile since there was no one to see. Jack figured they would have more success if they came back after dark.

As she had sat there and waited during the day, Laura thought about the last two months. She was beginning to worry about her job. She had taken an extended vacation after their violent first encounter with gangs and felt she had better return in the next week. The homeless food station project had eaten up an additional three weeks. Now this hunt for the facts about child slavery looked to take an even larger chunk of time. It was needed, and it was exciting, but she wasn't sure she wanted to give up the position and authority of her job as yet. She had gone to God in prayer to make a decision and had gotten a distinct feeling that her place was by her husband's side at the present time. God seemed to be preparing her for her place in His plans.

As she was waiting for evening to arrive she fell into a light sleep. The young man of her earlier dreams had aged but was still after her. This time she was running down a dark corridor and he was running after her. No matter how hard she ran or where she turned, he was always right behind her. She knew this was simply dream stuff and that the feeling of being at the man's mercy was something from her past that was bugging her. Then he yelled something at her which she couldn't hear. She looked back and he was stopped and she was pulling away from him. She turned back to the front and saw him ahead of her. He was just standing there as she ran toward him. She stopped running and . . . Jack shook her awake. He said, "It's time to go." Then as he looked at her he noticed her anxiety. "What's the problem honey, another bad dream?" She nodded and went to get her notebook. She wrote as they traveled downtown.

Night time in Denver in the early summer is delightful, most of the time. This evening was very pleasant. The temperature was in the upper sixties with a light breeze from the mountains and was in direct contrast to several weeks ago when they had shivered in the cold. There was a cloud cover and the reflected light from downtown illuminated the deserted warehouse area with a dim, unfocused light which was washed out by the occasional street light that was still functioning.

A half block from the entrance of the Banger's warehouse, Jack and Laura were sitting in a battered pick-up truck Jack had borrowed from a neighbor's son, in a deep pool of darkness created by a broken street light and building shadows.

It was almost nine p.m. and Jack was about to call it a night when he finally saw a group of people headed for the warehouse. It was seven boys and a single girl. She was being pushed and pulled by several of the boys toward the big ugly building. The group reached the building and opened the door and entered. The girl was not happy about going in there and tried to break loose and run. One of the bigger boys punched her in the face and she went down in a heap. He then picked her up and took her into the building.

Laura wasted no time in dialing 911 on her cell phone. The operator took the information and told her that a squad car would be there soon. As the operator tried to keep Laura on the phone, Jack reached over, broke the connection, shut off the phone, and opened the door to his side of the truck.

Laura got out and followed Jack to the side door they had scouted earlier that day. It was still unlocked. The young couple entered the building and homed in on the voices near the front of the large building. The going was slow because of all the trash and debris left all over the floor. Eventually they got close to the group that had entered by the front door. Peering around a large wooden packing case they watched the gang make fun of the young girl who had just recovered from the punch to the head. She was bleeding from a cut in her mouth and already showed a bruise where she had been struck.

The leader of this bunch was a teenager with a weight-lifter's build and muscle structure. Really bulked out in the arms and chest his well-maintained body and classic face were terribly at odds with his words and actions. He pushed at the girl kneeling on the floor. "Hey chippie, I bet the johns are going to request you over and over again. Especially the old fat ones! Yeah, you're going to be the pick of the litter for a long time to come." He laughed at his own joke.

Another young punk with a feral look said, "Jake, you said we'd all get a chance first."

Cursing, Jake threatened to hit the new talker. "You idiots, we got to make the deal with the man first! You know, undamaged goods bring higher prices. All the boys standing in a circle around the young girl laughed. She just hung her head and cried even harder.

Jack didn't want things to get completely out of hand. Turning to Laura, he said, "Stay here and call for help when I get in over my head." He then turned and walked away from the packing crate and directly toward the circle of boys.

The ferret-faced boy was the first to see him. "Look Jake, we got company."

Jake squinted and looked out of the circle of light cast by the single overhead lamp that was working and stared at Jack as he approached. When Jack was almost up to them he said, "I don't know what you think you're doing buddy, but you are on private property and you didn't ask permission."

Jack watched everyone there and then looked at Jake. "Let the girl go Jake. She isn't going to go with you." Jack was counting on boldness to carry the day. After all, these were still children, somewhat.

Jake laughed a hard laugh. "You need a lesson in manners mister." He walked toward Jack. He was at least six foot tall and weighed around 200 pounds. His chest and arm muscles rippled as he prepared to fight. He came in fast, tight, and centered and drove a mighty punch toward Jack's stomach with his right hand.

Jack rotated to his right and smashed Jake in the throat with the rigid fingers of his left hand. In this fight Jack wasn't pulling his punches. It was only the massive muscles of Jake's throat that saved him from a crushed throat. Jack continued to move to his right and came out behind Jake. Executing a quick rear snap kick between the legs he got Jake's undivided attention. He then stepped forward and lifted the leader off the floor in the bent over position and threw him head-first into one of the steel beams that held up the roof.

The 'clang' Jake made against the beam with his head suggested that he had opted out of the rest of the fight and preferred to lay on the floor and hurt, a lot.

Jack turned toward the other kids who all suddenly backed up and gave him room, lots of room. Jack stepped over to the girl and helped her up to her feet. He held her arm as they walked away from the ring of boys. After several steps he suddenly felt it was time to run and he took off pulling the girl.

A loud explosive noise slammed against Jack's ears and the girl tripped and fell to the floor. Jack looked and saw that she had been shot. The bullet had hit her in the side of the head and she never knew what happened. This was all apparent in less than a heartbeat and Jack let go of her now limp hand and dove to the floor. Just in time to escape two more shots that flew through the space he had been in a split second before.

Jack rolled several times until he came up behind the packing case and found a thoroughly shaken Laura. He looked carefully around the packing crate and could see the two men with guns angling to both sides of their hiding place. Jack knew it would be less than ten seconds before one of them could get a good shot. If they left the packing case they would expose themselves to the shooters, if they didn't leave, the shooters would be in position to shoot them any way. Jack prayed a quick three-second prayer to Jesus and prepared to attempt to lead the gunners away from Laura.

All of a sudden there was an amplified voice from outside the warehouse. "This is the Police! Put down your weapons and come out with your hands on your head!"

This distracted the shooters enough for the Malones to make an escape. They ran behind more cartons and angled for the side door. Just before they got to it, Jack grabbed Laura's shoulder and brought her to a stop. Looking around he pointed to a rusty metal ladder fixed to the side wall of the warehouse. The ladder started five feet above the floor and Jack lifted Laura up so she could grab hold of the ladder and pull herself up onto the lowest rung. He then jumped up and followed her five more feet. In the dark they both walked out onto a small platform above the side door. Crouching down, they were invisible behind the small half wall around the platform from the local area of the floor of the warehouse.

Suddenly, running footsteps heralded the approach of the gang and the shooters. The shooters were first and pulled the door open and ran outside. The gang followed. Suddenly there was a really bright light shining through the door and a flurry of gunshots rang out. Things got rather quiet for a while and then three policemen in Swat Team uniforms came cautiously through the door and fanned out through the warehouse. When they were halfway across the building, Jack signaled Laura and they climbed back down the ladder and peered out the door. There were police everywhere and the gang was being loaded into a police van. All except one of the shooters who was being photographed and covered with a body bag.

At the moment there was little or no attention being paid to the doorway and the two Malones walked slowly out discussing the shooting. Instead of trying to leave the area, they went looking for the officer in charge of the operation. Trying to get to see him was a hassle. He had ten other people who felt they were much more important that wanted to talk to him first. They waited in the middle of all the activity and kept being made to stand back while operations were in process. Eventually they had been moved completely away from the officer and the area near the door. Going with the rhythm of the police in the ebb and flow of the operation they eventually found themselves at the police line which was a band of yellow tape. Stepping under the tape they walked back to their truck and left the area.

When the police called to determine why Laura had made the cell phone call and not stayed on the phone with the operator and wasn't in the area when the police got there, she told them the truth."I was so scared I had to leave. I didn't want the gang to notice me."

Later the next morning, Jack was still down about the young girl being killed while they were running away. He told Laura about the sudden urge to run and then the shot and the girl falling away from him. Laura was sad about the girl losing her life too and offered Jack an idea. "Consider the urge to run that came over you. Was it experience in these kinds of matters that made you decide to run when the other boys were afraid of you and were staying away? Or, was it the Holy Spirit moving you out of the line of fire?"

Jack thought about that and said, "But God is a God of Love. He would not have wanted to sacrifice that young girl to save me."

Laura made a small face and added, "I don't know what God does or why he does it, but it might be that a bullet in the head was the best future that young girl had in front of her and He knew it and saved her a lifetime of pain and terror."

Jack had to concede the possibility and agreed that God is the only one that knows what God is doing or why. "I guess I have to keep reminding myself that I don't have to understand why he does what he does. I just have to have faith in Him and know that he is doing everything for good."

He wasn't sure of the logic but he did feel better about the situation.

After discussing the battle last night concerning one child, they agreed that they were in over their heads and needed some professional help. Jack got on the phone and placed a call to a new friend they had made during the Don Miland days, Mark Connelly.

After leaving their number on Mark's answering machine, Jack and Laura had a light lunch and a run on the bike trail behind their house. They had just finished showering and getting dressed when the phone rang. It was Mark.

Jack explained their recent history and the problems that they had encountered with the 'Bangers' the night before. He didn't go into great detail, just enough that Mark could understand the situation. Before he could ask Mark to join them in their investigation the professional interrupted him.

Mark said that he was working on a case in Chicago with some heavy backing in an operation that he could not drop at present.

Sensing Jack's disappointment he countered with a plan of his own. The Malones could join him and learn what was going on there. That way they could see the national picture and when he was done with his job here, perhaps they could all go to Colorado and apply any lessons they learned in Chicago to the local scene. Jack talked it over with Laura and they agreed to meet Mark at Chicago's O'Hare airport the next morning at 10 a.m. Jack called Bob Wexler and told him to run the company while they were gone.

Laura was even more worried about her job, so she again prayed for an answer. That night she got the definite answer that God wanted her to be by her husband's side. So, with sadness, the next morning she called her boss and tendered her resignation from the investment firm due to conflicting requirements. Her boss didn't like to lose her but grudgingly agreed with her. He did make the stipulation that if she wanted to go back to work, then she had to call him first.

Jack checked in one more time at TA and found everything running smoothly. The crew of Bob, his dad, and his uncle had worked out most of the bugs in the LifeCape project, but were still not satisfied with the reliability of the nanoelectronic molecular transfer mechanism of the heat cycle. The whole concept was being created on the molecular level. Seven molecular scientists had been hired on contract to handle the related physics. A unique laboratory had been built on the TA property to house the project and would soon include two nuclear tunneling microscopes and associated video gear.

The design concept required a new way of looking at molecular construction and nanoelectronic transfer devices. This is where the reliability question had come up. The transfer would work in both directions. Both heat and cool but would break down if subjected to high-vibration shock. The lead scientist had just tested a theory he had about the elements being used to hold the microelectronic transfer devices together. This new arrangement promised a much higher shock tolerance and a twenty percent boost in heat transfer as a bonus.

Jack finished the call and told Laura, "Maybe I ought to retire, too. I don't think they have missed me at my own company." They both laughed and started packing, again. Jack checked and found in his heart that he would like to take part in the research work but he was very aware that God had other tasks for him to do right now.

CHAPTER NINE

The girl looked around her and pulled her light jacket closed. The night was unusually cool for a Chicago spring evening. The temperature was just above 60 degrees and the streets were still wet from the soaking rain that had just let up. The wind gusted around the corners of buildings whose tops were lost in the dark above the glare of the carbon-arc street lamps. Clouds scudded across the large yellow moon and only added to the feeling of isolation. The clock in the window said ten-fifty-five and the streets were practically deserted. An occasional auto splashed through the wet streets and broke the silence of the canyons formed by the buildings.

The young girl in the powder-blue jacket stood shivering in the doorway of a closed business while she kept a wary eye on the streets. She shrank back into the shadows as a blue and white Chicago police car cruised down the one-way street.

A late-model, dark-blue sedan pulled over to the curb and a young man got out. He would have been at home on any college campus in his conservative pin-striped suit. He looked around and then leaned back against the fender of the car and waited quietly. It was almost eleven and the girl who had answered his advertisement said that she would meet with him at this place exactly at eleven.

The girl, Sandra Koffman, glanced around and moved away from the doorway she had been huddled in since six that evening. Fifteen years old, she had already passed through the gangly stage and was developing into an adult woman's body with no experience to match. But, she was three weeks away from a home she couldn't go back to, out of money, hungry, cold, and she desperately wanted somebody to care for her. The talk on the street was that the people this guy worked for had helped a lot of kids in the last year. Several kids that had taken the trip to Houston had decided to return to Chicago instead of going home. They had told stories of a beautiful ranch with good food and warm beds. She had no trouble finding the small advertisement offering shelter.

Seeing the young man in the suit just standing there waiting, she stepped out of the doorway and walked toward him. She was ready to run at the first sign of danger.

As she neared the young man, another car, going the wrong way on the one-way street pulled up nose to nose with the blue sedan. Three large black men got out of the car. When the young man noticed the black men, he frowned. His left hand was in his coat pocket. He carefully pressed the button on a small electronic unit. Slowly taking his hand out of his pocket he turned and faced the approaching men who had gotten out of their car. The three men closed with the pair silently. Their street-fighter training was obvious in the cocky way they held themselves as they strutted down the sidewalk. Hands held inside the jackets of the two flanking men indicated shoulder holsters and therefore guns. The trio approached the pair silently with a casual superiority. This was their turf and nobody had ever beaten them at anything yet. Stopping ten feet away from the car, the leader of the men pointed a beefy finger at the young man. "Don't move Sucker, the MAN wants to talk to you!" he snarled.

The young man was very careful not to make any sudden moves. A minute later, a late-model luxury car pulled to the curb behind the blue sedan effectively boxing in the sedan. A large black man in expensive clothes got out of the back after an even larger bodyguard got out from behind the wheel and opened the back door for him. Brother Riggs, who, at the moment, was the undisputed kingpin of vice in this part of Chicago, looked the young man over with contempt. As usual his thoughts were egocentric and ugly. "This white pimple was trying to muscle in on his business. HAH!"

Unnoticed by any of the participants of the late-night confrontation, a dark van running no lights quietly came to a stop in the end of an alley a block away. The distance made little difference to the electronically-amplified optical and audio systems employed by the occupants of the van. Unknown to Brother Riggs, this same van had been following his every action this evening. The rooftop bubble on the van concealed a pair of phase-locked audio "boom" mikes and an extremely powerful set of optical lenses feeding visual images to a color video camera. The combination allowed the driver and two occupants of the van to feel like they were standing right outside the small group.

As the local "power" Riggs had been small potatoes for a long time. He was always willing to sell anything to anybody at a profit to himself. Lately he had managed to become a central pivot point of greater concern. He had helped a left-wing radical group set up the robbery of a large quantity of military weapons. After the successful robbery, he had personally killed the radicals with one of the stolen rifles. He then made a small fortune selling the guns and munitions to other extremist factions in the Chicago area. Yet, even that wasn't the reason that the people in the van were interested in him and his operation.

He was making a real "killing" selling guns and children to the crazy brothers and even crazier honkies. His activities had gotten a lot of attention. First by the organized crime strike force operating in the Chicago area, and through them, via the President of the United States, the occupant of the van. Brother Riggs had taken his enormous profits from gun sales and started working a new racket. This was anything that debased children, both boys and girls, and made money. His source of supply was the runaway kids on the streets.

When he hadn't been able to get enough from the Chicago streets to satisfy his customers, of whom there were many, he turned to "importing" them from other cities, such as Denver. This is what caused Mark Connelly and the Malones to become interested in him. The Malones association with Mark turned out to be a real plus since it dovetailed with the investigation that Mark had already started for the federal government about the stolen guns, another "coincidence".

Brother Riggs poked his immaculately manicured finger against the young man's chest and his deep basso echoed between the buildings. "This gal is going to work for me, White Boy, not you! I'm tired of all you egg-sucking liberals taking all the local talent!" Riggs had fought his way up in one of the toughest gangs in Chicago. His men were smart and tough. A police car cruised by but didn't stop after seeing Riggs's car.

Suddenly, the three guards stiffened to attention as a half dozen white men came around the corner behind the couple and came down the street laughing and talking about a party. To prevent an incident, Riggs told the girl to come with him. She shook her head from side to side and moved closer to the young man. As Riggs moved to grab her arm, the young man put his arm around her and stepped backward. Apparently he stepped off the curb because he suddenly fell backward and downward, dragging the girl with him and falling between his car and Riggs car.

Due to this action the attention of all three of the toughs and that of the bodyguard were centered on the falling man and girl. This proved to be the worst thing that they could have done, just as it had been designed to do.

Taking advantage of the distraction, three of the six white men dropped with military precision into a prone position on the sidewalk, while the other three went down to one knee behind them. Six MAC-10 automatic machine pistols fired as one. Brother Riggs, his bodyguard, his three tough soldiers and his car all died without firing a return shot.

The shell casings were still bouncing on the pavement as a large, tarp-covered truck backed around the corner and up to the men. All seven men jumped into the back of the truck taking the young girl with them. The truck roared away down the street. Suddenly a screaming streak of fire shot from the back of the truck through the air and into the blue sedan. The explosion that followed shattered all three of the cars. The gas tanks blew up in sequential secondary explosions that threw pieces of cars and bodies everywhere. As glass fell from several stories of broken windows, the fire became a holocaust. In the aftermath of the explosion, the only sounds were the roar and crackle of the flames and that of a distant siren. An awed silence returned to the street as the truck disappeared in the distance.

The powerful motor of the van rumbled to life. The darkened van glided out of the alley and carefully skirted the flaming debris. As the van began to track the distant truck, Mark Connelly shifted his position and checked the readiness of his weapons. He was definitely puzzled as he drove away from the flames that had brought an early end to his most recent research project.

Mark reviewed the action in his mind. Superior military tactics and firepower had clearly eliminated a cannibal. But the use of those tactics and weapons had definitely caught his attention. As a military expert turned freelance professional anti-terrorist, Mark was an asset. He knew he was a "black operative" for the current administration in Washington and as such could take on tasks the federal agencies would not do.

Brother Riggs' men had been some very tough dudes, but this new group with the automatic weapons and the truck had suckered them and taken them out professionally. But, Mark wondered, "just who all of these new military-types were, and what was their part in all of Mark's stolen gun investigation?" Mark and his friends in the van intended to find out.

As they trailed the truck at a great enough distance to prevent being spotted, Mark thought about the situation into which he had placed himself. He used to work for the government of the United States as a Navy SEAL, doing dangerous and important things without a lot of pay. Now as a free-lance military consultant, he found himself working for the United States government, doing dangerous and important things but making a lot more money with a lot more freedom.

In his previous life as a Navy SEAL he had saved the life of a government official who had later became the President of the United States. A President who never forgot the man who had led the team that not only saved his life but that of his wife and children from terrorists bent on using them for regime change. That type of debt a man of honor never forgets.

Mark realized that as a new president, the man had backed laws to punish crimes against children and had worked on efforts that paralleled the conservative Christian Advocacy Group. He had invited them to discuss the situation and found out that many in the halls of power were extremely leery if not outright antagonistic against Christians as a whole. His own cabinet warned him not to get too chummy with Christians because he would endanger his political future.

Not politically "slow", the President agreed with the congressmen and his cabinet members and stopped his enthusiastic public endorsement of the Christian group. But he continued to have private meetings with selected 'non-tainted' members of the group. The fact that he was a Christian had helped get him elected. But now it seemed there was a concerted drive within the halls of power to have him distance himself from Christianity. Inside he knew that if they offered him the throne of the world, he would never renounce his Savior, Jesus Christ. And, he knew that God's commandments concerning his brothers and sisters in Christ were crystal clear. He would not compromise his Christianity to keep the role of President but it would be prudent not to stand openly against such power blocs because he could help Christianity more as President.

Sitting at his writing desk in the bedroom of the White House the President recalled one of the pivotal times in his life. His younger sister, Pat, had a little girl when his girls were just ten years old. Two months after the birth of his daughter, Pat's husband, a Boston detective was shot and killed in a sting which had gone bad. Pat mourned the loss of her husband and dropped into a massive depression. She was so demoralized by the sudden loss she fell into a coma and died leaving her infant daughter alone in the world.

During this time the President had been a minor official at the State Department. As the closest living kin he had been awarded custody of his sister's daughter, Tracy. Due to her young age he realized that he had become the little girl's only father. His two girls had always been the light of his life. Now it was as if they had a younger sister. Both the prospective president and his prospective first lady made Tracy feel like she had one dad and mom and two sisters. As his career grew he still made time for all three children. That was another of the reasons that he got elected, his devoted family life.

As his girls became teenagers and suffered through the hormonal wars, Tracy was just a loving little girl. She would come up and tell him, "I love only you!" And she meant it too. Of course she also told his wife the same thing and meant it then too. But she became the child his children weren't anymore. Even though the election and campaigning took him away for long periods, he and his wife always found time to buy her a present or have her join them on a trip. She was very special to them both. The President's two children had become young adults but had not as yet had any grandchildren for him to dote on.

Three weeks ago, Tracy had disappeared while on the way home from school. The disappearance hadn't been silent. The driver of the car assigned to Tracy had been shot and was recovering from his wounds. The two Secret Service agents assigned to her hadn't been as lucky. They had been machine-gunned to death in the first part of the attack. The driver described the people that took the little girl but the FBI had not been able to find her yet.

The President remembered trying to console his wife. He couldn't even console himself. He was supposedly the most powerful man in the world and yet he was unable to find and return his little girl. He placed special emphasis on the search and rescue to the FBI and the local authorities, but to no avail. She wasn't found and there were no clues to her whereabouts.

When he tried to use his contacts at the White House to get information about this particular case, many of the same people, well-meaning people, warned him of the political costs involved in such a high-profile involvement concerning his own vested self-interest. Again he agreed in public to let the law enforcement groups handle the case. After spending a sleepless night with prayer and concern for his innocent little niece, he called the one man he thought could help him find her, Mark Connelly, covert operations. He already had Mark tracking a particularly nasty gun-running case and he knew Mark would be hard-pressed to do both jobs. But he had to ask.

The President was pleasantly surprised when Mark agreed to help look for his niece. It seemed that the case tied into one Mark was interested in with some friends, Jack and Laura Malone. The President remembered their names from Mark's confidential report of the action in Colorado. The President privately prayed that Mark would be successful.

The President was trying to hold together a new coalition of Middle East countries to force Iran to stop backing terrorist groups. It was a real brain burner. He took a sedative and went to bed before his wife. While he was asleep he had a dream that showed Tracy walking with two people he did not know. She had one hand in that of a tall young man and the other hand in that of a young woman. Tracy was smiling broadly. Both of the adults wore military uniforms, full body armor, and carried assorted weapons.

The President didn't have any idea who the man and woman were or what they had to do with his niece but seeing her happy made him feel better than he had since she had been taken. He definitely felt it was a sign from God that she was alive and she would be coming back to him.

CHAPTER TEN

Mark Connelly had always lived life flat-out on the edge. Ever since he was a young boy he always wanted to join the armed forces and be a hero for his country. He earned a college degree in criminology paid for by a track and field athletic scholarship. After college he joined the US Navy and through a great deal of blood, sweat, and tears he managed to earn a place on a SEAL team. The Sea-Air-Land team operations were rigorous and he found himself learning to work as a member of a team where all members relied completely on the other members to handle their tasks professionally.

Mark worked hard and his natural athletic abilities helped him to achieve top marks from his SEAL instructors and the commanding officers he served under. He would study anything and everything about the equipment he was to use, the plans involved, and the enemy. He prided himself on being as totally prepared as possible.

On actual assignments he found that things seldom went according to plan, but, having all the pertinent data in his head allowed him to understand the situation and adapt and respond far more quickly than many of his teammates. Many times he was able to complete a mission without injury to anyone on the team because of the combination of acquired knowledge about the situation and his quick wits.

He knew he made mistakes. Some of them were real lulus too. But on the command and leadership qualifications he consistently rated at the top of his group. He became a team leader for several years in dozens of dangerous missions. To utilize his skill more effectively the Navy then made him a tactician and finally he was assigned to Combat Operations as a senior planner.

Mark had not been too happy about that, but kept quiet. He knew to refuse the promotion meant his career was over. No more promotions or higher rank. But, he had never aspired to sit behind a desk while other young men and women risked everything as they carried out his plans. Therefore he concocted a scheme where he was able to "accompany" the SEAL team or teams for front-line "observation" and first-hand feedback.

This machination worked until he got wounded helping to recover two nuclear weapons lost during the crash of an Air Force B-1 bomber near Cuba. The world never did learn what occurred in the race between the United States and a then powerful, Russian military navy.

Mark had been one of the first officers informed of the actual site of the downed weapons. His job was to determine how to secure the return of the bombs without allowing the Russians to either know what they were doing or beat them to it.

The bombs had been jettisoned in an effort to protect them from a crash and to lighten the aircraft just before it crashed into the sea. The Cuban radar had lost the plane fifty miles before it crashed and the Cuban and Russian search craft were combing the waters forty miles north of the actual location of the weapons. The problems were compounded by the fact that the weapons were actually deeper in Cuban territorial waters and the Russian-controlled Cuban press was having a field day hinting that the United States was conducting over flights of the island with live nuclear weapons. Now, if they could produce the US weapons they could use the liberal press to crucify the American government with embarrassment.

Mark devised a plan that involved a massive surface ship search twenty miles further north of the Soviet ships. This would hopefully draw the Russians farther away from the actual dump site and give a small salvage ship a brief chance to grab the bombs.

The SEALs were involved as protection for the operation and Mark "went along" to observe. The actual feint was more successful than supposed and drew the entire Cuban/Russian search force away from the site and incidentally, way into international waters.

Mark remembered the day was breezy but clear. The salvage ship, disguised as a fishing trawler, managed to locate the bombs on the floor of the shallow area of the sea within sight of the Cuban mainland. SEAL divers using deep diving rigs attached cables to the bombs which were to be drawn up to the ship through a hidden access in the hull of the rescue vehicle.

The first bomb was secured and the second was on its way up when a lone Cuban shore patrol spotted the supposed "trawler." Since it was operating clearly within Cuban waters without authorization Mark decided correctly that the Cubans would also assume correctly that the ship was a US spy ship equivalent to a Russian spy trawler. The Cuban boat charged at them to attack and sink them.

The second bomb was still fifty feet below the surface when Mark told the captain to order the ship underway. The two Navy SEAL divers had been given enough warning to allow them to reach the secret access and climb on board before the ship started steaming toward international waters.

The winch overheated trying to reel in the bomb and contend with the pressure created on the bomb by the moving ship. The bomb was being pulled parallel to the surface behind the ship and only twenty feet below the surface.

Mark watched the numbers come together as the Cuban ship sped toward the fleeing American ship and begin to fire their deck guns. It quickly became obvious that the disguised trawler wasn't going to make it. The movement of the rescue ship had spoiled the gunner's aim on the patrol boat but that would not last long. The unarmed American ship could not continue to run a zigzag pattern for fear of either losing the bomb or even possibly running into it.

Stepping into the small compartment where they kept the SEAL gear, Mark picked up a pair of LAWs. The weapon was designed to stop tanks but could be used for a wide variety of everyday, light destruction duties. He worked his way back to the stern of the ship and deployed the first LAW launcher. Two more of the SEALs saw what he was doing and took up positions and used their M-16s to keep the Cubans busy. One of the sailors on the Cuban ship spotted the action through his binoculars and ordered both of the light machine guns to open fire on the American ship.

Mark fired the first missile just as the trawler suddenly swung to the right in response to the incoming rounds. His missile missed the pilot house he had been aiming at and took out the port machine gun emplacement.

This caused the sailors on the second machine gun to target his position exclusively. He had just fired the second missile when one of the bullets hit him high on the right shoulder. The impact of the round was dissipated by the bullet-proof vest he was wearing but the force of the impact spun him off his feet and under the anchor chain housing. This probably saved his life as the gunner had found the right range by then and the bullets practically chewed the corner off of the American ship where Mark had been standing.

The second anti-tank missile tracked true directly into the window of the pilot house of the Cuban patrol boat. The entire pilot house exploded and sent shrapnel everywhere across the patrol boat. The second machine gunner was blown completely off of the patrol boat which suddenly veered to the right and heeled over with its starboard side under the surface of the sea. The pilotless craft righted itself and continued at high speed directly for the Cuban shoreline several miles away. The remaining Cuban sailors abandoned ship.

Mark had missed all of this because of the golf-ball sized knot on the top of his head. He had lost his helmet when the bullet hit him. The knot was where his head had impacted on the chain housing.

During the time they were battling the Cuban ship they had sailed into international waters. The American ship slowed enough to manually raise and secure the second bomb.

Mark was carried into a cabin and his shoulder and head wounds were treated. One of the other SEALs also got treatment for flesh wounds caused by wood splinters gouged out of the deck by the incoming rounds.

The Russian-trained Cuban Air Force had responded by that time but was driven away by a flight of Air Force F-16 Falcons from Florida. Mark learned all of this in retrospect from the other SEALs and the Captain.

When the top-secret action report of the events reached Mark's superior officer, he first awarded him the Navy Cross medal. He then added several new terms to Mark's vocabulary and grounded him for the duration of his career. This turned out to be only two months. Due for service completion after eight years, Mark left the Navy and set up an independent service as an anti-terrorist specialist and consultant. He had been involved in several major "consultations" before he was contacted by a friendly President of the United States.

This man had been an Assistant Secretary of State early in Mark's SEAL career and had gotten not only himself, but his wife and children kidnapped in a small Latin-American country. Mark and his team had rescued the family and the man had not forgotten Mark when he took over the highest office in the land. It was interesting to Mark how the man ever found out who he was. This was explained later when the President himself told Mark of his dedicated search and power politics when he became Secretary of State to make sure he knew who saved him. He found out just after Mark had left the service. Therefore he was even more grateful when Mark's name came up while the President's office was seeking a specialist.

Two years of contract work, sometimes with the covert assistance of the United States government, had parlayed Mark's initial value to the President into a full-time covert appointment. Except for the little excursion he'd taken to Colorado to help his Sensei, Jim Grady. There he had learned a hard lesson about God and the realities of this world and the next. He'd also met two people he'd die for if they asked him, Jack and Laura Malone.

CHAPTER ELEVEN

In Chicago, the homeless girl, Sandra, was still in shock. As the explosion and fire faded from sight behind them without any sign of pursuit, she watched each of the men in the truck sit back and relax. Sandra sat in the corner of the truck bed with big eyes watching the men quietly. She had seen men like them on television and in the movies. They called them mercenaries, men who hired on to the group offering the best pay. They were hard men and very efficient at violence. That made her even more scared to be a young girl alone with these steely-eyed men that smelled of gunpowder.

The young man, who she had originally met on the street, went to a chest sitting on the floor of the truck bed across from the girl. Opening the chest he drew out a military-style flight jacket. Moving over next to Sandra, he put the jacket softly around her shoulders. She looked at him with large eyes that held fear as well as tears. He smiled at her. Taking her hand he spoke quietly.

"Hi. My name is Bob Eastman and I'm terribly sorry that had to happen while you were there. Those men have been after the street kids for quite a while." He frowned and stood up, swaying with the motion of the truck. Knocking on the window separating the bed from the cab, he spoke to someone when the window opened. A few seconds later he knelt down beside her again and gave her a warm sandwich and a cup of coffee. As she ate the sandwich he continued to talk to her. "I had a better meal in the car, but, I guess that this will have to do for the time. You have been away from home quite a while, huh?"

As she wolfed the sandwich down she thought, "Turkey never tasted better than it does in this sandwich. I don't even like coffee and it tastes great." Looking at the other men in the truck she asked Bob, "Are they some sort of policemen? Is that why they killed those black men?"

Bob poured her some more coffee. "Yeah, sort of, don't worry about it, those men back there deserved everything that they got." The anger in his tone surprised her. Seeing her startled reaction he explained. "Those men take young kids like you and force you to become virtual slaves. Selling your bodies, even your soul, is all they want from you. They are the worse scum in the world."

Suddenly feeling warm and safe, Sandra also felt very sleepy. "Do we have very far to go?"

Bob smiled again. "Yes, honey, we have a real long trip ahead of us. Why don't you try to sleep for a while?" He took the cup from her limp hand. She was already asleep. Putting the cup in the chest he joined the other men in the back of the truck asked, "Anyone following us?"

The leader of the mercenaries shook his head. "No. We got away clean this time." He looked at the sleeping girl, "She O.K.?" The obvious concern on his face clashed with the freshly reloaded MAC-10 in his hand.

Bob stumbled with a swerve of the truck and grabbed hold of the back of the seat near him. "Yeah, she's all right, I slipped a knockout pill in her drink and she'll sleep until we're in the air. By the time she wakes up she'll think this whole night was a bad dream."

Bob stared out the back of the truck for several minutes at the mist being created by the truck tires. "I guess I had better let Mr. Lister know what happened tonight." Seeing the tight look on the merc's face he shook his head. "You and your guys did great tonight. I think that phony party gag was good." He slapped the other man on the shoulder and went to the front of the truck bed. Knocking on the window he told the truck driver to pull over at the next rest break area so that the men could avail themselves of the facilities. He took out his cell phone and placed the call. After filing his report he went back to the end of the truck to wait.

The gray Illinois countryside slid darkly pass the truck except for the occasional bright patch when the moon broke through the clouds. A swerve to the right announced the rest area. When the truck came to a halt he turned to the men in the back. "Keep an eye on her. We wouldn't want anything to happen to her now, would we?" He was pretty sure of these men, but, then it never hurt to make sure no one got the wrong idea.

"Mr. Lister will be very glad to hear how you guys saved her." Climbing out of the back of the truck he gave them something else to occupy their time. "I'm not sure that we got away that clean. I thought that I saw a vehicle pull out of an alley back there. Keep a watch on what cars come in here or go by. We'll only be here for a few minutes. If the guys have to take a rest break, try to remember to leave their guns in the truck." That brought a laugh from all of them. He got out of the back and went around and climbed into the cab.

Watching the vehicles approaching, the men in the truck took no special notice of the dark black van that sailed by on the highway below.

Mark had no trouble spotting the truck as he passed on the highway. He also saw the glint from something in the back, probably field glasses. He told the other two passengers, "These guys are being very careful." "Well, other people can be careful too."

Jack looked at Laura and spoke his thoughts, "Gee, I wonder why they're being so careful? After all, they just killed four or five people and blew up two blocks of downtown Chicago." His sarcasm made Laura smile.

Two miles further down the freeway, Mark pulled off on an exit ramp and stopped on the top of the crest of the hill. Aiming the starlight scope back at the rest area he could easily see the truck. Figuring that it would not be long before they were moving again, the former SEAL and his friends got comfortable and waited.

Having spent a good part of his adult life hunting and fighting the cannibals of the world, Mark Connelly was in his element. The war he waged on the violent animals of this world had left him little time for any restful periods. His memory of the recent warfare with Don Miland in Colorado reminded him that now he was also a warrior for Christ. This was a completely new concept for him. But, the demon that attacked them and the heavenly power that rescued them in the basement of Don Miland's mansion hadn't been a dream. Grateful that he was on the winning side, Mark was still troubled by the amount of information he lacked on spiritual warfare. He knew one thing for sure. The majority of the lustful, evil men he contended with in this world were not only responding to Satan's urgings, but were actively cooperating with Satan.

Back at the rest stop, Bob opened the window in the back of the cab. "How's the girl?" The leader of the merc's moved forward to the window. "She's still out, hasn't moved since you left."

After making sure that no suspicious vehicles had been spotted Bob told the driver, "Take us to the airfield." With a grinding of the gears, the truck moved out, back onto the freeway, heading south. Twenty minutes later they took an exit and went west for a short time. Turning to the right the truck left the pavement and moved over a dirt road for several hundred yards. A bright light flared ahead of the truck out of the darkness. Turning off the engine of the truck, the driver got out and approached the light. A few seconds later the light went out and the driver returned.

Starting the truck again he guided them around a stone barricade with two men holding M-16 rifles watching them. Three hundred yards further down the dirt road, the truck came out from under the trees into a large meadow. Sitting on the end of a grass runway was a ten-passenger, twin-engine aircraft. Moving quickly, the girl was moved into the aircraft. Bob gave the driver some more directions and then got into the aircraft himself. Seconds later the propeller on the left engine spun as the engine roared to life. The right engine followed immediately. The pilot tested his controls and taxied over to the grass runway. Three minutes later, the plane was only a rapidly shrinking pair of red lights in the sky.

The three friends sat in the van and watched the plane leave the field. There had been no way that they could have gotten near the truck or the plane with the guards watching the dirt road. But Mark had been able to get the registration number off of the tail of the airplane as it taxied out to take off. As he pulled back onto the highway he placed a call on his cell phone. One string leads to another, he thought.

Mark drove Jack and Laura back to their hotel so that they could get some rest while he researched the aircraft and tried to determine its real destination.

As they walked into their suite, Laura took Jack's arm and sat down with him on the sofa. She laid her head on his shoulder and sighed. "Do you think we will ever get back to just being a normal couple living at home?"

Jack thought about the question for a few seconds. He realized that the death, explosions, car chases, and guns and missiles everywhere were chafing his wife's view of life and her desire to have a quiet home life. In some ways, he agreed with her and would be glad to simply go home from work and relax, without having to look over his shoulder or worry about a package delivery. Yet, in some deep recess of his spirit he knew they were doing what they were supposed to be doing. He understood that the Lord had always had them in his plan to protect and help other people.

Perhaps his recent exposure to the spiritual world attuned him to a real sensitivity to what the Lord wanted him to do, and not to do. Still, Laura had a point. They were way out of their league here, what with machine guns and missiles on the streets of downtown Chicago no less. To follow the leads could put Laura in the line of fire again. Perhaps Mark can work better by himself on the rest of this project. After all, Jack's company could use some guidance once in a while. "Okay" he said as he hugged her, "I'll tell Mark that we are going to go back to Denver and rest up for a while."

Jack noticed the message light blinking on the phone. Agent Gary Rhodes of the Denver office of the FBI had called and wanted Jack to call him back immediately. As he dialed the Denver number Jack recalled his previous meetings with the aggressive FBI man. Jack had contacted the agent initially for gang-related information just before he and Laura's lives had been turned upside down by the affair with Don Miland. Part way through that melee this self-same federal investigator had been part of a state-wide manhunt to arrest Jack and Laura for murdering two policemen.

Jack shook his head. After Don Miland had bet heavily against God and lost and the truth came out that the Malones had been set up and were actually innocent, no apology had been offered and, in truth, none was expected. Gary Rhodes had been doing his job and he certainly didn't have to apologize for trying to bring them in. He had actually wanted to have them in safe custody while the FBI found out what had actually happened.

After it was over Gary Rhodes had taken them to dinner on his own money. He wanted to remain friends with them and he wanted them to tell him what really happened at Don Miland's estate south of Denver. In the few weeks since then they had formed a low-keyed friendly relationship. As the phone in the Mile High City rang, Jack wondered if this meeting with Gary would be good or bad news.

The agent was working late in his office and he answered the phone on the second ring. Jack knew that Gary had been tasked with coordinating the Bureau's operation to identify the voice on the telephone answering device from the Malone's home that Laura had discovered upon their return from the South Seas.

Jack could sense tension in the agent's voice. "Jack!" I'm glad that you could call back so quickly. I've got a positive ID on your caller, even though he tried to disguise his voice electronically." The agent stopped for a few seconds. "Do you remember a Sergeant Dalman at the Marriott in the Denver Tech Center when your house had been destroyed?" After Jack said he wasn't sure, the agent continued, "Really nondescript average type person. He has brown hair, is a little overweight, and rarely smiles. Anyway, it turned out that he was the inside man for Don Miland. We were able to match his voice-print to the tapes you, excuse me, the CBI was able to save from Jack's place and the tape you gave me. His full name is John P. Dalman and he was a highly effective policeman until money became his only goal. We were able to determine from the Don Miland tapes that Dalman was the person who killed both of the policemen at the safe house. It was really easy for him because they trusted him. Anyway, he's the one who called you and left that message."

"Okay," said Jack, "Have the police put him away?" Jack knew that the Denver Police department was acutely embarrassed by being suckered into chasing the Malones. They were attempting to jump through hoops backward to make amends.

"Well "Gary said, "I've got good news, not-so-good news, and really bad news for you guys." Without waiting for a response the FBI agent started running down their alternatives. "First the good news, every city, county, state, and federal officer has a mug shot of John Dalman and he is their number one priority at the moment. Second, the not-so-good news, while we have almost grabbed him twice, he's still on the loose. Now for the really bad news, Dalman's complete exposure by your operation lost him everything he had; his job, his source of illegal funds, his family, his retirement, and sooner or later, his freedom and possibly his life. He blames you and your wife for everything that has happened to him. You might say he has developed a really severe dislike for the both of you. Our staff psychologist referred to his emotional state where you are involved as 'extremely homicidal." The agent stopped to get his breath and Jack wondered if there was anything like 'mildly homicidal' and if it would make any difference to the victims. Jack asked him, "Is that the bad news?"

Gary sighed, "No." He paused a second, "The really bad news is that he found out somehow that you were going to Chicago and where you are staying. He left for Chicago on an early morning flight out of Denver International."

Jack shook his head. "Do you really believe that he will try to kill us?"

Laura was sitting on the couch next to Jack and was rather wide-eyed as she listened to Jack's half of the conversation.

Gary's voice got a hard edge on it. "You bet he'll try to kill you. Do you remember the soup kitchen you visited on Larimore Street before you got your "Lord's Lunchbox" up and running?"

Jack smiled, "Lord's Lunchbox?"

Gary chuckled, "Yeah, that's what the street name is for it. People on the street are telling everybody it's from God and his angels protect it."

Jack told him, "In a definite way they are right. It is from God and his angels do protect it, but what about that soup kitchen? Are you talking about the one that had a fire which killed a bunch of people a little while ago?"

"Yep, that's the one. It seems that you left twenty minutes before the 'accident'. Well, the accident was the work of Mr. Dalman. He put together some napalm, an accelerator, and some type of explosive trigger. The three staff people and the fourteen homeless people never knew what killed them. The explosion and fire storm was instantly lethal and it was meant for you two. So the answer is yes, he wants to kill you and will stop at nothing to do it."

"How do you know that it was us he was after, and how do you know he came to Chicago to find us?" Jack looked at the grim look on Laura's face as he asked these questions.

Gary Rhodes laughed. "He wrote us a book! That's how we got inside his head. Really, he did! He keeps a journal in a small notebook like most good cops so that he can jot down thoughts and ideas and be able to remember them later for his reports. John learned his lessons well and hasn't seen any reason to change them. We raided an apartment he was hiding in last night and he must have been going out the side window as we were coming in the front and back doors. Well, he left in such a hurry that right next to a spilled cup of very hot coffee was his journal."

Jack asked, "Did it give any clues as to how he was going to try to kill us?"

The agent was obviously reading from the journal as he was talking to Jack, "No, no, just a note saying, 'I've got them now!!!!!!' with six exclamation marks after it. We have alerted our Chicago office and they have warned the cops on the street, but remember, this guy has been a cop for so long he knows how to avoid capture." After giving Jack the local FBI telephone number, agent Rhodes hung up.

Jack explained the call to Laura and they prayed again for the lost souls killed on their behalf in the Denver soup kitchen. Jack was grieved by the needless killings and it helped to ask God to take the burden of those souls off of his heart. Laura also prayed that God would work a miracle in the soul of John Dalman and have him realize the error of his actions. They decided to leave the hotel to be on the safe side.

Making a quick sweep of their rooms, they checked the hall and moved down to the stairs and headed for the lobby exit. Jack began to feel Déjà Vu as they quickly ran down the stairs, echoes of their ordeal in Denver. They reached the bottom without incident and started to go out into a maintenance hall when a man came around a corner quickly and almost ran into Jack.

Reacting quickly, Jack ducked underneath the outstretched right arm of the slightly-built man and moved beyond him. As he moved he brought his own right arm up and, catching the other man's throat, he literally yanked him backward right off his feet. Since Jack was a teacher and did this sort of thing almost every week it was quite a natural movement and very fast. Still, because he had not sensed any hostile intent, Jack grabbed both of the man's wrists and stopped him from slamming onto his back on the concrete. The whole exchange happened so quickly the man didn't have time to yell.

The thin Hispanic janitor's eyes were absolutely huge in his face as he stared up at Jack. "Que?" he said. As Jack helped him back to his feet he shook his head and mumbled "Madre Dios." He quickly backed up from Jack and took off down the maintenance corridor the other direction as fast as his feet would carry him. Jack looked at Laura and shrugged. They found the exit to the alley and headed down the dark alley toward the parking garage.

A voice rang out of the dark behind them, "Hey, Malone!" The voice sounded cold and edgy. Jack and Laura turned to see who owned the voice when a bright light split the murkiness of the alley, effectively blinding them and concealing the holder of the flashlight.

The end of the barrel of a large-caliber handgun appeared in the light. It was aimed directly at Jack. The voice, which Jack and Laura assumed belonged to John Dalman, got even tighter with a hint of evil craziness. "I just wanted to see your face as I killed you for all the crap you've done to me!" Jack braced for the killing shot with a prayer to Jesus and tried to move in front of Laura. Then a new voice was raised in the alley. "Why don't you leave the nice people to us, huh?" The whole scene was suddenly lit by two sets of automobile headlights, throwing everything into sharp relief.

A small, sharp-faced man in a black leather jacket was standing about ten feet from the man with the flashlight. When the lights illuminated Dalman's face, Laura drew in her breath in a sharp gasp. Two more young men appeared on the other side of the rouge policeman. Dalman's expression got so grim that Laura thought his face would crack. "Back off punks, I'm a cop and these people are mine."

The sharp-faced man smiled a cold smile at that, "So you're a cop. Well, 'Whoopee-Do' I'm impressed." He didn't look impressed. In fact he looked even more irritated. "This is our alley Mr. Man, and we do the killing here. The only thing we like to kill more than hero tourists are slug cops At that point the street punk did a cross draw to pull out a handgun that he had in a holster on his belt. Things happened fast at that point. Jack grabbed Laura's arm and started running down the alley. John Dalman let them go because he had much more pressing business at the moment. He dropped down to his left as he turned toward the sharp-faced man. While he rotated to his left he lined up his shot and fired two rounds point-blank into the chest of his tormentor whose pistol had just cleared the holster. He continued to rotate and fall into a crouch. The other two thugs fired at him but their bullets flew above the crouching ex-policeman.

As he came around toward the gun-wielding thugs, he fired two rounds at each of them, taking them both down. He finished his spin and saw Jack and Laura running down the alley. He pointed his pistol at Jack's back and pulled the trigger. "Click", the hammer fell on a spent shell. Dalman remembered he had fired all six rounds and his .357 Magnum was empty. Standing up he grabbed for the speed loader on his belt. He suddenly heard a roaring engine behind him. Spinning around, his eyes widened as he made out a black pickup truck, running no lights, racing down the alley straight at him. Unable to jump out of the way in time, he closed his eyes and raised his arm to cover his face as the speeding truck reached him.

As he braced for the crushing impact, John Dalman noticed something completely out of place, a melodic sound like a blend of music and singing. The sound was so enchanting that his heart ached at the magnificence of it. None of the gunshots or the noise of the on-rushing truck could be heard.

He realized he was holding his breath. As he started to breath he became aware of a beautiful fragrance surrounding him. He felt a great peace and tranquility that seemed to move in him as total contentment. He slowly unclenched his eyes and looked around him. He was amazed more than anything had ever amazed him before in his life.

He was standing slightly bent backward at the waist with his left arm up as if to fend off the on-rushing truck with the empty gun in his right hand. Only, there was no truck, no alley, nor anyone else around. Then he looked into the distance. There was no end to the breathtaking vistas he could see all around him. The scenes were rainbow colored with muted light pastel mists and deep vibrant hues blended into ranges whose beauty impacted the mind like love and stayed in the memory long after the eye stopped looking at them.

There were things happening everywhere around him but he could not comprehend what it all meant. He felt like a young child looking in the middle of a hurricane. It was staggeringly beyond his ability to understand what he saw.

But, everything he could see worked together in perfect harmony. He knew intuitively that this was the way things should always be. He experienced a surge of great anticipation. It was like he'd felt as a child just before every wonderful Christmas and happy birthday but multiplied by a hundred and all happening at one time. He felt such elation that he wanted to shout and jump around.

There was an upwelling in his heart and soul of an unlimited future of marvelous possibilities that stretched out before him. He knew without a doubt that he was in heaven. He smiled because he had always known, regardless of the things he'd done in his life, that he would still make it to heaven, if such a place existed. Well, it did, and he had made it.

He sensed an overwhelmingly powerful presence and was suddenly aware of a magnificent being whose face was bright, shining like the sun, sitting on a great throne before him. He realized the joy, the peace, the hope, and yes, even the love that he felt came from being before him. John Patrick Dalman knew without a doubt that he was in the presence of Jesus Christ, the living God.

This knowledge shocked him to his core. He had always listened to other men who said that Jesus was a myth, and the Bible was just a fairy tale. He had never believed in Jesus, the Bible, or the prudish church people who had tried to tell him their truth. Now, truth sat before him.

Being in close proximity to the purity of God himself, John could see how worthless his life had been and he felt terribly inadequate. He, his life, and every unworthy thing he had done stood as an insult in front of God. Humbled, ashamed, and feeling completely unworthy of being in God's presence he wanted to fall to the ground and hide his face. Yet, without any conscious thought on his part, he stayed on his feet facing God, The wonderful face looked at him sadly, and he clearly heard, "I never knew you John Patrick Dalman, be gone."

It was as if the weight of the world suddenly dropped on him. The beauty, the joy, the peace, the limitless future, the love and the presence were gone as if they had never existed for him. John Dalman knew then that he had utterly lost everything, forever. He had an instant to wail as he regretted the folly of his life and then . . .BLAM! The truck smashed into him and John Dalman's spirit left this world while his crushed body was still airborne.

Unfortunately, things got much, much worse for him after he died.

Running to get into the side entrance of the hotel, Jack and Laura stopped and looked back in time to see the truck strike Dalman and throw his body into the air. Laura gasped. "That was the second man I was seeing in my dreams."

The truck slid to a halt and several men got out and helped the men who had been shot into the truck. It was obvious that they had been wearing body armor under their clothes. They left the cop's body where it had fallen. As they drove away, Jack and Laura entered the lobby of the hotel and Jack went over and had the desk clerk call the police.

When he rejoined Laura he asked her, "Are you all right? I'm so sorry I got you into all this mess."

Laura gave him a little smile, "Oh, I'm all right. I think I'm either becoming used to all the violence and death, or I'm too numb to react. Now I definitely think that we should go home." She paused and looked inward for a few seconds. "I don't feel sick or upset and I just watched one man try to kill us and then get killed himself after shooting three other men." Her left eyelid started to jerk and she began to tremble. Jack took her up to their room, and held her until she relaxed and he prayed with her until she fell asleep.

Jack looked at his sleeping wife and got down on his knees and prayed some more. One of his earnest prayers was to ask God to give her the ability to forgive herself for any guilt that she might be feeling about the violence that had just occurred.

That reassuring peace flooded throughout Jack's spirit. He relaxed and felt the nearness of the Lord. As he continued to thank the Lord for all the things that had left them alive and unscathed he was aware that he knew, without a doubt, that the Lord would give Laura peace and joy while she rested. He could sense that there were many things that God had in store for them and that it would be exciting, dangerous, but very fulfilling.

Continuing to praise the Lord, Jack told Jesus how extremely thankful he was that the Lord had worked things out in the alley. He knew that God was aware that he loved Laura more than his own life and would be really lost himself if he ever lost her.

That thought made him realize something he had never thought of before. Jack tried to imagine what Laura might feel if he were to be killed and she was left all alone. He did not like what he felt. But he felt a true measure of the love and assurance that definitely came from outside of himself, and he knew that God would watch over his love regardless what happened to him.

CHAPTER TWELVE

As Sandra Koffman slept in two of the comfortable seats, Bob looked out of the window and watched the clouds race by the twin engine Apache Turboprop as it flew southwest at 340 knots. Bob studied the other men in the aircraft. They were either sleeping or playing cards. After almost four hours of air travel, Bob woke the sleepers up for the landing at Houston's Hobby Airport just south of the city itself. Sandra slid into the window seat and looked at the expanse of the huge southern Texas City. She told Bob, "Everywhere I look there are homes, businesses, and lights. It stretches to the horizon in all directions. It looks even bigger than Chicago." She tightened her seat belt as the runway raced up to meet the plane.

After leaving the runway at the last taxiway, Sandra watched as the pilot continued to taxi until they reached a private hanger on the west side of the field. Entering the hanger, the plane came to a halt under the huge halogen lights, and the engines were shut off. By the time Sandra left the aircraft, the fifty foot tall hanger doors were closed and a new SUV crossover was waiting next to the plane. She and Bob Eastman got into the car and it left the hanger through a smaller door inset in the hanger doors.

Sandra looked out through the gray-smoked glass windows of the SUV and watched as dawn began to color the eastern horizon. Looking at her escort she asked, "How can you afford to do all this for runaways? Look, I don't have any money to pay you." Concerned that he might think that she was ungrateful, she said "But, I really want to thank you for all that you've done anyway."

Bob Eastman stared at Sandra's face for a minute and then looked out the window when he answered her. "What we did for you last night and today is more than repaid by the contributions that you will make to this country in the future years." Speaking with a real conviction, he turned to face her in the SUV's captain seats as they headed south on Interstate 45. "You don't know the talent that I have seen Mr. Lister save from an empty useless life. He is the man behind the saving of you young people and even though he is quite rich, he's personally involved in each and every case. I'm very proud to be working with him in this effort."

While Sandy thought that over, the vehicle left I-45, traveled around Loop 610 to the west and south and then headed southwest on US 59. Less than thirty minutes later they left the highway and reached a drive that left the frontage road. A sign next to the drive proclaimed in large letters, "THE LISTER RANCH - NO ADMITTANCE WITHOUT PERMISSION." Over the rise Sandra saw a gate and a guard. She quipped to Bob, "That's there for people who couldn't read, right?"

Bob showed the guard his identification and they were admitted to the ranch. He pointed out the security around the ranch was for the children's protection. There were a lot of less than honorable people in the world who would prey on kids if they could. Having had a three-week crash course in street relations Sandra could heartily agree with him.

As they approached the first buildings Sandra could see kids all over the place. Playing music on their mp3s, using ear buds. Some just walking around or playing games and generally having a great time. There were few attendants in view and partially viewed behind one of the buildings was a swimming pool which was getting a lot of use in the south Texas heat.

The SUV dropped Bob and Sandra in front of the reception building. Upon entering the main hall Sandy was surprised by the thought that this room impressed her by the pleasant decor with shag carpets and living room type furniture. The place didn't look like an office at all. One of two young women got up from a desk and approached them. Smiling, she held out her hand. "Hi! You must be Sandra", she said. "I'm Julie, come on over to the desk and let's get you set up for your stay."

Sandra felt a sudden fear. Turning to Bob she said, "How long do I have to stay here?" He just smiled "As long as you want to, no longer." Reassured, she went to the desk with the young woman to help with the paperwork. After giving some information on her real home (which she made up) she was measured and issued a basket of clothes including a swim suit and pajamas.

Bob came over and wished her well and hoped that she would decide to return to her home when she had a chance to think things over and talk to the counselors. He then left the building through a side door.

Sandra walked after Julie through a tree-lined footpath past several buildings and entered the fourth building they came to. Sandra was given a room on the second floor. The room had a large bed and two chairs along with miscellaneous dressers and a dressing table with a large mirror above it. There was a private, well-stocked bathroom off to one side of the bedroom and both a television and a radio were positioned where she could use them from either the chairs or the bed. Julie helped her to put her things away and then took her over to the clinic. After a thorough examination and several tests Julie took her out the door of the clinic.

Looking her in the eye, Julie said, "There are only six rules here at the ranch. The first is simple, enjoy yourself. The second is, don't cause trouble. Keep your relationships light, especially with boys. Remember, they will only be here until they decide to go home or on one of the work programs. The third is, stay inside the ranch, and don't go near the fence or the guard shack. The fourth is, being available if your name is paged. The fifth is, to report anything or anyone that bothers you. The sixth and last is, be on time for meals and curfew is eleven P.M. You understand all this?"

Sandra said yes and was given a detailed aerial view map of the ranch with big numbers on all the buildings so that she could find her way around. Julie walked her outside and reminded her to ask questions of any of the staff if she needed help or was confused.

As Julie started to walk off, Sandra called her back. Frowning she asked "Is this it? What do you want me to do now?" Julie took her by the hand and walked her out to a large grassy area. Smiling she said "Sandra we don't want you to do anything, sweetie. As long as you mind the rules, you can do anything that you want to. If you want help, just ask for it." Sandra wasn't prepared for that answer.

Julie continued, "Look, the main reason that you are here is to sort out how you feel about life and yourself, with our help if you want it. Once you have done that, with or without our help, then you can decide what you want to do. Normally, the kids here go back to their homes. Quite a few of them have serious problems in their home environments and decide to work for Mr. Lister. He has programs all over the world and pays the children well. Housing, food, and clothing are provided and some spending money. The majority of money earned is placed in a trust fund at a bank of their choice that is theirs to use when they reach eighteen."

Julie went on to explain about the younger kids. "Some of the younger children become adopted by families all over. What you need to do is enjoy yourself and unwind for a while. When you get bored or restless, come see me and we will talk, O.K.?" With that Julie walked off toward the office building.

Sandra looked at her map and slowly walked around watching the other kids. Most of them were about her age give or take a couple of years. There was an outdoor dance floor set near one of the buildings. Looking at the map she figured out that the building was the recreation center. About ten kids were dancing to the latest dance songs. The kids that were not dancing were drinking soft drinks and talking at the tables around the dance floor. Sandy noticed that the dancers were having a good time but there was little of the frantic intensity or competition that the kids dancing back home had when they danced.

Hearing a lot of yelling and cheering from the end of the building she walked over there and watched a spirited volleyball game in progress with a dozen kids cheering the players on from the sidelines. One black boy jumped high and spiked the ball over the net where it hit a big red-headed boy in the face. Sandra shrank back from the impending violence. But, the black boy just ducked under the net and offered his hand to the red-head to help him up from the ground. Even though he had some blood running from his nose, the white boy just grinned, wiped it away on his sleeve, and shook the black's hand. Then the game started again.

In the next two hours Sandra saw a couple of hundred boys and girls having a good time and enjoying themselves. Having a coke at the stand near the dance floor she struck up a conversation with a good-looking blonde girl. The conversation confirmed everything she had seen and heard. This was a resting place. Yet, something bothered her about the attitude of these kids. They did not plot to use the services, to escape (why would you?), or do any of the other normal mischief that kids her age got into. There didn't seem to be much interest in anything but having a good time and not getting into trouble. Sandra was a very curious and inquisitive girl. She thought that she would get bored pretty soon. The call to lunch was sounded. That was good because even though she had said she wasn't hungry while she was being admitted, she really could eat a horse right now. After lunch she would see about finding out why nobody was concerned about the way things were going at the ranch.

She found lunch to be great. They had all the hamburgers and fixings you could eat. Beans, milk, and desert were really good. Feeling full and sated she went outside and found a shady spot to rest. As she lay there looking up at the clouds she tried to remember that she had something to do after eating, but the thought eluded her. Oh well, she had all the time in the world to worry later. As she fell asleep she smiled.

Julie looked around from the TV monitor and smiled to Bob, "It's all right. She's made the adjustment and will be fine. We've run the DNA analysis on her blood and got a match from the missing kids division. I've put the proper information in her files. If she decides to go home we'll be able to facilitate the trip." Bob nodded and taking his airline reservations folder he headed back to Houston's Hobby Airport.

Back in Chicago at the Federal Building in downtown, Jack, Laura, and Mark were shown into a twenty-by-twenty foot carpeted room. There was a large-screen TV on the wall. A stocked wet bar and some very comfortable chairs arranged in a semi-circle in front of the TV. Mark winked at Laura and smiled. "You will like this, I guarantee it!"

A few seconds later the screen lit up and it was like being in the same room with the President of the United States. President Andrew McArthur Bollen was looking to his left at someone out of camera range and nodding. He turned and smiled to greet the three video guests. He came to a visual standstill and lost the smile. As he examined Jack and Laura more carefully his eyes widened and the smile returned. This set of facial gymnastics made the three of them exchange glances and puzzled looks.

President Bollen shook his head and waved his hand at the camera, as if to say "don't worry about my odd behavior." He explained, "I'm sorry to startle you all like that. I just was a little startled myself." He looked off camera. The visual clarity and depth was such you wanted to look where he was looking and couldn't understand why you couldn't see anyone there. He asked several people that were apparently there to leave the room. When they had done so and there was an audible 'thud' from the door of the Oval Office shutting, he turned back to the camera. Peering carefully at them again, he then looked at his notes on the table before him. The table in front of them was exactly the same table in front of him so that it looked like the table continued from the room they were in to the one he was in.

The President looked up again and said, "You are Jack and Laura Malone from Denver, right?" When they both said yes, he continued. "Jack and Laura, Hum." He sat back in his chair and relaxed. "The reason I was so taken aback when I saw you two is because I have seen you before." Andrew Bollen looked introspective. "I had a dream, no disrespect to Dr. King, but I really had a dream in which I saw both of you and you were on either side of my niece Tracy, holding her hands. Although you two were dressed in combat gear and had weapons, all three of you were smiling and walking in a park." There was no hiding the tears in his eyes. He took his glasses off and used a handkerchief to dry them.

When he had recovered and donned his glasses again, he looked serious. "I have read your reports about the girl that was killed in Denver and the one that was kidnapped, or rescued, there in Chicago. I like your style and your commitment to children that are in danger. I have also read Mark's report and I understand your feelings about placing your lives on the line and possibly estranging yourselves from your life at home. I asked Mark to get us together this way to see if I couldn't convince you two to continue on with him in pursuit of this lead. I assure you that the full resources of the United States government will be at your disposal to see this case to a resolution. I also felt that your lead on this girl might possibly have some bearing on my niece's disappearance."

The President became very animated at this point. "But, when I saw you and realized that you two were the ones I had seen in my dream. I knew it was a vision from God and that she will be saved by the two of you! I am probably the most powerful man on this planet and I can't do anything to help my little girl. So, I am begging you to stay the course and save Tracy for me, please." The last word was so soft you had to strain to hear it because it had real passion in it. This wasn't rhetoric or politics, the man was putting his heart on the table.

Jack looked at Laura and saw tears in her eyes. She nodded slightly and Jack looked back at the screen, "All right." That was all there was to say.

The President smiled a hearty smile and would have clapped them both on the back if they had been physically there, "Good, good. I hope that you will both come to see me in person, soon."

Mark nodded to the President. "Mr. President, I have the information on the aircraft that left here and on Mr. Lister the president of Lister Enterprises. I want to thank you for the quick service."

The President nodded back and said, "At your service Mark, at your service, and again, I owe you." The President wished them well, told them to check in frequently and said good-bye.

After he had disappeared, Laura wanted to make sure that what they had agreed to with the President was also God's will. "Jack, Mark, don't you think we should pray for guidance?" They formed a small circle and held hands. As they praised the Lord and worshipped they felt the peace come down all over them. As a definite sign that the Holy Spirit of God was with them it astounded Mark. Laura asked the main question. "Dear Jesus, we love you and want to do your will. Is it your will that Jack and I continue to follow Mark and do as the President asks us to do?" They were all still for a few minutes and in his mind Jack clearly saw a child's face smiling at him. It faded away and he again felt the confirmation of acceptance and love. He said, "In your precious name Jesus, Amen."

Laura looked up at him with a question on her face. He nodded, "I saw a happy child's face and felt the acceptance of our course." He smiled at his wife, "Another thing. The President saw us walking with Tracy, which means that we will come through this thing." He turned to Mark, "Of course you realize that he didn't specifically see you." Mark smiled, "That's okay, and I got my own confirmation that things will work out."

CHAPTER THIRTEEN

Maximillian Thornton Lister sat in a six-hundred dollar chair at a three thousand dollar desk. His thirtieth floor corner office cost six thousand dollars a month and none of that bothered him. His international corporation netted over a billion dollars a year and his special sales brought in more than two million a month. But, it hadn't always been this easy. Lister knew he had been born into the lap of luxury and as both a baby and as a young child he had been catered to down to his slightest desire. First money and then power became the only gods he cared about.

His parents had been wealthy and aristocratic. He remembered that they bought him the best of everything especially in nurses and nannies. Max shook his head as the memory of the severe shock he had suffered when he was six years old. It had angered and hurt him to find out that the woman that had always taken such good care of him was not his mother. He remembered even now that as a small child he had no idea what his mother looked like. It was three weeks after that before he actually met his biological mother for the one and only time in his life. She was no more interested in him than she was interested in a loving relationship with his father. He found no warmth or love there and realized at that tender age that he did not like his mother now that he was allowed to meet her. In his rage and anger at his mother for not loving him he believed that everyone hated him. The anger he had as a child built into a lifetime of bitterness and hatred of women.

He was seventeen years old when he finally saw his father as the cold, dead man laying in the elaborate coffin that had been as uninterested in him as his mother had been years before. He had everything material but it didn't bring him any satisfaction or love.

He inherited the five and a half billion dollar empire of his father's a week later when his mother was killed in a boating accident half a world away. The conservator that was assigned to handle his accounts until he was of age was not interested in the boy, only the money and how much he could get for himself. He'd made the mistake of telling young Max about what he was doing and that there was nothing that could be done about it. That afternoon Max hit the conservator over the head with a fireplace poker and committed his first murder. He'd reveled in the power he had over life and death.

The murder had been covered up and then money changed hands so that the conservator had been the unfortunate victim of an accident. Max was way ahead of the accountants this time. He found a lawyer who was willing to do things the way Max wanted them done and made him conservator of the estate. From that day on, Max ran things the way he wanted to. His education continued at the best schools but Max never spent one day in any of them. His stand-ins were well educated but undocumented because of the deceptions. Max's private tutors were able to bring him up to a level of high school graduate before he rejected anything except the trappings of an educated man.

As he grew toward manhood, the evil he carried in him grew and hungered for more gratification. He rejected women and turned his sexual drive into a drive for power. He let nothing stand in his way. If he couldn't get it with money or power he arranged for break-in, a mugging, or an accident to befall the hapless person.

Max knew he didn't need anyone, especially a clinging female. Oh, "How" he hated his mother. The anger burned even more deeply as time went by. He wanted to make every woman in the world pay for the pain he had suffered. One of the best ways to hurt a woman was through her children. He hired experts and professionals and created a massive corporation that dwarfed that of his father. But he wasn't satisfied. He had the most expensive, biggest, and best of everything. That included a jet plane, a yacht, and four mansions on three continents, but they didn't satisfy him.

He went to many parties where his wealth drew syncopates and lackeys like a magnet. At one party he met an emissary of the new regime that was running Egypt. The emissary made him an offer that intrigued him more than anything had for quite a while.

Lister remembered meeting with Libya's new ruling leader, Mahout Mohammad, of the ruling Muslim Brotherhood. Lister was delighted to find someone who was more of a power junkie than himself. He came away from the meeting with the feeling that he had met a master of control. A man who felt his life was far more important than any nation you could name. After his meeting with Libya's new leader he was wined and dined by the emissary who discussed a private arrangement that the leader of Egypt couldn't be a part of, at least not openly. Lister knew that there were some major power politics going on in Libya but he left with the assurance and the funds to do a major operation. He also came away with an agreement to share in the rule of the world. First though, he had to destabilize Israel's major backer, the United States of America.

Max worked up a suitable scenario and presented it to the emissary. The man was very pleased. Max's plan was not only doable, but the multi-billionaire was going to fund a lot of it himself.

Max had hired Ike Morris as his director of operations for his Children's ranch. Ike was, in reality, an ex-Soviet spy who was looking to improve his lot and he blended into the legal and illegal Lister operations very well. He also brought with him a host of other talents. Like cryptanalysis and subtle wiretapping.

Max had a translation of the emissary's encrypted phone call to Mohammad. He listened as the emissary told Libya's ruler that he, the emissary, knew Allah would allow him to use the infidel billionaire Lister for his own purposes and then Max Lister would follow the proper path of elimination necessary for all infidels.

Max chuckled. They didn't know that he knew their plans. Lister was sure that once they were in control of the majority of the world, he would eliminate the emissary and the "Brotherhood's" new desert madman.

His secretary reminded him of his meeting and he departed his office still chuckling about the affair with Mohammad.

CHAPTER FOURTEEN

Maximillian Lister observed the people around the table as he walked into the large conference room on the sixty-seventh floor of the Listex Building in Houston, Texas. The heads of the various Lister Enterprises were conducting an overview report of the many businesses that the multinational company controlled. The shipping line, the hotel franchises, the diversified holdings and the banks had each taken their turn at presenting the profit and loss picture. The directors of these businesses were excused and the foundations and grants were allowed to outline their present status and plans. The last enterprise to be considered was the Children's Ranch.

The director and Max Lister listened to the tax write-offs and the daily operations summary. The last quarter's number of children rescued was 631. Children processed back to their homes out of the group was 345. Adoption agencies accepted and placed 67 of the younger children that had no extreme problems. That took care of 412 children which left 219. Six had turned out to have been involved in serious crimes and had been turned over to the authorities.

The remaining 213 children were inducted into the various Lister enterprises around the world. They would be taken care of and trained until they were of age and then allowed to join the different businesses if they desired. 39 were carefully tutored and then returned to the cities that they had been saved from and spread the word that there was a better way than living on the streets. This increased the number of runaways that made it to the ranch.

The Operations Director, Ike Morris, casually watched the billionaire as Lister listened carefully to the disposition of the children. He saw a large man with a full head of wavy brown hair who was good looking in a dark way. His eyes were an intense slate gray that made many other men look away when he glared in their direction. Women were equally attracted by his wealth and looks and repelled by an aura that made them shiver when they got too close to him. His powerful build was contradicted by the damp clamminess of his hands and fingers. A careful observer like Ike noticed the restlessness of his whole frame.

Ike liked the fact that the money and power that Max Lister controlled made for a very obedient and orderly world. The man was constantly managing and reviewing his plans and corporate activities. He did not like trouble in achieving his carefully planned goals. After reading the report of the Chicago action against his personnel, he turned to his Director of Operations for the Children's ranch who was in control of the recovery actions.

Lister's deep bass echoed in the huge room. "Well? Have the trouble-makers been completely eliminated or do we need to take further steps to sanitize the Chicago operations area?" Ike scanned the papers he held and looked up to meet his leader's eyes. Ike didn't flinch from the glare. He knew he was dead the minute that Lister wanted him dead. Being already technically dead made for a strange peace of mind. He had nothing to lose. Ike was aware that his attitude is what made him the ice cold soldier that is an unholy terror to his enemies. He who has little regard for his own existence would have none whatsoever for theirs.

Ike was good at what he did and he knew that Lister knew it too. "As far as our intelligence can determine, the main problem, one Brother Riggs and his two main supporters were killed in an explosion of unknown origin late last night. The police files have buried the incident as an inter-gang dispute. The remainder of his crowd is fighting over the leadership of what remains of his activities. Since they don't know what killed Riggs, there is every indication that there will be no further disturbance from that group."

The heat in the room had begun to edge upward as the sun climbed in the eastern sky over the Houston skyline. The micro slat shades rotated in response to a command from a microprocessor which in turn sensed the level of sunlight through a series of sensors. The level of light never dimmed in the conference room as the interior illumination was also computer controlled. Completely heedless of the technical marvels maintaining his environment, Max Lister had the other directors leave the room with the exception of his bodyguard and Ike Morris.

Leaning back in his chair Lister folded his fingers together and inquired about his two favorite operations. "How many packages are we shipping out tomorrow?" Ike looked at his documentation. "Sixteen prime packages", he answered.

Lister smiled and got up from his seat. Walking around to Ike he patted him on the shoulder. "Good! That will bring in around three million dollars to finance our other operation and give us some leverage on more lustful Arabs!" Are the blackmail teams in place with the proposed buyers? Lister was smiling as he paced the floor. After receiving Ike's nod, he asked the only other important question that had been on his mind the whole morning. "Are we ready?"

Ike relaxed as he had a good answer for this question. "Yes, sir, we're ready! In exactly eighteen hours the freighter leaves the port. Three hours later the mercenaries hit the armory. In less than four hours, the militant rabble in Houston will have the firepower to take over, destroy, and loot most of the city until the Army moves in to shut them down. This should cripple the city or destroy it completely. The radio and TV feeds are in place to spread the story of the dissatisfaction across America like it has never been done before. There is nothing that can stop us now. Ike, an ex-Communist didn't believe in the power of any western God, either.

CHAPTER FIFTEEN

Twelve hours after watching the private plane leave the grass field outside of Chicago. Mark Connelly stepped from the transfer tube of the commercial airline at Houston's Intercontinental Airport several miles north of downtown Houston. Mark had traced the aircraft registration to the Lister Corporation whose headquarters was located in Houston. The twin engine aircraft had settled on a southward course after gaining altitude so it was probable that the trail lead to the big oil city fifty miles north of the Gulf of Mexico. After their conference call with the President was over, Mark and the Malones grabbed the first flight to Houston.

Mark arranged for a rent-a-car, they picked up their luggage and walked out the pneumatic doors on the lower level of terminal C to wait for the bus to the agency lot. The heat and humidity struck them almost forcefully as they stepped out of the air-conditioned building. Mark had gotten used to the same type of steamy heat in the jungles of South America and was nonplussed by the change in environment. He noted that the Malones weren't quite as quick to adjust.

Jack drove the nondescript Chevy Monte Carlo on the Sam Houston Toll way west and then south as they bypassed downtown Houston. As they drove, Mark reviewed the information that had been received from his intelligence agency contact concerning the Max Lister organization.

Mark read, "While being one of the bright lights of Houston society and a mover and shaker in the community, he isn't as clean as his publicist makes him out to be. In the first place, he only appeared on the scene four years ago as a wealthy man with big ambitions. Under CIA/NSA review his past fell apart as told and an on-going investigation is in progress. The details are classified but enough information was released to determine that he was very rich. His other corporation efforts brought in over two billion dollars a year. But the source of the eight hundred million dollars for purchasing and constructing a ranch for runaway children southwest of Houston was evidently supplied through a Libyan middleman by Matrice Mujahid."

Laura asked, "Isn't that the crazy military man who is holed up in the desert?"

Mark laughed, "Yeah, Mujahid is a spin-off of Sierra Leone's Fokay Sankoh terrorist group. Matrice managed to make himself a General and carve out an enclave in the eastern Libya desert. Mahout Mohammad claimed he had nothing to do with the General. Although Mahout Mohammad didn't associate either himself or the Libyan regime with Mujahid, he also hasn't kicked him out of the desert base he'd made for himself within Libyan territory. That means Mujahid has the tacit approval of Mohammad for whatever he is doing."

Reading on, Mark smiled. "A similar, but completely different investigation has the FBI digging into Lister's activities in an effort to prove that he is the brains and money behind the racial tensions and small scale riots in the fifth ward over the last six months. The problem for both intelligence groups is that there is no substantial proof that Lister is Mujahid agent or that he was directly connected to the organization behind the unrest. Until they had something solid to show in court, there was little or nothing that they could do except watch him."

Mark continued, "The business with the girl in Chicago doesn't fit into the scope of the activities that the intelligence agencies have tagged Lister with at all. The Lister Ranch for runaways is completely on the up-and-up on the surface. The investigations into that operation show nothing except an exceptionally beneficial activity. The kids he and his organization rescued off the streets of America's cities were mostly returned home. There was no apparent brain-washing or creation of in-place agents. The FBI had even used a youthful agent and he processed through the ranch like hundreds of other kids and returned home. The only hidden thing he had found was that they tended to use a mild sedative to keep the kids in check at the ranch. A forensics analysis of the substance showed nothing harmful. "

"The whole operation could simply be a cover for his other, less honorable activities, but if it is, it is an expensive one and that doesn't wash. I knew other Libyan-connected terrorist agents in the US and they never spent any time or money that didn't directly help their operations."

Mark thought about the Chicago action. "Now the military operation against Brother Riggs did fit a Mujahid type operation, but why do it to rescue the child from the gang? Lister wasn't the type to provide a major operation for altruistic reasons, especially if Mujahid money was being spent. That's why the President gave us the go-ahead to see if we could find out what was really going on in Houston."

After they checked into a two-room suite at a hotel on Highway 59, southwest of the city, near the Sam Houston Toll way, Mark laid out a plan so that they could investigate Lister's activities in the least amount of time. "I want to call Washington for more information, and then, based on what I learn I want to do a soft probe at Lister's headquarters in the Listex Building.

Jack and Laura decided to see what they could learn about Lister's Ranch. The threesome had a quick brunch and split up.

Mark made a call to his covert intelligence contact at the CIA. The agent took the call on the second ring. Normally, the agent could be arrested for being involved in clandestine operations within the borders of the United States. But, Mark knew the agent had his directions from the highest levels and even though the agent knew that plausible deniability was his fate if anything went public, he apparently enjoyed his job. The relationship between him and Mark had endured through the old harsh administration. Now, the sitting President was privately in favor of anything that destroyed organized crime and terrorism with the effectiveness of a military operation. Mark knew that while the President could not openly endorse his operations, he had personally endorsed Mark.

Mark thought about his tacit backing by the government. He didn't like to have to answer to anyone, but the assets and perks that came with the association were more than worth a little pride.

Mark knew that the President was aware that this type of operation was a potential danger to his career, but the man did it for the country anyway. The forces Mark Connelly and others like him countered were extremely worse for the entire country. Mark realized at their first meeting he had rated very highly with this President because of his outstanding military career and his successes as a free-lance operative for the government. Equally important was the fact that Mark had saved the life of not only the President, but, his wife and kids, also. The deciding factor was that Mark had shown that he was morally responsible. In his line of work that went a long way with the head of state.

Agent Bill Reynolds briefed Mark about Lister's organizations and the Intel that he had secured from the data banks of the various intelligence agencies. It was primarily a recap of what he had heard before with two significant additions. It seemed that there was a freighter owned by Lister that was about to sail from the Houston port the next morning. The hint Reynolds had tapped into was that an extremely important and secret cargo was to be shipped out of the U.S. directly to Tripoli. Rumor also had it that there was to be some sort of major disaster in Houston tomorrow. As to the type of disaster there was no information available at the present time. Except that Lister and his people could be very deeply involved.

The Agent finished by saying, "Mark, I can't give you much solid Intel on whatever Lister is planning. But some of the projections that I have worked out on the computer regarding the rise in the number of attacks, riots, and confrontations in the Houston minority communities indicate that the whole city could blow up in civil war in the next forty-eight hours. The rumors indicate that Lister is set to inspire an incident which will most probably act as the trigger for the upheaval. The only advantage the city government has is that most of the dissidents are poorly armed."

"Why would Matrice Mujahid finance a riot in Houston Texas?" Mark was sure there was more to the package than simple unrest for the American public.

The agent sighed, "There is no official explanation as to why Lister is pushing the race riot angle, but I have an idea of my own. I think that this will just be the tip of the iceberg. I think civil unrest, starting in Houston will suddenly flare up all over the U.S. As the internal conflict grows and becomes an army responsibility, Mujahid can do pretty much what he wants to in the Middle East. In my view, the paramount interest of the General is the quick elimination of Israel."

Mark smiled, he had seen what the Israeli intelligence apparatus, the Mossad, could do let alone the Israeli military machine. "I think the General would bite off more than he could chew if he drew down on the Jewish nation."

91

"Yeah, but this civil unrest is right up his alley as a distraction to keep the U.S.A. too busy to pay attention to things in the middle east until it is too late." Bill Reynolds still regretted that the U.S. hadn't gone in and blown this particular desert crazy away when they had the chance.

"Thanks, Bill" said Mark. "I'll do a quick recon of the Lister headquarters this afternoon and that freighter tonight. What you've given me tells me that the numbers are falling fast."

As he drove toward downtown Houston, Mark felt a feeling that he hadn't had for quite a while. He knew that the Lister organization was probably a terrorist creation. He also knew that Lister's organization was probably involved in fermenting a riot in the giant city, pitting group against group. These were standard subversive tactics employed by terrorists everywhere they wanted to destroy the existing system. But if the Children's Ranch was actually an honest operation, front or no, that means that a substantial portion of Lister's employees could be innocent of any wrongdoing against the country. They probably believed in what they were doing and in their work. Mark Connelly did not wage war on innocents. He had to get some hard intelligence on the numbers involved or he was operationally hamstrung. Even a cannibal knows that he can surround himself with innocents and prevent an honorable warrior from striking him for fear of destroying the wrong people.

Parking outside the Listex Building, the specialist considered his options. First, he had to do a soft penetration and recon of the operation until he could identify the rotten parts and excise them from a possibly healthy body. Just like a surgeon. Mark smiled at the comparison. It was one that he had made many times before as a sniper.

Twenty-five miles to the southwest of Mark's location in downtown Houston, Jack pulled their newly rented four-wheel drive onto a small side road at the perimeter of the Lister property known as the Children's Ranch. They had prepared by getting an off-road vehicle and added a variety of vision aids such a binoculars and night-vision glasses from Mark's supply. They each also had a silenced pistol which was probably very illegal if they were caught with them. This was supposed to be a recon of the ranch, but you never knew what might happen when you work around terrorists.

They headed out on foot to a low hill just above the fence that surrounded the ranch from the rest of the scrub land this far away from Houston. Staying below the top of the hill they circled around until they could crawl up to the top and see the majority of the ranch laid out before them while still remaining hidden. Jack knew that he and Laura were in good physical shape because of their constant exercise programs and their outdoor activities not to mention their youth. They moved through the foliage easily because they were used to the effort and enjoyed it.

After scanning the entire area around the buildings and the buildings themselves, the couple took twenty minutes of video tape so that they could show Mark on their return. Nothing looked out of place or even remotely like a terrorist organization ran the camp. After two hours Laura said, "This is getting us nowhere. We need to find a better way to check this place out." Jack agreed in his best imitation of a British snob. "Yes my dear, you're absolutely correct."

They were just about to climb out of the little camouflage nest they had erected when Jack put his hand on Laura's shoulder and indicated with a finger over his lips that she should be silent.

Following his line of sight, Laura saw someone slowly crawling up the hill toward them. Covered in a light brown and green camouflage cover, the person was making steady progress up the hill but seemed unaware of their presence so far.

Lowering themselves back down to the ground, Laura and Jack split up and waited for the crawler. Just as the person crawling up the hill reached their location, Laura pointed her pistol at the person and said, "Don't move!"

For a second things seemed to be going as Laura wanted them to go, then in what seemed like high-speed motion, the crawler rolled over at Laura and grabbed her pistol. Another pistol appeared out of the camouflage cover and was pointing directly at Laura. A motion of the barrel indicated that Laura should let go of the gun. All these actions stopped as Jack dropped directly on top of the person under the tarp and shoved his pistol's barrel roughly into the back of their head. He wasn't taking any chances either. His finger was on the trigger of the cocked pistol and he meant to shoot the instant anything happened.

The person under the tarp seemed to realize the situation and held up both hands with the pistol held by the trigger guard in the right hand. Taking the pistol, Laura recovered her gun and told the intruder to take off the tarp, carefully. Jack stood up and backed away slightly.

The crawler slowly sat up with their hands still in the air and shook the tarp off. When the tarp fell it revealed a rather pretty face and shoulders of a young black-haired woman. She was watching Laura very carefully but was still mindful that there was someone behind her who was also armed. Keeping her left hand in the air, she unhooked the front of the tarp and let it fall to the ground.

With almost no indication of impending action the woman launched herself backward in a rear roll intended to knock Jack down and give her a chance to get his gun. She almost succeeded. Jack was able to throw himself to one side and avoid her grab for his pistol. In one flowing motion the woman grabbed at her throat with her right hand. In a blur her hand snapped out directly toward Jack's face. Jack had seen this action before, many times. His eighteen years of martial arts had trained him well in the use of, and defense against, throwing stars.

Jack snapped his right hand upward past his face with the correct timing for the full sleeve on his camouflage jacket to catch the whirling object and bat it down. Out of seemingly nowhere the woman produced a throwing knife. The position they were in would have been perfect for a throwing knife with the sun at her back. As her hand snapped back to throw the slim blade, she stopped, she lost Jack in blinding gold light. She turned her head, and finally lifted her left hand in a protective manner in front of her eyes. The bright, glaring gold light sprung from the other young woman's chest and she couldn't see past it!

Laura's gold cross pendant was reflecting the sun, and the angle was perfectly aligned with the attacking woman's eyes. Tears in her eyes, she switched the knife to an attack position and stepped in to thrust at Jack.

Unfortunately for her, Jack anticipated the maneuver, blocked the knife thrust with the pistol in his left hand, grabbed her right wrist with his right hand, and disarmed her. He continued to twist her wrist to the right while rotating her arm in a big circle over and to his right. As the positions changed the force on her shoulder blade increased exponentially and it gave her a choice. She could fall to the ground face first or suffer a dislocated or broken shoulder. As she fell to the ground Jack quickly kneeled over her back, released her arm, and slammed her face down into the dirt. He then screwed the silencer on his pistol into her ear. Then he whispered to her. "If you stop trying to kill us for a minute maybe we could talk."

Lifting her face out of the dirt slightly she nodded her head. Jack handed his pistol to Laura and stood up away from the prone figure. He hadn't had this good of workout in weeks. The adrenaline was flowing and he was ready to keep going. He said, "Get up", and offered her his hand expecting some more tricks, but this time she had apparently resigned herself to talking. She ignored his offered hand and athletically pulled her legs under her and sat down Indian style with her legs crossed under her. She carefully scrubbed the dirt from her face and hair.

Jack squatted down across from her and about four feet from Laura. He made sure that Laura had a clear field of fire in the event she had to shoot. Looking at the woman he stopped to breathe deeply to settle his voice before he talked to her. She was a darkly Caucasian with short-cropped black hair and an unusually penetrating set of blue eyes. She looked to be about five-foot, six or seven inches tall, one-hundred and thirty pounds and a shapely but firm female body. Jack suddenly heard the word "Esther" in his mind.

Remembering what he had learned, he formed a thought, "God. What do you mean by this name, Esther?" In his mind's eye he saw a shining six- pointed Jewish star which was overshadowed by an indistinct woman shape wearing a cloaked cape and holding a knife. Thinking quickly, Jack chuckled to himself. "Right... a Jewish cloak and dagger Mossad agent." He felt a warm glow of correctness. Jack quickly reviewed what he knew concerning the premier Israeli intelligence agency. "The Mossad Merkazi Le-Modiin U-Letafkidih Meyuhadim, which was Jewish for Central Institute for Intelligence and Security. The Mossad was the most important of five Israeli intelligence agencies. They handled espionage, intelligence gathering, and covert political operations in foreign countries. The Mossad reported directly to the Israeli Prime Minister. He looked up at the woman.

"Central Institute? Special Operations Division? Metsada, right?"

Irritation flared in the woman's eyes but she didn't say anything. So, Jack decided to take a risk. "If you are who I think you are then we are on the same side."

Smiling for the first time the woman laughed softly. She had a warm contralto voice with no accent. "And what side would that be?"

Jack was still working on his feelings from what the Holy Spirit had given him. "On the side that thinks there's something evil in anything of Max Lister's and wants to find out just who that might threaten, especially if it is innocent children." Jack explained about the girl that was taken from Chicago apparently to the ranch and the means used to secure her.

For several minutes the woman thought about what they had said. Then she came to a conclusion and held out her hand. "I'm Sarah Cohen." She looked closely at Jack. "You are a very perceptive person." She worked her wrist and smiled slightly, "And a good fighter. I would guess you would be from your CIA, but I don't expect you to tell me if you are."

She looked back at the ranch spread out below them. "You're right. There is something wrong with Lister's operations but that child you're talking about is not part of the real problem involving Max Lister, at least, not yet."

Sarah straightened out her legs and leaned back on her elbows. "How much do you know about Max Lister?" Laura shook her head, "Not enough but we're trying to learn how the Children's Ranch figures into his less-worthy activities." Sarah shook her head, "You don't have time to learn about him in the usual ways."

Laura held up Sarah's pistol and raised an eyebrow at Jack. At a nod from him, Laura handed both Jack's and Sarah's pistols back and holstered her own. The other two followed suit.

Sarah looked at them quizzically for a minute. "I know you probably can't tell me anything about what you are doing here either, but I think we might be able to help each other, if our organizations would agree.

Jack smiled a small smile and agreed, "Could be."

Sarah studied both of them for a few minutes and came to another decision. "I sense an honesty and openness with you two that I haven't felt since I was in high school. Therefore I am going to share some information with you that I will deny if it ever comes out, understand?"

They both nodded. Sarah continued, "Israel has been concerned about Max Lister for about five years now. He was a cruel and ruthless taskmaster over the employees he had working for him in Germany. He assumed control of his father's business when his father and mother died while he was a pre-teen. Somehow he gained control through an executor of the estate until he was of age. Regardless, his businesses prospered because he had excellent managers and a staff that was interested in corporate growth, regardless of Lister's personal knowledge or capabilities. You know he's not very well educated even though he holds degrees from some of the best universities."

Jack could agree with that. When he had been a student at the University of Colorado in Boulder, Colorado, he had seen many students party their way through four years of college. And still receive their degrees. Most of them could not even tell you what courses they were supposed to have passed to get that degree, let alone use the knowledge real students learned in those classes.

Sarah continued, "Several years ago, Lister met with General Mujahid in Libya and became life-long buddies with the terrorist." The cool professionalism slipped a little when she was discussing Mujahid because of his extensive campaign to kill anything Jewish.

"Suddenly, Lister up and moves from his ancestral home in Germany and relocates to here in Houston, Texas. This is very strange. We watched and waited to see what he was up to. He flourished business-wise and he started this ranch for lost children. We were almost ready to dismiss him as a threat to Israel when we got a report from a source in Greece. It seems that our boy Max is stirring up racial tensions in Houston. Then we get additional information that he was involved in a clandestine purchase of highly illegal and dangerous materials from the Russian Republics. The problem is that we can't trace where the materials have gone and that is of the greatest concern to my government. We are not sure what the racial games are for and that also concerns us. Now, what can you share with me?"

Laura shook her head, "Not much I think. We only know that he is doing something shady with the children and that he is fomenting a riot very soon, here in Houston. But then, you already knew that."

Sarah glared at her for a few seconds. "Your government doesn't have any more information on Max Lister than that? What type of intelligence operatives are you?"

Jack shook his head. "We're not officially connected to the government. We are simply a concerned couple that has been given the chance to uncover something shady with Lister's operation concerning the children."

One of Sarah's eyebrows rose for a few seconds as if to say "Sure." But something about the way they presented the information confirmed the fact that they weren't American agents. She struck her forehead with the palm of one hand. "How stupid of me, here I am risking my career by revealing information to amateurs who don't know what I already know." Her look wasn't very kind and she started to stand up when Laura asked her to stay for a few minutes. She eased back to the ground with an irritated look on her face. Laura took a breath and jumped in with both feet. "We said, we're not officially connected to our government. That doesn't mean that we don't have some very high level contacts that are requesting our involvement in their investigation of Max Lister."

Sarah thought for a few seconds, "How 'high-level'?"

"The President of the United States," Jack answered. "We have some history at this business even though we haven't had any formal training. And we have an associate that is quite good at your game working with us." Jack felt the need to keep this brief alliance going. "We should have a great deal of new information when we regroup this afternoon. If you want to join us then I can guarantee that you will be in on that information."

The Mossad agent slowly nodded, "Alright, I am at a dead-end here anyway. I believe that the ranch is tied into the stolen nuclear material but how, I don't know."

Jack went to get the four-wheel drive while the women walked back together. Laura was intrigued with a woman involved in a spy occupation and asked her about different aspects of it. Most of these bordered on things Sarah wasn't allowed to answer. One question she answered quickly. Laura had asked her about the glamour of the position. Sarah laughed and told her about the 'life' she led.

"Movies and books have glamorized the "secret agent spy" she said. "Actually the largest amount of intelligence work is a very unromantic search of public information performed by university-trained research analysts in quiet offices. Most of what they distill is sent to action coordinators and they never know if the information is used or not. The occasional field agent, like me is a rare item anymore. Most of what we do can be done by satellite surveillance or communications intercept operations." Sarah's face became stony and cold. "The job of the field agent is most often a painstakingly tedious or even at times a disgustingly immoral and distasteful occupation. I have served my country at times when I questioned the morality of my actions. It's not a very pleasant thing to have to do."

They finished talking just as Jack met them. They took her to where her car was hidden. Then the two car caravan pulled back onto Highway 59 and headed back to the hotel to await Mark.

As Sarah drove along in silence, she thought she saw a car tailing them. But, they turned off and she dismissed the idea. The memory of a recent operation in this country thrust its way into her mind. In the crystal clarity of the memory it was as if she was there again.

-------------------------------******-------------------------

The snow lay quiet on the countryside. The light breeze brought a faint chill with it as it blew across the snow in the darkness. Sarah was well prepared for the conditions and was not concerned about frost-bite on her extremities as other agents had warned her about. This was her first field assignment in the northern tier of the United States and she was alert and alive to the slightest sound. One of the slight sounds she was listening to was the 'squeak-crunch' of someone's footfalls through the ankle-deep snow in the field near her.

Dressed in arctic military camouflage she blended into the snow and bushes she was hidden in. She practiced field craft very precisely because that was the type of person she was. If she was going to do something, then she was going to do it right. So, she moved her eyes and not her head. That way her silhouette did not change but she was able to scan a much larger area. She spotted the walker about ten meters away. The temperature was about -10 Celsius and the snow was cold enough to squeak when it was stepped on no matter how careful you were. She watched the guard breathe out and a cloud of ice crystals appeared in front of his mouth. He stopped and looked in all directions. Sarah stayed completely still. Not seeing anything out of the ordinary, the guard slowly moved off to her right and eventually went out of hearing range.

Sarah remembered the map and knew just where she had to go. It was apparently where the guard had come from. She checked in all directions and then double-checked with night glasses. No hidden watchers were revealed by the infra-red device. She slowly rose into a standing position and moved out of the shrubs backward toward the guard's tracks. As she backed up, she used a piece of cloth to obliterate her tracks in the snow. Reaching the much larger footprints of the guard, she stepped into two of them so that she was facing backward to his path of travel. When she was sure that there were no visible signs of her path, she started walking backward in the existing tracks.

Eight minutes later she spotted her target. A smallish chateau set back against a heavily wooded hill. The tracks led directly to the door of the chateau and that would not be a good place for her to be. Fortunately there were many more tracks where she was. She switched paths and ended up behind a small shed or barn eighty meters from the house. She quietly dropped into a snow bank near the building to reduce her silhouette and to blend into the snow with her white camos. Watching the house she was certain it was inhabited but not sure if it was the man she was sent to get. She slowly slid the Galil rifle in its arctic camo sleeve off of her shoulder and set up its bipod to keep it out of the snow and provide her stability if she had to use it.

Ahmed As'adat Alkar was a Palestinian with a gruesome past. In the name of national honor and for the goal of peace he shot, stabbed, and blew up twenty-seven Israeli children in a school in the disputed zone. None of the children were older than eleven and none of them survived. He was supposedly killed in the blast that decimated the school after his shooting spree. That turned out to be a lie because he made the mistake of being seen last week in Fargo, North Dakota in the United States by a reliable informant. Thus her assignment was to track him down and resolve the problem of his freedom, one way or the other. The Mossad was clear on the philosophy of dealing with killers and terrorists that have committed crimes against the Jewish nation. Her orders were to locate Ahmed, identify him positively, and eliminate him. After all, he was already dead, right? They had a martyr's funeral for him in Palestine. Along with all the angry press that pointed the finger at Israel for causing Alkar to commit such crimes.

She forgot the hype and anger when the front door opened in a blare of bright light and a man walked out onto the front porch and lit up a cigarette. Sarah carefully pulled the light amplified glasses out of their pouch and studied the man. In the magnification of the glasses she could see the beard, the bushy eyebrows, and most importantly, the scar that ran from his right cheekbone down across his jaw line and into his throat. That scar was a gift from an earlier meeting with another Mossad agent. Unfortunately the cut was all the Palestinian got. The Mossad agent died in the exchange.

It was Alkar all right. She slowly moved the Galil rifle and brought it up in front of her. She centered the magnified scope on the man's forehead. He was only part way through his cigarette so she had plenty of time. She pulled the trigger and the Palestinian was slapped completely off of his feet. The built-in CCD camera and miniature CD recorded the entire matter. The silenced shot was right on target and another butcher was on his way to his flock of virgins in the garden of delights as promised by a stone statue.

She looked around and still saw no one. Sliding backward she turned around and crawled thirty feet past the building into a small group of bushes and trees. No alarm had been raised yet. She stood up and slung her rifle over her shoulder. Walking quickly away to the north she reached a barren rocky area with no snow. Tracking snow onto the first part of the rocks, she then stepped backward in her own footsteps until she reached the bushes again. She picked up a loose pine branch and then started walking backward and covering her tracks as she moved to the west. Eventually she reached the same rocky escarpment and was able to make good time toward the snowmobile she had arrived on.

Slowing down as she reached the snow again she walked into a line of trees that separated her from her destination. Easing up to one of the trees, she scanned the area with her night glasses. Seeing nothing she was tempted to bypass other checks so that she could complete her retreat. But, her stubborn pride in doing things right would not let her take shortcuts. She used the infra-red glasses to carefully survey the entire area again. As she scanned the horizon she saw a slight glow of heat over one hill. The hill wasn't near her hidden snowmobile, but it was only two hundred yards to the south of the location. Something wasn't right! There shouldn't be any heat source in this rugged hill country. She slowly slid back down into the snow and checked again. It was still there. Just a slight glow, but definite.

Sarah tried to come up with an explanation for the anomaly, but couldn't. So, tired though she was, and running away from a possible manhunt she might be but, it still needed to be checked out if it was going to be done right. She backed away from the tree line, down a small slope until she was hidden from the area she wanted to go to. She then traveled south until she was past the area of the glow and still two hundred meters west of it. She had to negotiate several slippery hills and go around impenetrable areas of trees and deep snow, but she still got to a hilltop overlooking the area the glow seemed to be at in less than twenty minutes. She lay just over the hill getting her wind back and resting. Then she heard the sound of a dog braying on her backtrack toward the chateau. "Uh oh!" she thought, "The fat's in the fire now!"

She slowly lifted her head over the ridge and looked down to see the cause of the glow. She almost gasped. Slowly sliding back down the slope on her side she let out her breath in a sigh. On the other side of the ridge were two large trucks with canvas-covered beds. The problem wasn't the trucks, but what they had brought. There had to be forty armed men standing around or leaning up against the trucks in complete silence. They were the backup for whatever trap had been set for her at her snowmobile!

The dog yowled again, closer this time. She was caught between forces and nowhere to go. Her control knew what she was doing but was three hundred miles away and didn't know about this little complication. She knew if she had waited for backup, they would probably have missed Ahmed Alkar again, but, what to do now?

She calculated her chances and determined her course of action. Easing back up to the top of the ridge she pulled a small radio transmitter out of her backpack. She flipped up the cover and, holding her breath, she pushed the button. Two hundred meters away the snowmobile exploded in a tremendous explosion, lighting up the nighttime sky for a mile around. The men in the area below her formed up into ragged queues and started running toward the area of the explosion. Two guards were left behind to watch the trucks.

Sarah patiently and carefully used her IR scanner and checked the area in the hills around the trucks and was rewarded with four very much muted glows in widely separated places. Pulling her light amplified field glasses to her eyes she was able to spot two of the four 'hidden' gunners protecting the trucks. If the people that were smart enough to set the original trap hadn't taken this precaution she would have been surprised. She carefully aimed six shots with the silenced Galil assault rifle and less than eighty seconds later had a clear shot at the trucks.

She quickly slid down the hillside below her and dashed zigzag to the first truck. She pulled a package out of her backpack and magnetically attached it to the frame behind the cab but up by the cargo area. Most intelligent military type personnel will look 'under' a vehicle to see if it has been booby trapped, but very few would think to look up high. She set a timer for ten minutes and ran to the second truck avoiding the bodies of the two guards lying in the snow. Checking it out quickly and finding nothing low or high, she climbed in and started the vehicle. Quickly backing it around, she took off for the southern road that was easily visible in her night glasses.

She checked the time and was mildly surprised to see that it was after midnight already. As the truck lumbered as quickly as possible to the south she calculated the response the Palestinian group might be able to muster in the deserted hills of North Dakota at this time of the morning. She didn't like the answer. She had been driving for a while when there was another explosion behind her in the hills, probably the other truck. She kept on driving at the limit of the big truck's ability to stay on the trail.

Watching her mirrors she saw a glint in the sky and correctly interpreted what that meant. She pulled the hand throttle all the way out, opened the door and, watching for her opportunity, dove off the running board of the truck and rolled three times before coming to her feet as she stopped rolling. The truck continued down the trail at full speed. She moved quickly into the woods at the side of the trail and pulled another package out of her backpack. This one she put on, including the hood. The hood and cape would reduce her infra-red heat signature so that most airborne detectors would not find it. She hoped that the chopper didn't have the newest American Forward Looking Infrared or FLIR detector. That one could find her even with the aluminum shield she had on.

She set off to the east through the woods as the truck still lumbered south held on the road by the ruts. She stopped next to a tree when she heard the helicopter's blades race by behind her. Three seconds later the tell-tale sound of a rocket propelled grenade or RPG ended in a bang and the truck stopped going south. The grenade did not destroy the truck, just blew off a tire and riddled the engine with shrapnel. It would not take them long to find that she wasn't in it. She hurried to the east looking around her with her night glasses. Finding what she was looking for she went ahead for a half-kilometer and then took care of nature's call. She then added another half-kilometer to the east and finally she backtracked and covered her side tracks again. She ended up at a small opening in the side of an only slightly larger hillock. It was so small she wasn't sure she could fit in it. But she did. Covering any sign she had been there, she made sure her weapons were where she could use them and covered the entrance so that it did not look like an opening. Then she settled down and went to sleep.

An hour later she came quickly awake when she heard footsteps nearby. Watching carefully she made out three armed men as they followed her trail to the east. Eventually they were gone and she went back to sleep. Dawn came and sunlight woke her up. She wanted to stretch and yawn, but training and instinct kept her quiet as she carefully scanned the surrounding country, seeing nothing. "Well," she thought, "they could be gone, or they could be laying low waiting for me to pop up."

Carefully, she got out an American power bar and a concentrated drink. She slowly ate the bar and drank some of the drink. Checking the time she was sure her control or backup would be in the area since she hadn't checked in last night. She pulled out the small code transceiver and turned it on. The message light glowed. She pulled out a small earpiece and plugged it into the transceiver. Pressing the play button she heard Aaron's voice, "Sabre one, Sabre one. Respond at the hour." That was all. It was enough. She waited the sixteen minutes until the hour and pushed the code button. Several seconds later the message light lit up again. "Sabre one, we have your location, stay put, repeat, stay put, hostiles all over the area. We are bringing in local help, will signal when clear."

Sarah was glad she hadn't tried to leave the cave. She settled down and waited. About an hour later a helicopter went over. Then a bull-horn was used south of her but she couldn't make out what was said. Time was wearing on her in the cramped hole and she needed another potty break real soon too. Finally the message light lit up and she heard the good news. "We will be at your position in two minutes. Wait for us."

She waited and then heard a vehicle approach from the south. It stopped somewhere to her right and people got out. Then she heard Aaron calling to her. She tore down the stuff in front of her hideout and crawled out into the sunlight. Aaron and two other men saw her and came over to help her with her gear. They all hustled to the four-wheel drive and headed south. She gave the CD disk to Aaron and he played it on the portable player he had in his briefcase. He nodded, "Alkar is no longer a problem." He saved the CD and pulled out the issue recorder. Her debriefing was over by the time they reached a real road and headed for Fargo and an airplane.

-------------------------------*****-------------------------------

The memory faded and was replaced by the urban sprawl and rush hour traffic of Southwest Houston.

CHAPTER SIXTEEN

Entering the lobby of Lister's headquarters building, Mark played an old role he had perfected numerous times before. The obvious is usually overlooked and the person that acts like they belong are normally not asked questions. He walked across the lobby to the desk of a cute young blonde. "Hi there", he said, "I'm with the Washington Post working with the article that we are doing on the Lister organization. My name is Michael Black."

The blonde girl looked uncertain for a second. "Article? I didn't know that the Post was doing another article so soon on Mr. Lister. I mean, they just finished the other one last week didn't they?"

Mark thought, "Ouch. I walked into it this time." He smiled at her "Actually this time we are going to profile the entire group of operations, especially the Children's Ranch angle." He took a pad out of his shirt pocket and started to write in it. "What is your name?" he asked. She smiled and blushed. "Tammy Lou Holten" she replied. I think it's great that your paper is giving us so much exposure. I know that the story will help the thousands of runaways out there." "Who did you want to see?" she asked as she reached for the phone on her desk.

Mark's mind raced. "How about the Head of Operations for the Children's Ranch?"

Tammy Lou thought for a minute and decided. She picked up the phone and punched in an extension. After getting connected by his secretary she spoke into the handset, "Mr. Morris? I have one of the Washington Post reporters at my desk for their next article. Yes sir, his name is Michael Black. No sir, he would like to see you to discuss the various operations of the Children's Ranch for a general profile." Yes sir, I will. Thank you."

Tammy Lou smiled as she hung up the phone. "Ike Morris will see you in about five minutes in room 5310 on the fifty-third floor. Just take the elevators over there and see the receptionist on that floor." "Here, take this badge, everyone has to have one." Saying that, she got up, came around the desk, and as she pinned the badge onto his lapel she leaned against him. The not-so-subtle reminder that she was a healthy young woman wasn't lost on Mark. He smiled warmly at her. She obviously liked his tan good looks and wanted him to remember her when he wrote his article.

Mark thanked her and headed for the elevators. Suddenly he found himself in trouble. Like most major corporations that faced the possibility of terrorists, this one had installed magnetic detectors, artfully hidden in the shrubbery and plants in the lobby. He was almost at the first one when he noticed it. The silenced automatic in its shoulder holster would be pretty hard for a newsman to explain. But to suddenly turn away when the guard on the other side of the barrier was already watching him would also be too obvious.

As he stepped through the barrier it buzzed loudly. The guard put his hand on his pistol and got up from his stool. Smiling broadly, Mark reached into his shirt pocket with his right hand. Pulling out a micro cassette recorder, he waved it at the guard and walked pass him into the open elevator. The guard looked uncertain, but then the guy didn't match the image of a terrorist and he had a proper visitor badge on, yet? But, by the time he decided to make sure, the elevator doors had closed and the matter became a non-issue as far as the rent-a-cop was concerned.

As he rode up in the elevator by himself, Mark pressed the buttons with 50, 51, 52, and so on through 60 on them. He just stood there as the elevator stopped and obediently opened its doors at each floor. He got off on the 52nd floor and turned to the left. Seeing a sign indicating the stairs, he opened the door and stepped into the stairwell.

Climbing up the stairs, he passed the 53rd floor and came to the maintenance deck above it. This five foot tall floor was full of machinery and pipes. Twenty seconds later the lock on the door snapped open. Exploring the area quickly, Mark found a central well that contained all of the phone lines and other major wiring for the building. Small landings made out of steel mesh marked each floor. Carefully shutting the access door he duck-walked down the steel mesh floor. He examined the cable entrances for the various offices.

Finding the one marked "5310" he traced the wires to a duct that ran directly east. Smaller air return ducts branched off of the main tunnel in each direction, smaller, but, still large enough for a determined person to move through. This was because the vertical tunnel also acted as the main air return plenum for the air-conditioning system. The wind raced past Mark as he slid into the east bound duct. Moving carefully so as to not disturb the people below him, he worked his way the twenty five feet over to the downward pointing air return ducts over the largest office served by the duct. This turned out to be Ike Morris's office as Mark had surmised. Carefully lowering his head to just above the outlet of the duct he was able to see most of the office.

Ike Morris was sitting at his desk writing on some papers. Mark's blood ran cold at the sight of the man. His name wasn't Ike Morris. It was Anatole Korpov. Anatole had once been a rising star in the older KGB, an absolute ice cold killer, of high intelligence, but no morals and the compassion of a snake. Korpov had fled to Libya after the fall of the Soviet Union.

Mark knew then that the presence of this man just about sealed the terrorist identity of the organization. It could also mean that Korpov was keeping a close watch on Lister and his activities for his Libyan master. It also provided some problems. He and Korpov had met once over rifles in South America. It was doubtful that either could ever forget the other. Mark remembered that event clearly.

-----------------------------*******----------------------------

In the steaming jungle with the humidity over 98%, Mark watched as Korpov arrived, apparently with an order from the KGB specifically to eliminate Mark and his team on the orders of the Kremlin. Korpov's plans had been well laid and almost perfectly executed. The bait had been a particularly nasty rebel Major who specialized in torturing captured Latin American and United States Special Forces personnel. The trap had been baited when the rebels had overrun a forward military base and captured a U.S. Army Special Forces instructor. The fact that the Major would interrogate the prisoner immediately while still in government territory was just too conveniently timed to the availability of Mark Connelly's SEAL Team.

Mark chuckled to himself quietly. Unfortunately for Korpov, the SEAL Team was much more efficient than even he expected. By the time Korpov climbed the tree where he would watch for the approach of the Americans, he was already in Mark's crosshairs. The SEAL Team had risked a HALO parachute insertion to beat the Major's timetable for torture. They had been in place for over an hour when Korpov went around and installed the "hidden" soldiers and other elements of his trap for the American rescue effort.

Billy Joe Lanier was in place behind the hut the prisoner was being held in before the trap was even set. Peering through the small slit he had made in the thatch, he watched as the Major prepared to work on the prisoner. Hot pliers and a hand-cranked generator were a large part of his equipment. His obvious satisfaction in injuring and deforming a captive enraged the Special Forces man, but he held his fire until Mark created a disturbance to draw off the troops outside the hut on the front side.

Mark watched as the Russian climbed the tree and took his position. He was using an American rifle, a Remington Model 700 ADL with a twenty-power scope almost identical to the weapon that the specialist had fixed on his back right then.

Taking a deep breath, Mark let most of it out and held his sight picture. He squeezed off the shot and chambered the rifle while still riding out the recoil of the first shot. The range had only been two hundred yards and the impact of the bullet slammed Korpov right through the limbs supporting him. He fell limply twenty five feet to the ground. Mark tracked his sight picture onto the two mines that the enemy had placed near the trail he was supposed to come down. The troops reacting to his shooting of Korpov were swinging around to get a shot at his location. The explosion of the two mines, one triggered by the other, killed at least four soldiers and wounded several others. The third round came slamming in from Mark's rifle and eliminated one of the noncoms trying to organize the troops. That took the starch out of the other troops and they scattered into the jungle to escape the rain of death.

With the first shot, Billy Joe fired one shot out of his silenced pistol into the hutch. The Major looked surprised at the hole in his chest as he fell to the floor. Billy Joe then slit the remainder of the wall and slid into the hut. Cutting the ropes holding the prisoner to the chair, he led him out the back of the hut and into the jungle.

Mark Connelly took a final scan of the scene before he left the shooting position he had selected. He was distinctly unhappy when he saw Korpov standing in the middle of the clearing sighting his rifle directly on the Mark's face. For several seconds the two men looked at each other and then Korpov fired. He was thrown backward as his rifle exploded. It had apparently fallen into the mud and the barrel had become blocked. The bullet couldn't get out the barrel so the receiver exploded instead. The specialist slid out of the tree and headed for the LZ to meet the other team members.

--------------------------------******--------------------------------

As the memory of that time in the jungle faded away, Mark found himself looking down on the miraculously alive Korpov. Mark surmised that the Russian had been wearing body armor and that was what saved him from the rifle shot. There was some evidence of plastic surgery on his face, probably from the exploding shrapnel of his own rifle.

Mark slowly retraced his steps until he was out of the door and back into the stairwell. Dusting himself off, he went down to the fifty-second floor and entered the elevator. Taking it up one floor he walked pass the receptionist who was busy on the telephone at the time. He walked confidently back to the office holding the Libyan agent and opened the door. The terrorist was facing the other way when Mark opened his door. He hung up the phone and turned around to find the end of a silencer being pointed at his head.

The specialist said, "You should be dead. Now, whether you live or die will depend on what you tell me about Max Lister and his organization in the next two minutes."

Korpov thought furiously and tried to stall. "Hah! You should have been the dead one. If my rifle hadn't exploded I would have rid the world of you those years ago. I remember..."

Mark cocked the pistol. Korpov realized that he had to offer something or lose it all, "All right! Max Lister is planning to..." As he talked, he slid open the drawer in his desk and reached for the pistol he kept there.

Seeing the move, Mark slammed his pistol against the left hand side of the terrorist's agent's head with sufficient force to turn his lights out for a while.

Mark quickly looked over the paperwork on and in the desk of the involuntarily sleeping vice president of Lister's organization. Not finding anything of interest he searched Karpov's pockets and found only a small notebook inscribed in Russian.

Pocketing the book he went to the door and opened it a crack. Seeing no one in the area, he slipped outside and retraced his steps to the front desk. The receptionist was not there. He punched the button for the elevator and was standing there when the woman returned from another office. She looked at him and asked, "Are you Mr. Black? Here to see Mr. Morris?"

"Yes I am." Mark Connelly smiled at her. She seated herself at the desk and pushed the intercom button. When she got no reaction, she said, "I'm afraid that Mr. Morris is out at the moment, would you please wait over there." She had pointed at some chairs by the elevator. Mark walked over to the chairs and sat down. A few minutes later the phone rang and the receptionist got busy. The elevator decided to arrive at that time. Mark stood up and entered the elevator. Getting off on the second floor he found a stairwell that let off into the lobby directly rather than through the metal detectors. This door was secure since it could only be opened from the stairwell inside.

About the time that Mark Connelly was pulling out of his parking space at the curb, Korpov came to on the fifty-third floor of the Lister Building and was violently mad. But, when he found his notebook missing he began to sweat. He decided to immediately put his plan for his escape from the U.S. into operation. He wasn't dead, though he should have been, but he was sure that Max Lister would straighten out that little oversight when he found out about the notebook. Thinking to himself, Korpov decided that it would be far better for his life expectancy if he disappeared without notifying Max or General Mujahid.

Twelve blocks away from the Lister Building Mark found a FAX machine at a Western Union office. Faxing the sheets of the small notebook to his CIA contact took only five minutes and twenty dollars. He had written on the final pages so that the contact would let him know the results via his cell phone.

Finding a local hotel and renting a small room, he cleaned up and took a cat nap until his cell phone rang. It was Bill

Reynolds. "Mark that was quite a piece of Intel you got. I don't think I've ever seen a more comprehensive layout on such an ugly scheme before. Underneath all the legitimate operations of the Children's Ranch, it seems that Lister selects a small portion of the children he rescues and ships them overseas to the highest bidder. They are almost always nine to fourteen years old and both sexes.

Mark Connelly clenched his fist so hard the phone receiver audibly cracked. He was definitely going to rain on one Max Lister and the despicable parade he had created. Children were innocents and not cattle to be terrorized and sold as slaves, slaves that would never see their families or loved ones again.

Mark listened as the agent told him about the other big surprise that the little book had disclosed. He decided to return to the hotel on I-59 and share his information with the Malones.

Back at the hotel, Laura continued to talk to Sarah about her life in the intelligence business. "How did you get into this line of work?"

Sarah sat back on the couch and thought back. "I think I first wanted to get involved during my mandatory military service. I was eighteen and I was very good at the things that the Central Institute needed in their people. They watch the military services for potential employees you know."

Sarah looked directly into Laura's eyes. "I was able to kill without having a severe reaction to it. I was able to compromise other people so that they would do or say what we wanted, and I could perform as necessary to get the job at hand done." She obviously wasn't thrilled about any of these capabilities. She just wanted Laura to know that she could and had done them in her occupation. "We are extremely dedicated but are also very cautious in what we do. For me, this seems to stem from the 1973 mistake in Lillehammer, Norway." When Laura obviously did not know what she meant, she continued. "Several of our agents were attempting to track down Hassan Salameh, a PLO intelligence chief who masterminded the slaughter of the Israeli athletes at the Olympics. They thought they had him and rather than lose him by checking further, they did a drive-by shooting and killed a Moroccan waiter named Ahmed Bouchikhi in July. They were caught and sentenced for the murder in Norway.

They got out after a few years and just recently Israel mended relations with Norway by paying Bouchikhi's widow a large sum of money. They still haven't admitted that it was Mossad agents that did it, though."

Laura shook her head. "That must have been terrible for everyone concerned." Sarah nodded. "It was and the aftershocks linger on in the service. We look three times if we can before we act." She looked Laura up and down once, "You know, you could probably qualify for a job in the field if you wanted to." Laura smiled and shook her head. "Thank you for the compliment, but I couldn't do what you do. I have enough trouble keeping Jack and I out of trouble."

Sarah smiled, "You two are very much in love aren't you? I hope I can find a man like that when I retire from field work."

Laura showed surprise, "You get to retire from the field? I thought you died in the traces or something like that." Sarah laughed, "You've seen too many movies."

Mark picked up on the sound of voices as he reached the door to the room. One voice he did not know. This could be from many sources because he didn't really know the Malones well enough yet to predict their actions. Checking the corridor and finding no other residents he drew his silenced pistol and held it behind his leg as he unlocked and opened the door quietly. Obviously, he didn't do it quietly enough. All three people were looking at the door and there were three pistols aimed his way. Noticing the relaxed atmosphere he smiled and holstered his pistol. The others did likewise and introductions were made.

Mark sized the Mossad agent up in two glances. He knew she would be an effective fighter and she was obviously intelligent, not to mention beautiful. Mark realized that she had an attraction for him that extended beyond the physical.

After Jack vouched for her concerning their present operation, Mark decided that he would watch and evaluate her and make a real determination later. He explained the phone calls and the information he had gotten at Lister's headquarters. His identification of Anatole Korpov made Sarah sit up straight on the couch. "Are you positive it was Korpov?" When Mark nodded she pulled out a cell phone and speed dialed a number. After making connection she talked excitedly in Hebrew for a few minutes.

When Sarah finished using the phone she smiled at Mark. "That's very good identification. My people have been looking for that snake ever since he slithered out of Russia and into Libya. He worked for Quaddfi for a few years and then, when the Brotherhood and Mahout Mohammad ousted Quaddfi and took over, Anatole Korpov bailed out of Tripoli and signed on with General Mujahid. We've got a chance to get him now that you got him running." Mark raised an eyebrow, "He's running because of me?"

Sarah thought about it for a minute and smiled at the good-looking American. "Oh yeah, if what we think is right, added to what you discovered, your actions have probably placed him in a failure position that would not look good to Lister or Mujahid. At least that is my professional guess."

Mark smiled at the thought of Karpov's distress. He reached into his pocket and brought out the notebook. "I did take this off of him while he was 'napping'. It's in Russian and I'm not sure what it says, but it's very detailed."

Sarah held out her hand, "Can I see it?" Mark looked at her for a few seconds making a determination. Then he decided that he trusted her enough to provide the Mossad with the information. It seemed that they had a pretty good handle on Lister as it was. After he handed it to her, she placed it on the table and slowly leafed through the first half of the book. She looked grim when she looked up. "I can read and speak Russian and German. This little book is a time bomb that I think we can use to ruin Lister's plans." She looked back at the book. "And I think that we had better ruin some really quickly or there is going to be thousands of Americans hurt and killed very soon."

She looked at one set of recent pages. "Before we deal with this rebellion or uprising, I think we need to get a handle on this ship he mentions in here. There are sixteen children they are going to take to sell on the sex slave market in Libya and the ship sails tonight!"

Mark reached over and started unzipping one of the carryalls with the weapons in it. "I know where the ship is and you're right. We need to stop that before it happens."

Sarah came over and inventoried the arsenal. Arching an eyebrow and smiling in appreciation she commented to Mark, "I like the way you dress up for a date."

Mark smiled a lop-sided grin and handed her an Uzi and a bandoleer of 9MM ammunition. Sarah quickly field-stripped the Israeli submachine gun and reassembled it after checking the operation. Snapping a 30-round magazine into the mag. "Well", she cocked the weapon and announced, "Let's go!"

Thirty minutes later, Mark noticed that the moon had already set by the time they reached their destination. A moonless night sky made the darkness over the Houston Ship Channel more complete in the area of the Algerian-flagged Libyan ship.

CHAPTER SEVENTEEN

Mark watched as their shadows slid quietly from one dark area to another as they approached the ship. The creaking of the ropes and wood around the docks was loud tonight due to the rising breeze coming in off of the gulf. The humid air was alternately foul with rotting and fresh fish and fresh air from the open sea.

Mark held up his fist and everyone stopped in place and kneeled down. Mark tracked the dock's night watchman as he checked in at his third station exactly at 2 a.m. The watchman turned and surveyed the length of the dock. He then moved off up the ramp to the next dock. As he moved on Mark moved quickly across the dock to the side of the cargo ship and used hand signs to direct the others. Mark turned his attention to the rope hawser leading up to the ship. He examined it closely. It looked perfectly normal. But then, Lister had been taking no chances and even though he was probably a terrorist, he wasn't crazy.

Slipping a small electronic field sensor out of his pocket, Mark moved it close to the hawser. Careful not to touch it, he slowly moved the device around the bulk of the huge rope. As it passed the very bottom of the hawser, the sensor vibrated in his hand and a shrouded, pin-head, light-emitting diode lit up. There was a small current being drawn on the hawser from the dock to the ship. Any one even touching it would cause an alarm to sound on the ship, bringing the wrong type of attention to their entrance.

Abandoning the hawser, Mark moved to a point fifty feet back from the bow of the ship, where the curve of her bows was the greatest. The shadows that were Jack, Laura, and Sarah moved with him, being careful to stay in the darkest shadows offered on the dock. Each person was dressed in a black nylon body suit with a variety of pockets and implements hanging on them. Their faces were covered in battlefield cosmetics and blended into the darkness.

Laura felt thrilled and very silly at the same time. She looked at the dark visage of Sarah a few feet from her. That's pretty close to what she knew she looked like at the moment, a very spy-like, deadly image. She didn't feel very deadly at the moment. Her stomach was doing a flip-flop about the danger of getting caught, especially dressed like this and with all the weapons she had on her body. Her thoughts were a mixture of concerns for herself and for Jack. She knew that Sarah and Mark were in their element but she was just a housewife and her husband was really a displaced executive trying to emulate their companions. This was not what she was trained for nor expected either of them to be doing. As the concerns tightened her stomach, she thought she heard in her mind. *"You asked me if this was what you should do. I said yes. Be at peace daughter, I am with you."* Laura smiled in the darkness knowing no one could see it. A silent prayer of thanks met a peace that settled over her like a warm embrace. She was filled with confidence that she could do whatever it took to do God's work. She remembered hearing a saying, "Whatever God brings you to, He will see you through." She relaxed and watched Mark as he improvised a way onto the suspect ship.

Taking a small package out of his combat suit, Mark quickly assembled a miniature fiber/ceramic cross bow. Constructed of the latest space-age materials the little device was stronger than steel and only weighed one pound, five ounces. Cocking the crossbow, he brought out an equally small black quarrel. Fastening a four-armed, rubber-coated hook with an attached leader line to the quarrel he quickly loaded and aimed the crossbow almost directly straight up. Estimating the distance to the rail on the deck above him as forty feet, he adjusted the distance setting on the side of the crossbow. Looking through the sight on the crossbow he sighted on the rail high above him on the deck. Careful to hold the angle and range he pressed a small button on the side of the cross bow. A mechanical linkage inside the precision device was affected by the distance setting he had made, the angle of the crossbow, and the weight of the quarrel. This linkage adjusted the tension on the crossbow so that the quarrel would travel the right distance. Mark pulled the trigger and the quarrel, with its attached hook and line, silently shot up a couple feet higher than the rail.

Running out of momentum, the quarrel fell backward. Mark had aimed slightly over the rail toward the center of the ship. When the quarrel fell backward, two of the four rubber-coated hooks dropped slightly over the rail. All four raiders stood quietly holding their 9mm Berettas in a two-hand grip.

As instructed by Mark, Laura and Jack each held their pistols at full extension with its silencer aimed at the deck in the event someone had heard any noise. After a minute had gone by without an alarm, they holstered their guns and Mark began pulling the leader line through the hook suspended above him. Connected to the leader line was a light, black nylon climbing line. The climbing line snaked up the side of the ship, through a small pulley and back down as Mark continued to pull on the leader line. Checking his watch he found that he was right on time, collapsing the miniature crossbow he quickly put it away.

Careful not to let any of his equipment strike the ship, he began to pull himself up the double line, hand over hand as he walked up the hull. In addition to the silenced Beretta, Mark was carrying ten pounds of communication equipment, two hand grenades, and miscellaneous knives and garrotes. Some men would have had trouble climbing stairs with all that gear draped over their frame. Mark smoothly pulled the entire assembly including himself up the ropes to the deck of the cargo ship. He had been in intensive training over the last dozen years and wasn't even breathing hard when he reached the deck. Surveying the deck and surrounding superstructure before rising above the edge of the deck, he slid quietly over the rail and rolled onto the deck of the hard-site ship. Signaling the all clear, he stood watch as Jack easily pulled himself up the ropes to join Mark on the deck. Sarah was right behind him. Jack signaled to Laura and she tied the rope around her waist. Sarah kept watch as Jack and Mark pulled up on the ropes and Laura soft-shooed it up the side of the ship.

Suddenly Sarah raised her right arm with her hand in a fist. Everybody froze in position. His eyes searching, Mark found the reason as the dock guard walked quietly back down the dock. He would not be able to miss seeing Laura in just a minute. The position she was in had her standing out from the hull of the ship. If she moved closer to the hull he would see the movement even more quickly.

Jack carefully let go of the rope and moved back from the rail. He quickly slid Japanese "Shuriken" out of the pouch he had on his belt. He carefully aimed and threw the star with a forceful snap of his arm and wrist. The little star whirled out from the ship and down the dock behind the guard. It hit the wooden barrel that Jack was aiming for with a solid thud. The guard, hearing a noise behind him, reversed his direction and moved slowly down the dock away from Lister's ship.

Pulling mightily, the two men and Sarah quickly got Laura up to the deck, pulled the ropes in, and crouched low to the deck just before the alerted guard came back. After not finding anybody where he thought he heard a noise he was definitely on the alert. After he had passed on down the dock, the foursome coiled the ropes and Mark removed the hook from the rail and placed the whole thing in a shadow by the rail, just in case they needed it for a quick escape route.

Drawing their silenced Beretta 92Ss from their holsters, they padded across the deck and moved along the starboard side of the superstructure. Stopping every fourth step, they listened carefully for any sounds. Mark tensed, his combat sense flaring. He quickly dropped and rolled forward as a metal hook whistled through the space where his head had been a second before. Twisting around, he brought the Beretta into target acquisition. But, before he could squeeze off a three-shot burst, the metal hook caught the barrel of the pistol and wrenched it out of his hand.

Raising the hook over her head for a killing blow, the attacking woman was vulnerable to a rising roundhouse kick from Mark. The force of the kick slammed her up against the metal bulkhead of the ship with a meaty thud. The woman grunted as the air was knocked out of her lungs. She had dropped the hook when she was kicked. The heavily muscled woman shook her head, pulled in a big breath and started forward again. Jack stepped into the fray and delivered a devastating chest-high kick that slammed the woman completely off of her feet and head first into the metal bulkhead. Her body went limp and landed on the ship's deck with a loud thump. This time she didn't get up.

Sarah stepped forward with a combat knife in her left hand and reached for the woman's hair with her right. Her training did not encourage leaving live enemies behind her.

Jack stopped her with a hand on her knife hand. He shook his head and said, "Don't kill unless you have to." Sarah contemplated his interference for a few seconds and nodded. She then put the knife away, went to the rail and got a life vest and walked over to the unconscious woman. Squatting, she tied the vest onto the lax body. Sarah then did a dead man lift with the woman's body and before anyone could stop her, she dropped the woman over the side of the rail into the water. As she walked by Jack, she whispered, "There, I didn't kill her, satisfied?"

Jack looked over the rail and saw the woman's head above water, floating away from the ship and under the dock. Shaking his head he joined the rest of the group as they continued to search for the children Ike Morris' notes said would be somewhere on this ship.

They heard footsteps coming from the aft end of the ship. Spreading out they hid behind anything they were near. For Laura and Jack it was a bulkhead riser. Sarah and Mark disappeared into the shadows near the corner of the bulkhead. A large young man came around the corner in a relaxed attitude. Suddenly he stopped. Even in the dim light he could see that the woman guard was missing. As he reached for his assault rifle, a powerful arm closed off his windpipe in a solid choke hold. Even though he tried to fight, darkness came swiftly. Mark laid the unconscious man on the deck and secured his hands and legs with plastic riot cuffs. He then taped his mouth shut with a piece of duct tape. Looking at Sarah he asked her, "Is this good enough or do you want to throw him off the ship too?"

Sarah smiled and checked the bonds. Nodding she said "yes, he needs to be removed from our business, but I won't this time. He'll stay here and not bother us." Then she led the little group further aft on the starboard side.

Carefully looking around the next corner, they found four more men lounging against the hatches to the middle holds of the ship. The taller of the two men was Mark's height and probably didn't weigh much less. Even though his back was toward Mark, something, perhaps a shuffle of a foot or other small noise, alerted the tall man to the approaching danger. Stepping suddenly to his left, he opened the distance between himself and the group of raiders. These mercenaries were professionals, not easily fooled street punks.

At that point, an almost silent brawl broke out between the four crewmen and the raiders. Laura was the most out-classed fighter on the deck. Her partner for the dance closed quickly with her and threw a right-hand roundhouse punch that would have broken her jaw if it had connected.

Using the training that Jack had been drilling into her, Laura ducked under the punch and shoved the stun gun against the man's belly. Triggering the 50,000-volt device caused the man to freeze and suddenly collapse. Laura said, "Score one for technology!" as she put the stun gun in its holster and used plastic cuffs and tape to secure the man's hands, feet, and mouth.

Tracking the tall man, Mark threw a steel ball bearing the size of a golf ball at the man's head that caught him moving forward. The ball hit him directly on the forehead and knocked him out cold. Most of the sounds of the one-sided battle were covered by the near-by blare of a ship's horn as it maneuvered through the ship channel.

The two other mercs split apart and attempted to bracket Jack and Sarah. Jack threw himself forward and down and did a quick sweep with his legs to catch the merc just above the ankles and dump him onto the steel deck. But the soldier of fortune jumped up and avoided Jack's sweep. As he dropped back down he snapped a front kick that caught Jack in the stomach and knocked the wind out of him. Knowing what was coming next, Jack threw himself down and to his left while he tried to get his breath back. The spinning heel kick that would have ended the fight for Jack whistled past his head. The merc straightened up and came at Jack again.

Still hampered by the kick, Jack tried to react fast enough to block the furious assault by the heavier man. Blocking a right-hand roundhouse punch brought the two men together face-to-face. Jack was almost gagged by the stench of the mercenary's breath.

The merc got in a punch to the ribs and a partially blocked palm heel strike to the side of Jack's head. The mercenary started to capitalize on the advantage he had due to the beating he had already given Jack. This fight became a pivotal point in Jack's transition from Dojo player to real combatant. Dazed, winded, and matched in ferocity he came to the point of realizing this was not a competition but a life or death struggle. The mercenary would surely kill him if he dominated the fight. The pain throughout his body was trying to make him quit, which would be fatal. In his extremity he called on the Lord for strength and control. Interestingly he did not ask God to let him win, just for the ability to continue the struggle.

The mercenary threw a haymaker left that shot over Jack's head as he ducked away from the punch to his left. The separation gave Jack a precious few seconds to recover his breath and his control. The merc charged back at him and tried a front snap kick, which left him on one leg. Blocking the kick past him with his left arm, Jack drove a straight-fingered shuto strike to the man's throat. He had practiced this strike for so long his fingers were like a solid piece of metal. He felt the larynx collapse and the merc threw both of his hands up to his throat to try to clear the obstruction. Jack spun around to his right and snapped a full-power, right-handed back-fist to the left temple of the struggling man. The thin tissue of the skull at that point collapsed and the mercenary was dead as he fell to the deck. He just didn't know it yet. Jack sagged against a cabin wall and looked around him.

The last merc slid over the hatch he had been in front of and dropped out of sight. Not physically capable of chasing him, Jack could only watch. Then he saw a really strange sight. The merc suddenly stood up and slammed his face into the hatch cover directly in front of him. Jack thought that this was a really odd thing for anyone to do. He understood when Sarah stepped out from behind the hatch.

They all stood still and listened to the ship around them. Quiet had returned to the area and the muted thumps, chugs, and thwacks made by the dispatching of the mercs had not raised any alarm as yet. Tying up the two men that had been disabled took only a few seconds. Sarah came to the man Jack had been fighting and knew from the open-eyed face that he was dead.

She looked up at Jack with compassion, knowing that this was probably the first person he had ever killed with his bare hands. Jack looked back at her and smiled through his pain. He whispered, "I guess you don't have to throw that one overboard."

Laura and Mark came over and Mark checked Jack's injuries. Not finding anything worse than possible bruised ribs and some facial contusions, they waited several minutes until Jack was up to continuing. Running lightly to the next passageway, the little group one-by-one turned right and moved into the center of the ship. Exploring passageway after passageway they found no more of Lister's people. No alarm had been raised so far and Mark was sure he knew why. The crew was probably under orders not to create any fuss while they were in port that could bring the authorities on board. That would account for the woman's silent attack on Mark rather than just shooting him in the back. It also explained why most of the other mercs didn't have rifles. Mark smiled at the crew's need for silence complemented the speed and completeness of the raider's strike.

Dropping down a level, they struck pay dirt when they found the holds reconditioned to carry patients like that of a hospital ship. Ten girls and six boys, ranging in age from ten to sixteen, were strapped into the bunks and had gags taped to their mouths. For some reason, the crew hadn't sedated them with drugs. Mark could see panic or resignation in the eyes of each child depending mostly on their age. The younger kids didn't understand the fate they faced as well as the older ones. Sarah and Laura quietly and quickly moved from bunk to bunk, removing the kid's bindings, and taking the gags out of their mouths. Cautioning each one to be very quiet, they hugged each one and gathered them all at the hatch to the upper deck while Jack and Mark stood guard.

Released from captivity the children were very willing to do as their rescuers told them. Mark and Jack went out and checked the deck between them and the gangplank. It was empty. They returned to the middle deck and the children. While Mark was helping the children across the deck, he noticed a porthole aglow toward the bow on the port side of the ship.

Hearing voices near the source of the light, he moved toward the portal. According to Sarah's Intel, there should be at least ten people on the ship. So far they had only found six.

Slowly moving to the side of the porthole he peeked inside. Four of the crew were playing cards. On a bunk on the far side of the cabin, the remaining mercenary was sitting on the bunk next to a young girl who was tied to the bunk hand and foot.

Most of these guards had pistols and two Kalashnikov AKS-74Us leaned against one wall. Checking the time, Mark motioned for Laura to join him. After estimating the odds, Mark decided that they only had time for a direct frontal assault. Sliding the Beretta out of his holster he huddled with the others. Mark made assignments based on the situation. Laura and Jack were to escort the kids off the ship and out of sight if possible. He and Sarah were going to rescue the girl in the cabin and then join them.

Jack, Laura, and the kids moved off in a silent rush. Mark waited until they were on the downward gangplank before he turned to Sarah. "I know that the quickest way would be to waste the human garbage in the cabin, but I have learned through bitter experience that unless God Himself tells me to do it, I should only kill as a last resort or in true self defense. Do you understand what I mean?" He wasn't sure that the Israeli agent had the same compunctions he did.

Sarah sighed, "Yes, Mark, I know what you mean. I actually agree with you. I'm just not sure we have that liberty in this case."

Mark thought for a second. "Look, there is no other way out of that cabin other than the one door. If we can get the drop on those guys and get the girl out of there, then we could seal them in while we escape."

"How do you plan to seal them into the cabin?"

Mark pointed at the small chain hanging near the door from a divot. Sarah smiled and with a wry look said, "Okay, you second, me first."

Mark didn't play the male hero, he'd seen how this lady fought and he was just as confident in her ability as he was in his. They moved to the sides of the door and risked a second peek to make sure nothing had changed. It hadn't as yet. Turning the handle slowly they inched the door open. Taking a deep breath Mark yanked the door open and followed Sarah into the hot, stinky cabin. As Sarah moved toward the man and child, Mark aimed his pistol at the people at the card game. To show that he meant business, he triggered a silenced shot that blew up the vodka bottle on the card table.

The players raised their hands to ward off the flying glass and vodka. Mark told them "Keep them high if you don't want to die." The silly thought went through his head that he had made a dumb rhyme while staring down four armed sailors. No one made a move. It was obvious that he meant what he said.

Sarah had her pistol pointed at the man on the bunk and saw him start to grab the girl and pull a knife out of the pocket of his pants at the same time. She calmly shot him through the left hand, knife and all. His scream made everything tense but the little drama didn't fall apart, yet.

Sarah walked over and carefully picked the damaged knife up off the floor. Using it to cut the young girl loose she suddenly slammed it into the mattress between the man's legs, very close to him. Even with the pain of his hand, his eyes grew very large and he forgot how to breathe for a few seconds.

Sarah pulled the girl with her and backed out onto the deck through the doorway. Telling her to stand still, Sarah grabbed the light chain and was ready when Mark backed out the door and slammed it. She quickly wound the chain around the handle and stretched it tight, locking it over a pin on the rail. They quickly drew the girl away from the cabin in the event the men inside started trying to shoot out the porthole.

Not knowing what shape she was in and not having the time to check, Mark pulled the girl up from the deck and over his shoulder as they ran away from the cabin. Jumping down the stairs he headed for the gangplank. The girl, hanging over his left shoulder and facing backward, screamed. Mark dodged to his right, into a passageway as Sarah went the other direction.

Unsilenced AKS' spit Russian-made 7.45mm bullets through the space they had just occupied. Looking aft, Mark saw four men that the intelligence information must have missed, running toward them. Using his free hand he pulled his pistol and sent several shots their direction. The silenced rounds didn't make a dent in the roar of the AK-47s but one man took a round in the chest and flipped over backward to the deck. The other three men took shelter behind a ventilator and continued to shoot at the black-suited intruders and the girl. Mark realized they didn't care how much noise they made. Startled from their sleep, dozens of gulls took wing from the masts of the ship, screaming their displeasure at the din. In the early morning lull, the noise of the full auto fire was ear-splitting.

Pulling a grenade from his belt Mark arched it over the deck so that it came down behind the men. The grenade exploded and drove all three men to the deck in an attempt to avoid the shrapnel. None was seriously injured but all three had lost their hearing and had small cuts.

As Mark and Sarah ran with the girl to the head of the gangplank, one of the three remaining guards grabbed a grenade of his own and pulled the pin. As his arm went back for the throw, one of the other men spun around, to run to the rail to shoot at the invaders. As he turned, the front sights on the barrel of his AK-47 struck the man with the grenade in the face. The grenade holder staggered backward and dropped the grenade and put his hands to his face. The grenade fell down the hatchway directly behind them. The grenade took a crazy bounce down the aisle and fell through a second hatch down into the engine room.

While the three men squabbled amongst themselves, Mark and Sarah finished running down the gangplank to the dock. Mark was carrying the young girl. The grenade bounced under the primary fuel feed for the engines and exploded. The fuel cooked off and blew the entire back end of the ship out of the water with huge gouts of flame and noise.

Mark saw the watchman who had been running to see what was causing the gunfire and explosions. He was only eighty yards from the ship when the explosion happened. Mark knew he couldn't believe his eyes as the whole 38,000 ton freighter rose up above the dock stern first. Then the blast caught him and hurled him into the air. He came down in the channel in time to be slammed around by the miniature tidal wave generated in the ship channel by the explosion. Doggedly he swam back to the dock.

The roar went beyond hearing and tremendous sheets of flame shot straight up from the deck into the sky. Knocked off of his feet by the explosion, Mark managed to get his body under that of his charge and cushion the girl from hitting the dock. Sarah did a tuck and roll, and escaped damage by ducking behind a large crane on the dock. When the ship slammed back into the water it had more holes in it than a pegboard.

Mark could see where the three men had been was only a gaping hole and roaring flames. Turning to run he saw the unconscious woman in the life vest as she was lifted up by the wave and dumped on the stern deck of a harbor tug.

Mark noticed people were just starting to arrive at the dock in response to the gunfire and now, from the explosion. One of the first on the scene was a Houston Police Officer. Taking one look at the black-suited man coming down the dock covered with weapons and holding a young girl in his arms, the cop reached for his revolver.

Suddenly, secondary explosions racked the wrecked ship. The explosions threw debris and flaming oil over the dock near the ship. A large quantity of ammunition started cooking off and rounds were going in every direction.

Mark yelled at the officer. "FBI, get your squad car back to the entrance of the dock and don't let anyone down here who isn't with the fire department, police, or the FBI!"

The young officer was not convinced yet. Mark glowered at him. "This is a federal case Sonny. If you don't want to be walking a beat on Montrose Boulevard by next week, you'd better move it!"

That did it. Nobody except a federal officer would use that type of threat on a local police officer. He ran to his car and backed up the dock to the entrance. Watching him go, Mark was glad he'd read up on Houston before this little exercise.

Seeing Jack waving to him from the other side of the dock away from the furiously burning ship, Mark ran over and down a flight of stairs. Sarah came charging down the stairs right behind him. Jack had scrounged along the small floating dock and found an inter ship shuttle that was big enough for all of them. Mark hopped in, followed closely by Jack, Laura, Sarah, and all the other kids. Putting the girl into Laura's hands, Mark hot-wired the ignition, Sarah let go the mooring lines, and Jack handled the helm as they pulled out between two berthed freighters and away from the doomed freighter and the burning dock.

The activity at the dock was frantic as many other ships were trying to get underway to escape the fire, the fire department was trying to get at the burning wreck, and everybody screaming to get someone else's attention. Mark looked back and saw ten or so crew members jumping over the front bows of the burning ship into the channel. Just then the first of the news helicopters arrived on the scene.

Still being wracked by internal explosions and tied to the dock, the cargo ship settled to the bottom of the ship channel tearing out the moorings as it went.

CHAPTER EIGHTEEN

Mark and Sarah took the children into the Israeli Consulate. They could not take them to the police or the FBI because they didn't want to be detained while the local forces sorted everything out. Max Lister would not be waiting around while they explained everything to everybody over and over again.

The Consulate personnel made the kids comfortable and let Sarah use a secure communications channel to talk to her superiors in Israel. After a quick debriefing Sarah was frowning when she came out to where Mark was waiting. After she confided in him the information about Lister and the military armory in south Houston that she had just learned, Mark asked for and was allowed to use an untraceable line to contact the FBI and the Navy. When he was done, he grabbed Sarah's arm and quietly said, "Let's go!" They left the children at the Consulate to be turned over to the U.S. government tomorrow.

Jack and Laura changed clothes and went to an older downtown hotel to get some rest because they didn't want to return to their rooms in southeast Houston in the event the room had been somehow compromised. While Laura tried to get to sleep, Jack checked the windows and doors and just to be on the safe side, he wired a flash-bang grenade to the door handle of the room the way Mark had shown them. If anyone forced their way into the room, the mono-filament wire on the door handle would pull the pin and release the 'spoon' on the grenade.

Jack used Mark's phone cutouts to place an emergency call to FBI agent, Gary Rhodes, who was in Washington, D.C. When the connection was finally made Gary was almost beside himself with the urgency to talk to him. "Jack! Both of you have got to get out of that hotel and out of Houston if possible. We just got a call from an informant in the Houston riot probe. In the last thirty minutes someone in Max Lister's organization has stirred up an ugly mob and given the leaders descriptions of all four of you and the location of the hotel you're at right now. They could be there in any moment. Get this! Most of the people in that mob are simply dissatisfied citizens who think that you guys are of the main leaders in a movement to commit genocide on the Black and Hispanic races in Houston. They are confused and acting illegally, but they aren't your enemy. You understand?

The frown had continued to deepen on Jack's face as the federal agent had talked. How had Lister gotten to them so quick? They probably were tailed from the raid on the freighter. That would account for the quick response and identification. But, how does a civil rights riot tie into Lister and his obviously malevolent aims? Jack and Laura couldn't fight the mob that was coming for them because they really weren't the enemy. All this raced through his mind while he listened to Agent Rhodes. Moving to the window he looked out. There already were quite a few people milling around outside the building. They definitely didn't look like an early morning Houston work crew. But nothing indicated that the attack was underway as yet. Jack gave Agent Rhodes a question of his own. "Where is Mark Connelly?"

Gary thought for a second. "He knows about the attack on the armory and he's trying to get help from the military to protect you. Can you and Laura get out of the hotel quickly?"

Jack smiled at that. "Sure, what choice do we have?" He thought "None, but, we have lots of it." Hanging up, the young husband went into the bedroom to wake Laura. Hearing the spoon fly off the grenade at the door he spun toward the door to the living room. Three men in black body suits and ski masks were rushing through the door brandishing silenced pistols. Even though they were professional in their actions, they still had to acclimatize their eyes from the bright hall to the dark room. Before they could find their target in the dark room Jack dove behind the couch and rolled to the other end where he tried to become part of the carpet.

The flash-bang went off right at the front side of the couch. Jack had his hands over his ears and his mouth open to equalize the pressure from the explosion. The force of the explosion still slammed the couch against him and blasted all the glass out of the windows in the room. Since he was ready for it the blast did not disable him and he jumped to his feet to counterattack the gunmen. As he stood up he realized that he had lost his pistol in the explosion.

None of the attackers had seen the grenade, nor had they expected it. Caught unaware, they suffered greatly due to their proximity to the blast. Unarmed, Jack didn't let it slow him down. He charged into the men and disarmed the first man and then hit him across the left temple with a Shuto strike. This helped relieve the man's pain by making him unconscious. Jack then spun to his right and delivered a strong cross-body heel kick to the chest of the second man. This caused the man to stop trying to stem the blood flowing out of his ears and nose and casually fly into the nearest wall with enough momentum to knock him out by smashing the back of his head against the wall.

The third man got off ten shots by aiming at the blur that he thought was Jack in his almost totally blinded eyes. Two shots struck the upright, unconscious attacker in the head. Jack knocked the gun from the shooter's hand and drove an elbow strike into his solar plexus that knocked the wind out of the man. Turning, Jack chopped the edges of both hands against the sides of the man's throat. The simultaneously heavy blows on both sides forced the arteries running up both sides of the neck to collapse momentarily, cutting off blood to the brain. At the same time the blows hit the Vega nerves under the arteries. The combined shocks drove the man's brain into a complete shutdown and he fell unconscious to the carpet.

With parts of the wall paper torn off the walls by the explosion floating down on fire through the air Jack stopped to evaluate the situation. The first thing he had to do was beat out the fire on the front of the couch that the grenade started. He could hear people in the hall trying to get up the nerve to look into his room.

Squatting next to the fallen man Jack quickly confirmed the fatal condition of the assassin who had been shot twice by his buddy. Concerned about the tracks of those bullets Jack hurried into the bedroom with a fear in his heart. The other eight bullets had punched their way into the bedroom from the third man's gun. Some of the bullets had been on the level of the bed that Laura was in when the attack occurred.

"Laura?" Jack whispered.

"Jack?" came from a shaky whisper in answer. Laura climbed out from under the bed and stared wide-eyed at what she could see of the carnage in the other room. The flash-bang grenade explosion had caused her to instinctively roll off the bed and onto the floor. She was learning combat. Of course, the fact that the explosion had pretty much blown her out of the bed didn't hurt her time-to-the-floor speed. Jack moved to block her view of the dead man. His wife had seen enough in this situation without seeing dead people every time she turned around. Jack stepped over next to the bed and opened the door on their side of the adjoining room. He then did a spinning heel kick against the door from the adjoining room. The door flew open with its lock scattering over the carpet. Jack quickly scanned the hotel room and found it empty. Grabbing their few belongings, he led Laura through the anteroom door and to the door of that room which led to the hall away from the crowd gathered in front of their room.

Another explosion suddenly rocked the old building to its very core. The people in the hall started yelling and screaming. The smell of cordite and smoke started wafting up the stairwell as Jack and Laura hit the stairs to the roof three at a time. Their fight wasn't with the idiots attacking the building but with the man that sent the killers after them. Jack felt the anger build within him. Jesus would judge Lister's actions with the children, but that was after he died and met God. Jack felt that their job was to expeditiously arrange that meeting.

As they climbed the stairs, Jack recalled the Bible passage about children that haunted him when he thought of what Max Lister was doing to them. It was Mark 9:42 *"And if anyone causes one of these little ones who believe in me to sin, it would be better for him to be thrown into the sea with a large millstone tied around his neck."* Lister's meeting with God would not be a good one for him.

Reaching the roof, Jack motioned Laura to stay on the steps while he slid the door open a crack and scanned the roof. It was deserted. The mob hadn't expected him to go up because the building was four stories above the next closest building. There was nowhere to go. Scanning the skies, Jack began to think that they were probably right. With nowhere to go he scanned the horizon praying for a solution. "Dear Jesus, I thank you for all the things you do for us every day. You know the evil we are faced with and the desperate situation my wife and I are in. Please show us the way to serve you. We are . . ."

Suddenly something moved across the stars toward them. Drawing the pistol he had recovered, he snap-aiming at the movement Jack felt a little foolish when he was able to make out the shape of a rope ladder dangling down from the skies. Thinking that the Lord sometimes works in strange ways he reached for the ladder. As the ladder came to rest next to him, he helped Laura grab the rungs. As she and the ladder were starting to ascend, he jumped to the second rung of the ladder and felt himself being drawn upward into the night. As they drew away from the roof of the hotel, Jack prayed again. "Thank you Lord Jesus! It is in your name I pray all things."

Below he could see flames coming out of most of the first three floors of the old building. Hoping that the other residents had gotten out of the way of the flames he looked outward. He watched other buildings and towering smokestacks rush by in the night. They were still lower than the tops of a whole lot of things. He checked on Laura and saw her clutching the ladder in a very determined manner.

Looking up, he could see the almost invisible belly of a helicopter thirty feet above him in the dark sky. It was very hard to see and it was also very silent as far as rotor and motor noise were concerned. There was no reflected light from the body and the customary whop-whop of the rotors was missing altogether. As they were drawn up closer to the bottom of the helicopter Jack could see racks of missiles and the two ugly snouts of Vulcan cannons under the front of the cockpit. This was a military chopper and loaded for bear. Jack knew then that the pilot was flying the helicopter using night goggles that amplified light sufficiently so that no spotlights or other exposing light was necessary for him to see.

The ladder continued to be drawn upward by the winch until Laura was just below the level of the cargo bay behind the pilot. Two arms reached out of the bay and grabbed Laura by her arms and lifted her into the cargo bay. Jack drew himself up and in turn was helped into the compartment. A curtain of soft black material covered the hatch. One of two men who had helped them pulled the ladder up and stored it in a net next to the hatch. The hatch was closed and locked. Then a red "ready light" lit the area. Jack wasn't surprised to see Mark Connelly dressed in a U.S. Navy Seal combat night suit and heavily armed. The other man pulled the dark hood off of his head and turned out to be none other than Sarah Cohen. Mark squatted on his heels and offered his hand to his friend. "I'm so glad you could make It." he said with a lopsided grin.

Jack shook Mark's hand while he kept his left arm around Laura. He relaxed with his back against the bulkhead and smiled. "You two look like you're going to war." he said.

"Yes, we were," Mark replied with a tight smile. "If you weren't on the roof, we were going to go down it to find you regardless how many people we had to wade through. We don't leave anyone behind." Sarah smiled and nodded her agreement.

Nodding to them both, Jack smiled, "I couldn't have asked for a better rescue either." Jack meant ever word of that statement. There wasn't a better team he knew of to come to his rescue. If Mark and Sarah had set out to find and rescue him and Laura, they would have done the job or died trying. Jack also knew that neither Mark nor Sarah would die easily or unnecessarily. "Mark, Sarah, will you two look after Laura for a minute?"

Mark nodded. Sarah got a blanket out of a compartment and offered it to Laura to ward off the chill as the helicopter raced through the night air. Jack moved up to the hatch into the pilot's compartment and slid through. He was a bit surprised to see the pilot was a U. S. Air Force Major. This particular Major was the same Mike White who had flown them into Israel, and he was flying at tree top level and avoiding low flying aircraft, police helicopters, tall buildings, and water towers.

At the same time he was talking on two different radios and bringing the people on the other ends of those secure radio frequencies up to date. In the midst of all this activity he was still able to nod at the young green-eyed man he had just plucked off the roof of a burning hotel. His nodding was a feat not diminished in the least by the fact that he was wearing a pair of night goggles and applying body language to his flying.

After a while he switched on the marker lights on the aircraft, grabbed some altitude and things settled down. Major White removed the goggles and shook hands with Jack. Jack smiled as he shook the pilot's hand. He turned and sat down in the second pilot's seat and put on the headset he found there. Jack began looking for a mike button or something to activate the intercom feature. The Major showed him which switch to use. Keying the intercom button Jack said, "You sure dropped in at the most convenient time."

Shrugging his shoulders, the Major said, "Ah, Why not? I was just passing through the neighborhood and it looked like you could use a lift."

Looking around the space-age cockpit of the advanced helicopter Jack asked, "Did you also just happen to have this little buggy at hand or did you special order it?"

The Major rubbed his hand on the weapons console and smiled. "She is a beauty, isn't she? I was allowed to take it for a test spin since Mark was there. The lady General in charge of the base obviously thinks a great deal of Mark. I also have some very unofficial contacts with the alphabet agencies, you know, the FBI, CIA, and NSA that are very interested in all four of you. It seems that a high official in the government wants you taken care of and he's insisting on constant input as to your progress. The way I hear it, that's the highest level."

Jack grinned and told the Major a fact he already knew. "A lot of people think a great deal of Mark."

CHAPTER NINETEEN

As the helicopter settled to the tarmac at Ellington Air Force Base, south-southeast of Houston, Mark talked to Major White and then hopped out onto the runway next to Jack as Sarah and Laura were bringing each other up to date.

Mark looked evenly at Jack. "I know that you two just went through a real meat grinder back there but there is a great deal more that needs to be done right now. Are you guys' game?"

Jack had been amazed at his wife's resiliency in the decidedly abnormal lifestyle they had been thrown into recently. He found that he needed higher advice than his own with this decision and had already been praying to Jesus about this. He felt the answer was; they could, they should, and they would. He told Mark as much.

Mark smiled an extremely grim smile. All right! They were moved aside as two crews hustled to refuel the chopper. After moving to safer ground, Mark continued. "We finally got a break and a jump on Max Lister!" It was hard to hear as a pair of F-16 Fighters engaged their afterburners and roared down the runway and into the air. "The kids were able to tell us about the secret operations at the Children's Ranch. We need to set up a raid for about two a.m.! It will take coordinating the police, the FBI, and the military that are going to participate in the raid. The President himself is flying in here but has asked us to run the raid! I want you, Sarah, and Laura to take charge and organize it." Mark had to smile inwardly to himself as he watched Jack's face as he came to grips with the responsibility involved.

Jack thought of many things in just a few seconds but his first question to Mark was the obvious one. "Why are you not running this show?"

Mark shook his head and started to check the guns and other things strapped on his body and tilted his head at the helicopter. "We've got to head off the major riot that Lister has been brewing for the last couple of years. He's all set to initiate it in about thirty minutes if we can't derail it!" He waved at Jack and ran back to the helicopter that had been refueled and was already powered up again.

The silence of the liftoff still surprised Jack. The chopper was quickly lost in the night sky. Jack turned to the women and explained their priorities as spelled out by Mark. They hurried to a waiting Humvee and headed for a hanger that would be the first-stage headquarters for the ranch raid.

Pulling into the hanger in the Humvee they sped over to a group of men standing by several tables. Other men were spreading out maps and drawings on the tables and preparing a large communications linkup. In the background there were various groups of police, military, and oddly enough, several men in western wear.

As Sarah, Laura, and Jack piled out of the vehicle, several men walked quickly over to them. One was a U.S. Army Major and the other three were dressed in civilian clothes. Jack had just about straightened up when all four men started to talk at once. Listening to the babble for several seconds Jack held up his hands and brought everyone to silence. He pointed at the Major. "Who are you and what is the problem?" When the three civilians started to protest, Jack again held up his hand and glared at them. "Quiet, one at a time. You each will get your turn. Major!"

The Major glared at the three civilians and turned to Jack. "I'm Major John Wolfman, Mr. Malone. I am in charge of the U.S. Army Special Forces detachment that is to assist you in this raid." He glanced at the other men. There seems to be a jurisdictional dispute as to who is running this show."

Jack pointed at the next man, a tall black man with a steady stare and a look of self-control. He was blunt as well as tall. "I'm agent Roger Tasker of the Federal Bureau of Investigation and I understand that we are also to work this raid. As of twenty minutes ago a federal court indicted this man Lister as a federal fugitive. That makes this a federal case! End of story gentlemen."

Jack nodded and pointed at the next man, a large man with a weathered face and a decidedly western getup. He also stared directly into Jack's eyes. "Ranger Harvey Pultis of the Texas Rangers. The ranch involved is in our jurisdiction and we are not pleased with a military or federal raid in Texas."

Jack pointed at the last man. He just shook his head and held out his hand. "I'm Ben Williamson of the Park County Sheriff's Department and I'm obviously way outgunned here." He stepped back.

Jack started to say something and Roger Tasker spoke up. "Just who are you and what experience do you have that gives you the authority to risk my men's lives?"

Jack looked at the FBI man for a second. "I assure you gentlemen that I am relying on you all for advice since I am far less experienced than any of you. . ." At that the FBI agent threw his hands up in the air and said, "Great! That's all we ne..."

"MR. TASKER!" Jack's voice was ice cold and sliced through the FBI agent's complaint like a blade of hot steel through whipped cream. The agent stopped in mid-whine and glared at him. Jack continued, "As I said, I expect to rely on your advice. I did not open the floor to any personal opinions or derisive comments! Now! All of you hear this!"

Jack could stand up to any man in personal combat. So, if they took personal umbrage or wanted to settle it one-on-one he wasn't worried. This gave him a necessary freedom when it came to heated discussions. As the owner and manager of his own company he had developed the aura of leadership and the ability to project that aura. He also wasn't concerned about hurt feelings when more than a hundred children were at stake. As he talked he stared at each man in turn.

"The President of the United States of America personally put me in charge of this operation. If you don't like it, take your complaint to him or wait a few hours and tell him in person that you didn't agree with his decision! As long as I am in charge you will whole-heartedly cooperate with me and everyone else involved or pack-it up right now and get out of here! We don't need this kind of confusion! There are literally more than one hundred children's lives at stake at this ranch. We have less than three hours to plan it, approve it, and be ready to launch it! There is no room for ego-trips, personal agendas, or team politics! I hope I am perfectly clear because there are no second chances from this point on! Now, who wants to participate and who wants to go home?"

After that each man contributed what he thought that their team could do and what they personally thought should be done overall. Personalities were put aside for the moment and the raid took the importance. Jack settled any disagreements.

After considering all the inputs, Jack broke the raid down into four elements. The actual tactical elimination of the security perimeter and external guards would be by the military Special Forces. The Sheriff's department and the FBI personnel were to round up and secure the children since they had the most experience and were most likely to be accepted by the younger children.

There were only three Texas Rangers. (Harvey Pultis did mention that they had probably brought two too many using their philosophy of "One riot, one Ranger"). So, Jack decided the actual assault on the hidden and fortified "holding area." Included would be Ranger Pultis, a six-man elite squad of the Special Forces, Major Wolfman, Roger Tasker, Ben Williamson, Jack himself and one of his team. When some quick looks were exchanged between the FBI agent and the Sheriff's Deputy, Jack reminded them that a good leader leads from the front, not the rear. Major Wolfman nodded at him, winked and headed back to his men to make assignments.

Harvey Pultis ambled over to Jack as everyone left to prepare and asked him in a whisper, "Are one of those pretty team members of yours really going in there with us?" He was looking at Laura and Sarah.

Jack smiled and called the ladies over. He introduced them to the Ranger Pultis who was very gallant and courteous. Then Jack gave them their assignments. "Laura, you've got mobile communications like you had on the last raid. Get them straightened out quickly." At this, the left eyebrow on the Ranger went up a notch. Jack turned to Sarah, "You're in charge of the six-man Special Forces team. You need to communicate that to Major Wolfman and to the team members." Jack's look suggested that she needed to establish her authority quickly and decisively. Sarah smiled and headed over to the army group. The left eyebrow on the Ranger went up two notches at that.

Jack turned to the Ranger and said, "Hit me." Both eyebrows went right to the top of his face at that! Harvey looked at Jack and said, "What?"

Jack stood there and said, "Hit me!" The Ranger lowered both eyebrows and squared himself up with the taller but lighter man. He faked a left cross and snapped a quick punch to the ribs with his right fist. He was very fast.

Jack sidestepped the punch to his body with ease and stepped behind the Ranger. Harvey spun around and executed a credible front snap kick with his snakeskin cowboy boots.

Unfortunately his target wasn't there. Jack sidestepped the kick and closed with the Ranger. Reaching out with his left hand Jack pulled the eight-inch hunting knife out of the Ranger's side sheath and in a blur brought it up to the Ranger's throat.

Time froze. Jack smiled at Ranger Pultis and stepped back and inverted the knife and handed it butt first to the baffled lawman. "I just wanted to make a point with you that everyone on my team can handle themselves."

The grim line of the Ranger's mouth softened and he re-sheathed his knife. "I guess you can at that."

While Jack and the Ranger were getting their priorities straightened out, Sarah walked up to the Major and explained what Jack wanted her to do. The Major didn't like the idea of his men being led by a non-military type, but had decided that the people on Jack's team deserved to be taken seriously. He candidly remarked to the smaller woman, "I can order the men to follow your orders, but I'm not sure they will think well of it."

Sarah looked at the Major for several seconds. "Pick your best man and have him drop his gear. I'll see if I can't convince you that they should listen to me." She smiled as she said this. The Major didn't look too convinced. So she sweetly added, "Don't worry, I won't hurt him." That was a challenge that a male ego could not let pass.

The Major nodded and called over a young solid-looking Sergeant. "Sergeant Kelly, this 'lady' here wants to go through a few falls with you. No weapons, just unarmed skill. She says that she won't hurt you." Even though the Major delivered it deadpan, there were some snorts and muffled laughter from the other men. The Sergeant looked over at Sarah who had taken off her jacket and stood loose limbed in a cotton sweater and loose pants with soft-looking black boots. Sergeant Kelly just dropped his gear and shrugged out of his camo jacket. He was a real specimen of the finely tuned Special Forces personnel. The rest of the army unit formed a large circle around the two of them.

He didn't say a word but slid up quickly to Sarah and feinted like he was going to grab her around the waist and throw her to the floor. Instead he dropped to the floor and swung a quick left-leg sweep which should have knocked her feet out from under her. Sarah watched the maneuver proceed and automatically went into the counter for this type of tactic. She flipped herself backward and landed on her feet behind the sweeping leg. She executed a quick snap kick to the muscles in the front of the leg that was on the floor and stepped back. The Sergeant took the kick without much notice and rose to his feet. It still looked like a major mismatch between the beefy, rock-solid American soldier and the slim Mossad woman but Sgt. Kelly approached her with a new sense of wariness. She wasn't the easy job she looked like.

As he approached this time he adopted the wide stance of a wrestler yet kept his hands one behind the other in a karate position. Sarah knew this trick also. She had spent several months in the Mossad's physical combat boot camp and advanced hand-to-hand combat courses and had worked many times with men bigger and faster and even sneakier than Sergeant Kelly, many, many, times. She knew she had to resolve this challenge quickly because of the urgency of the crisis. She also knew that the man would not respond to any female charms or cut her any slack because she was smaller and female. At least she didn't feel like he hated her and things like that. Making her decision, she acted on it. As the Sergeant feinted with his left hand, she acted like she was going to drop to the floor and take a shot at his groin with a foot.

Sergeant Kelly immediately dropped his right fist into a defensive position in front of his groin which was what she knew he would do. Her apparent fall to the floor was stopped by her right leg while her left leg shot through the gap where the Sergeant's right hand had been and the solid leather heel on the soft-looking boot on her left foot connected solidly with the man's jaw on the right side. There was a collective gasp from the soldiers surrounding the couple.

Sergeant Kelly went backward, propelled by the kick and fell to one knee. He was about to roar back into the fight when he realized that the woman had not stopped where she was after she kicked him. She was right behind him and had an extremely tight hold on the front of his throat with her right hand and a solid block on the back of his head with her left arm. He started to do a forward roll to shake her off when he heard a very pleasant voice say, "I wouldn't do that if I were you." While he knew he had the strength to break out of the hold, something intuitive in the situation made him freeze.

He could feel the contours of the woman against his back, and he then heard softly in his right ear. "The muscles in your neck are too strong for a mere woman like me to break. But...my hands and fingernails are more than strong enough for me to rip out your throat if you continue this battle."

Sergeant Kelly wisely patted the floor three times. Sarah was glad that he stopped fighting because she'd had to eliminate one enemy soldier with that technique and wouldn't have really done it this time. Besides, it had an extremely messy result.

Sarah let go of the man and stepped in front of him and offered him her hand. He didn't use it for leverage to get up but he did shake it as he rose. The Sergeant smiled a lopsided smile at her and went to get his gear. She walked back to the Major and said, "See, I told you I wouldn't hurt him." The Major looked at her with a new respect and said, "Thank you." and he meant it.

Sarah waited while the Major picked the team and noticed that there was no lack of volunteers to be on her team. She wasn't at all surprised to see Sergeant Kelly as the point man. Actually, she felt rather flattered. They got down to planning the actual raid of the ranch.

Jack called everyone together and went over the plan again. They had two hours until they deployed outside the ranch and he wanted to make sure the communications were working and that everyone knew their signals. He checked in with Laura and the mixed crew that was manning the communications trailer. Everyone was working quickly and efficiently and in great harmony. Jack had been worried that he might have to repeat the message he gave to the team leaders to the communications teams. But it looked like Laura had everything under control.

Still, he called her aside and asked her how she was doing. She smiled, "Great." Then she pulled him aside and whispered, "They were going to be a little less than cooperative until I told them about the kids on the ship. They realized at that point just how important this whole thing is to each one of them personally."

Jack smiled. Laura gave him a personal radio and showed him the channel selects and the hands-free voice-operated-relay switch or VOX switch. Jack looked around and gave her a long kiss. After that she looked really sober and hugged him tightly. Her mind flashed back to the time in their lives where she didn't have to send her love off to do battle or to go in harm's way. They once had a quiet but enthusiastic life, filled with joy, laughter and each other. This whole thing was so alien than what she had expected her life with Jack to be like. In her mind she cried out to God, "Oh my God, why? Why does he have to go?"

Laura sensed the presence of the Holy Spirit and a feeling of rightness, a sense of absolute correctness filled her. With it came the conviction that they were doing God's will. If her plans and expectations did not match what the Lord wanted for them then she needed to revise them and accept the will of God. Her heart ached to please God more than anything. She thought the thought that true Christians kept in their hearts as Jesus himself had said in Luke 22:42, ." . .not my will, but yours be done." A feeling of conviction and peace flooded her from the top of her head to her toes. She smiled a peaceful smile and let Jack go realizing that she could never protect him for one second. It was in God's hands, in fact, it always had been.

Jack looked around at the hectic but organized activity going on everywhere with the comment, "I hope Mark gets back here in time for the action. I'm still playing this one by ear." Laura hugged him and told him it would work out, "All in God's time."

CHAPTER TWENTY

Lister was feeling pleased. Twenty miles away his plan was coming to fruition. The money and subtle drum beating of his agents in the various Houston communities had magnified the months of carefully planned incidents and confrontations. The minorities had finally reached the boiling point and there was no talking left. The only thing that kept the city from going up in smoke was the uneven advantage in weapons the police had combined with a lack of suitable firepower for the disadvantaged to take the city.

Lister's plans were going well. He had subtly angered the minorities until they were frustrated, irate, and burning for revenge. The weapons would be available in the next hour along with plenty of ammunition. Lister smiled to himself. All the weapons and ammo was to be the courtesy of the U.S. government. The guerrilla war that he started tonight would burn for days and destroy any semblance of government by the people or for the people. After the minorities had overrun most of the affluent neighborhoods in a self-righteous blood bath of the have-nots putting it to the haves, the military would come in and restore order. But that would not be easy or painless on either side. And, most of all it would take serious time to accomplish.

Lister remembered assuring his Libyan source that the Houston action would keep the U.S. federal government and the state and local governments busy for a long time, not to mention even more restrictive gun control laws, maybe even martial law. Lister recalled being a supporter when the gun control lobby had asked for two hundred thousand dollars to buy legislation to restrict handguns. He gave them five hundred thousand dollars. An unarmed populace is an easy target to control.

The recruiters he was using were paid mercenaries. Like the men that would be supplying the minorities with real weapons, they were cold men, cannon fodder that could not be traced back to Max Lister's organization. They kept attending meetings, buying drinks, proving to everyone that there was a secret government plan to eliminate the minorities. The demands for explanations from the local government were met with disdain and disregard because there was no such plan. Just as Max Lister knew they would.

Now, in the heat of a Houston summer night, a crowd of several hundred angry men had been swollen to twice its original number by gang members and others who heard that there would be automatic weapons made available to any who wanted them. Freedom wasn't exactly what the gang members wanted the heavy weapons for but, it would add to the general melee.

At his headquarters Max used a hand-held radio with a scrambled signal to give the go order to his troops waiting near their target. The time was now. He couldn't wait to make that old American cry of rebellion come true, "Burn Baby, Burn!" Then maybe the Libyan madman would honor him.

The helicopter screamed through the night sky. The engine exceeded the maximum RPM redline and still continued to push the weapons platform over the Houston skyline like a bullet fired in anger. Major Mike White watched the outlet temperature gauge on the turbine as it stabilized at a point well over the maximum safety rating. Having urged every possible iota of speed out of the craft, he concentrated on keeping the helicopter in the air and on course.

The advanced avionics helped immensely in allowing him to do just that. He wasn't watching the view out of the windshield of the helicopter. The augmented heads-up-display or HUD was highly active in multiple colors and images. It was a lot like playing one of the arcade games. The only difference was that this was a very deadly reality. If you crashed and burned here, you didn't get to try it again for two quarters. His threat board was clear, which one would expect over an American city. The worst thing he had to worry about was the odd civilian aircraft that operated below normal altitudes. Like the radio station Bell helicopter just ahead of them. It was going through the night almost in the same direction but with just enough of an angle to intersect their path.

The problem was one of relative speeds. The civilian chopper was traveling level at 105 knots. While they, on the other hand, were traveling at 330 knots. Mike eased their path to the right slightly so that they would pass behind and to the right of the other whirlybird. After they flashed by the other chopper wobbled around in their jet wash for a few seconds. Mike's auto scanner locked onto the transmission of the radio traffic commentator in the other chopper as they rapidly pulled away from the slower craft. "Whoa, what was that? Hey, Bill, did you see what just blew by us?" The rest of his comments were lost as the scanner locked onto a closer signal.

Momentarily unable to be anything but a passenger, Mark Connelly tried to visualize the layout of the armory. The lights of the city racing past just two hundred feet below was full of buildings but still reminded him of countless similar rides over the jungles of South America. The reason it reminded him of his jungle warfare days was the memory of the little girl he had just helped to rescue from the ship. Like many of the little girls he had seen in Latin America, she had been no more than thirteen years old. Haunted eyes that no longer knew how to care sat in a cute face that had lost its animation. Years of tender loving care and professional help could possibly put some hope and love back into her life and maybe God would give her back the peace of her lost childhood. But what of the other children Lister had already gotten his hands on? Taken to foreign lands and sold as slaves or forced into prostitution, never to see their loved ones again. They were beyond his help. But the white-hot anger he felt crystallized his purpose. NO MORE! Using his anger he burned away all thoughts except the ones concerning the on-rushing conflict.

They hadn't been able to reach the armory by phone, so, something was wrong, probably something caused by Max Lister. The Army was sending a flying squad to the armory but they were still twenty minutes away and wouldn't make it in time.

Mike pointed ahead and slightly to the right. "That's the Armory." He started dumping speed so that they wouldn't overshoot the target too badly.

Speaking into his hush mike, Mark told his friend, "Bring us in low and fast. Remember, they have weapons too." Mike smiled a grim smile. "Good, we wouldn't want to shoot unarmed men would we?"

Suddenly they shot over the Armory building and grounds. Traveling over two hundred MPH the view was brief but enough.

"They've just broken through the main gate." Mike noted as he pulled the helicopter through a high-G turn to the right.

Mark could swear his internal organs shifted position from the forces involved.

The leading officer of the mercenaries, a Captain, snapped his head around in a quick arc following the chopper that raced overhead. Another merc yelled, "What was that?" The captain answered in a grim tone. "Military chopper loaded for bear."

"Ours or theirs...?"

The captain shook his head and urged the men forward. "Better hope to hell that it's ours, I didn't like the looks of what it was carrying."

Hanging on tightly, Mark told Mike as they crunched through the high-speed turn. "Put us right over the top of the main building, facing them." Shedding speed quickly in the gut-wrenching turn to the right, Mike flared out the path of the war machine. With military precision he dropped the tail as he brought the chopper to a dead standstill directly over the front of the armory building facing the mercenaries.

More than one hundred and thirty soldiers of Lister's mercenary army were spread out between the gates and the building the helicopter hovered over. More than half were still in the trucks while three primary strike squads moved in on foot. Facing them were two men. Mark had chosen their position carefully so that the lights of the building were directly behind them. Being a military tactician, he used every possible advantage.

Looking up the forty feet from the ground, one of the mercs said "Oh, my God!" What he saw opposing him was a fully-equipped military Cobra Gunship painted flat black with the snouts of 20mm Vulcan cannons pointed at him. Fifty air-to-ground missiles were racked in clusters on and about the skid plates. The shrill scream of the turbine was matched by the tremendous heat waves from the exhaust that the carbon-arc lights on the building made into a shimmering, swirling cape as the downdraft blew it around.

Realizing the awesome danger they were in, the Captain yelled "Freeze! Don't shoot!" But several of Lister's mercenaries, who believed that they were invincible, begin to shoot at the helicopter. Squinting into the building lights they fired their assault rifles in a vain attempt to knock the Cobra out of the air. The pilot's HUD identified all the weapons in use but did not detect any radar or laser lock-on that would have meant shoulder-mounted missile launcher or a truck-based weapon. The visual scanner had not detected any Stinger missiles or similar weapon being brought to bear on the craft. The mercenaries obviously had not expected this level of response. Before anyone could fire a 40mm grenade launcher the weapons platform replied.

As the first bullets smashed off of the bulletproof windshield, Mark pushed down on the flashing red button on the console in front of his position. Although the response was almost instantaneous, Mark knew the sequence of events that quickly transpired. When he had pressed the red button, the computer-controlled weapons system was activated. Using two specially designed cameras located in the chin pods between the 20mm cannons, the computer developed a three-dimensional pictorial model of the entire area within its range of fire. This area was roughly four thousand square yards. The computer model was maintained in a memory map approximately one thousand pixels by one thousand pixels. A pixel, being an abbreviation for: "picture-cell."

The development of the computer model took approximately 2/100ths of a second. The computer also assigned a matrix of numbers that corresponded exactly to the brightness of each pixel. This only took 3/1000ths of a second. At that point, its military programming was explicit. "If….The model changes, shoot it." Of course, things moved, six trucks and sixty or so men.

Using a predetermined priority system, the computer picked the most dangerous movements. Bigger, closer, faster, shooting at, or moving toward the helicopter got you points in this contest. Two laser aiming systems pinpointed the selected targets, the 20mm Vulcan cannons, each with eight barrels, moved independently and fired one to five 20mm explosive rounds, depending on the size, speed and relative direction of the target. Aiming and firing of both cannons took less than one-tenth of a second, most of this was the mechanical aiming of the cannons. If the target was big and persistent (suggesting a tank) the computer also threw a missile at it.

Reducing Lister's army took less than twenty seconds. Large pieces of truck that flew the wrong way were killed again. Mike held the helicopter in position as it shook and vibrated like a demented roller coaster during the firing. The force of the cannon fire tried to push the copter backward but the auto-stabilizing circuitry of the avionics kept it locked into target acquisition.

Clouds of gun smoke were ripped away from the cannons by the rotor downdraft as Mark deactivated the weapons system. He stared at the carnage he had wrought. He had a flashback to the remains of the gangster's estate in Castle Rock, Colorado after a massive explosion. This scene was similar with nothing left standing with the exception of one man. Mark hoped that God would understand what he was doing had to be done to protect thousands of people in Houston.

A tree to the left of the battle scene, which had the audacity to move during the one-sided slaughter, slowly toppled over to the ground with a sigh. There was only one small limb left attached to the trunk. The cessation of the screaming fury of the cannons and the missile explosions brought a strange quiet to the entire area.

The local population had sought shelter when the mercenaries had piled out of the trucks and stormed the gates to the armory. None ventured out at this time either. Many of those gathered nearby to take possession of the guns that Lister promised them melted quickly into the night and reevaluated their idea of taking on the government. Robbed of their chance at new weapons, the gangs turned to attacking anyone in the area. Since that was mostly other gangs, the night wasn't so much different than a normal one for them. But the ravening maw of death that had anticipated thousands of victims had to settle for the mercenaries.

Three men lived on the field. Only one was basically uninjured. The Captain didn't look up or move a muscle until the black helicopter settled to the ground. He then, very carefully, laid his rifle on the ground and put his hands on top of his head. Bleeding from the nose and ears from close explosions, he nevertheless smiled as the two men in the black helmets and visors approached him. Looking around at the destruction scattered everywhere he just shook his head. "We surrender, I guess."

Mark Connelly stood there for a minute. The Ruger .45 was pointed directly between the Captain's eyes. He flipped his visor up with his left hand. His icy blue eyes bored into the merc. "Why?" was his only question, the Captain smiled again and Mark could have sworn he could see Satan in the Captain's eyes, "Pays good and it's exciting."

Mark shook his head. "Too bad you signed on with terrorists against your own country." The Captain looked introspective for a second and then frowned. "America used me in the Gulf Wars. This is all I know, all I am good at. The glint of red death suddenly flared in his eyes. "Kill me or die!" he said. Reaching down he quickly drew his .45 Colt Commander and started to aim it. The merc was too quick and Mark was forced to shoot.

Shaking his head as he stood there looking at the utter waste of another good soldier, Mark heard the sounds of the police response drawing close. Mike put his hand on Mark's shoulder. "We need to be out of here right now."

Sirens screaming, police cars converged on the armory grounds, but by then the black helicopter was disappearing over the tree line into the night. As he readjusted his hush mike, Mark turned to his friend. "How are we going to cover our backsides on this one? We just pumped several hundred 20mm rounds and forty-plus missiles into a basically civilian target within the continental United States. You know everybody in the military, the government, and probably the news media will want to know who did this."

Mike White smiled and concentrated on driving the bus. "Don't you worry about that, the guy who signs the checks for all us military types told me to support you without reservation. He was the one that arranged for me to have this chariot. Remember the Anti-Terrorist Legislation passed in 2001 after the World Trade Centers and the Pentagon strikes? Well, one of the provisions of that legislation provides for the limited and controlled use of military assets within the continental U.S. if it used against a terroristic threat. This was as close as a requirement can be matched to a law. The President said he knows you and what you need to do. He also told me to 'wring this beauty of a whirlybird out real good." Thinking back on his intention of flying right into the gates of hell for Mark... "I think that we did that, don't you?"

Grimly the specialist nodded. "Yes, I think so, and the guys back there certainly can't complain. Thanks again Mike, I couldn't have done any of this without your help."

CHAPTER TWENTY-ONE

The combined strike teams were assembled at an open area hidden from state highway 59 but only two miles from the ranch. The midnight hour quiet was filled with the sounds of men preparing for war. The muted sounds were like a melodic background to the movements of the various teams as they prepared their equipment and weapons.

Laura adjusted the throat microphone and ear-piece of Jack's communications set and VOX switch, as she ran her fingers across his shoulders she whispered quietly to him. "I'm getting tired wiring you up and sending you into dangerous places by yourself. Next time, I'm going with you!" She kissed him on his cheek.

Jack put his arm around her waist and hugged her to him. She briefly rested her head against his chest and hung on for a second. Letting him go she turned at a familiar sound and watched the black helicopter that had rescued them four hours ago, drop out of the night sky and settle lightly to the ground near the armored personnel carriers which she had learned were called APCs. Mark jumped lightly to the ground and headed toward them. Most of the troops stopped to admire the craft.

As Mark jogged over to them Jack noticed the nicks on the windshield and that the barrels of the Vulcan cannons were streaked with gray powder. Also, there were only four missiles left on the skid plate launchers. Mark had definitely seen some heavy action. The rotors on the chopper had never slowed and with a surprising lightness the craft jumped into the air and quickly disappeared in the early morning darkness.

Laura signaled two of the support team members who hustled over with Mark's gear for the ranch raid. As Mark strapped on the body armor she tried to get his comm gear attached. Snapping on the swat-style, quick- access holster he locked the Ruger into place and looked grimly at Jack who was already decked out to go to war. "What's the plan?"

Jack outlined the roles of the various teams and their activities as far as planning would go. A lot of what was going to happen tonight would be improvising as the situation developed. "I have gone over the transcripts of the children we rescued from that ship in Houston. Most add little detail to what we already know, but two of them really gave us the clues we needed to make this raid work out right." He led Mark over to the makeshift table on the trunk of a patrol car. "Tommy Avril was able to accurately describe the rooms and the layout of the furniture as he last remembered it. Samantha Collins gave us the number code to the secret floor on the elevator."

Mark tipped his head to one side. "How did she accomplish that?"

Jack grinned, "They thought she was unconscious and didn't cover up the keypad when they entered. Of course it didn't hurt that they messed up twice and one attendant had to talk the other one through the numbers."

Jack showed Mark the floor plan of the so-called 'holding area' where the kids scheduled to be sold as slaves or sex objects overseas were taken to be prepared for the trip. He said, "Read that to mean tranquilized and strapped into coffin-like containers for the trip to the ship." There were three rooms in all. The main room was the biggest and held the most interest for the team. This is where the children were kept. One of the other rooms was a lounge where the security teams could relax and the other was a bathroom. He turned to Jack again, "What's with the body armor? Is there something I don't know?"

"Possibly," Jack nodded as he explained, "There is the probability that the most-heavily armed security is located in the basement. Every person the kids remember in that area was armed. The complete subterranean floor was missing from the blueprints of the building. "Apparently they were able to build this secret basement for their clandestine operations even though the water table and ground level are at the same height in this part of the country. As far as the children can tell us, it only has one entrance or exit and that is the elevator. Makes sense to keep access to a minimum if you're trying to hide the area. But I still think that they will have a rat hole or two to jump out of if the heat is applied from the front." His last words were almost lost in the revving engines of the APCs as two of them left the area headed for the ranch. "Let's go." Jack shouted to his team and led Mark to their armored carrier. Jack looked back and watched Laura as she ran to the communications trailer and went inside.

As Mark and Jack were leaving the staging area, Sarah was already completing the roundup of the security personnel that had been guarding the grounds of the ranch estate. When the guards saw the military troops and hardware, there hadn't been a great deal of resistance and most of the guards became willing captives.

There was one that was a bit tough. The security personnel they had already captured told them about this one guy. He was an ex-military and a fitness junkie. He looked a lot like Sly Stallone at his Rambo peak and it was an image he tried to maintain. As they headed toward the area with this particular sentry she turned to Sergeant Kelly, "You want this one?" The muscular Sergeant nodded and pulled his communications headset off. Handing his rifle and pack to one of the other soldiers he flexed his massive arms and shoulders as he walked toward the guard shack. The rest of the squad took concealed positions and covered him. As he walked into the lights of the guard shack he shouted, "Hey, inside... you up to it?"

Nothing happened for a few seconds while the sentry determined that his radio and telephone communications weren't working. Realizing that this challenger wouldn't be alone he left his weapons inside and walked outside to face the soldier. As he stepped outside Sarah had to admire his physique. He did in fact look a lot like the actor and even had five inches in height on him. His shoulders and arms were muscled even more than Kelly's. It looked to be a real match. The man who walked out of the guard shack took a stance directly in the center of the lighted area and shouted back to Kelly, "You can call me Cory and I am up to it."

Kelly walked up to the big guard and took a stance directly before him. Cory feinted left and stepped toward the soldier with a quick sucker punch to the jaw. Kelly moved his head down and to his right which caused the punch to pass behind his head. At the same time he put all of his energy into a stomach punch which connected squarely into the other man's midriff. Cory was lifted off his feet by the punch and lost a lot of his wind. But it didn't stop him. His heavily muscled abdominals took most of the strength of the punch. He dropped down and punched a straight left punch at Kelly's face. Kelly blocked the blow to the left of his head with his right arm and again scored on a body blow. This one staggered the mercenary. Following up quickly, Kelly dropped to his right knee and used his left leg to sweep the feet out from beneath the other man.

Cory fell straight down and got mad. As he started to rise, Kelly used his right hand and came up from below Cory's chin. The blow from the palm heel strike lifted Cory into the air and into an arc that left him unconscious on his back. Kelly stood up and waved the troops up to his position. While he was putting on his gear, Sarah smiled and said, "Impressive!" He smiled back and patted her on the shoulder, "I only learn from the best." He then keyed his radio on and told the comm. center that the perimeter was secure. The other team of Special Forces personnel had already secured the entrances to the two buildings.

Monitoring the comm. net, Jack told Mark that Sarah and the Special Forces troops had secured the perimeter and the front entrances to the two main buildings. The Sheriff's department and the FBI were moving into the children's dorms as he spoke. Jack watched as their APC roared through the front gate and he saw two of the Lister security force on their knees with their hands on their heads and several Special Forces troops watching them. A minute later they arrived at the main building and disembarked from the armored carrier.

Jack took this time to introduce Mark to the rest of the team. Even the FBI agent was impressed. Jack had to admire Mark's image. The body armor looked like it had been custom made for him and he carried himself with the no-nonsense, self-assurance that indicated a lot of experience.

While everybody checked each other's equipment to make sure they were ready, Jack talked to Laura about the timetable and the other operations. When he was done he returned to the assault team. He noticed the Rangers seemed peeved by the requirement that everyone on the raid had to wear the body armor. They seemed very uncomfortable in it. Jack made his announcement. "All the other operations are essentially complete without a shot fired. The children are almost all off the property and the staff is being held outside the front gate."

The two a.m. quiet of the Texas gulf coast area had returned to the scene and the big moon looked down on the fourteen men left in the compound. It was a pleasant night to be alive. Still, Jack knew there was work to be done and he was ready. "Lady and Gentlemen, let's do it!"

Major Wolfman nodded and added, "The rest of my people are spread throughout this building and the grounds in the event they do have a rat-hole somewhere." Jack nodded and took the lead to the elevator. As they suspected, no more than six men could get in at one time. The remaining eight would have to cycle through after the initial six had established a beachhead of sorts in the assault area. As determined prior to the raid, Major Wolfman, Roger Tasker, Jack, Mark, and two of the Special Forces Sergeants would make the first trip.

Crammed together on the elevator as they were, Jack hoped that the security force was still unaware that they knew about this elevator. If they started shooting while all six men were still in the elevator it would be like shooting fish in a barrel. Jack punched in the five digit code that seemed appropriate for Max Lister, 13666. The elevator dropped quickly and stopped at the basement. You could have cut the tension in the elevator with a knife. The doors opened onto a darkened room that was absolutely quiet.

Mark eased out to the right and went to one knee behind a couch with his CAR-15 rifle up and seeking a target. Roger Tasker went the other way and went prone on the floor with the same armament. Both men covered the others as they exited the elevator car. Everything stayed quiet. Jack walked over to the wall next to the elevator and switched on the lights. The big room lit up with the glare of florescent overhead lights. There was no one in the room. The rest of the team got up and dealt with the let down experienced when you're geared up for action and it doesn't occur. Mark sent the elevator car back for the others.

While the others looked around the room and checked out the lounge and bathroom, Roger Tasker went over to a row of file cabinets on one wall and started looking through the drawers. Finding DVDs he looked around and found a TV/DVD player and powered it up. He inserted the DVD he had pulled out at random and punched PLAY. The resultant promotion sickened everyone in the room. The despicable and callous use of small children in the most degrading sexual perversions was highlighted and sold as a wonderful thing in a glossy production that had to been made by professionals.

Jack re-evaluated Roger Tasker in his mind as he watched the hatred and loathing eat at him. Suddenly, Mark cut through the spell the horrible video had cast on everyone. "Listen, what is that?" Roger turned off the TV and everyone fell silent. A heavy mechanical rumbling and drone could be heard at the low end of the spectrum, almost a feeling, rather than, a sound. Everyone looked at each other with the question.

Jack ventured, "It almost feels like a train track that you can't see with a train coming toward you." Several people nodded in agreement. Then Jack keyed his combat microphone. "Laura, got anything from the people on the site, or in the building?" Laura came back quickly. "Nothing outside, one person inside hears or feels the vibrations you do. I don't kn. . ." A droning sound cut her off. Special Forces Sergeant Morris looked up from the communications readout he had, "We're being jammed."

The vibration was getting heavier and louder. Jack said, "Where is the rest of our team?" Major Wolfman tried the elevator door. It was locked. "Don't know, I lost communications when you did. They were still waiting for the car to return to the first floor."

Mark's subconscious had been chewing on an inconsistency and the thought suddenly popped into his conscious mind. "Wait a minute. How could they ship out those kids in those 'coffin-like' containers you were talking about? They would never fit in that elevator."

A sudden feeling of impending disaster came over everyone in the room, as heavy clanking noises became apparent behind the far wall of the big room. Jack headed for the side of the room yelling, "Kill the lights!" Mark ran by the switches and shut off the overhead lights with one swipe. Everyone dove to the floor on one side of the room or the other.

In the sudden darkness there appeared a bright line of light across most of the far wall which quickly grew thicker and brighter. Jack's mind made the logical jump from fantasy to reality and he watched as the entire wall opened up into a large freight elevator with half of the door going down into the floor and the other half up into the ceiling. Inside the elevator fourteen men stood with bulletproof Lexan shields in front of them. Most were armed with assault rifles but at the front was a large black man with a black T-shirt that had a 'No Fear' logo on the front. He held a strange device in his hands. It looked like a cross between a fire hose nozzle and a small rocket launcher. Stepping forward in the elevator he spotted Sergeant Harmonand a ball of bright blue energy with an angry orange center sprang from the device. The ball of energy hit a chair next to the Sergeant and the chair literally exploded into fragments. The other troops bailed out of the massive elevator and started shooting at the raiders.

Furniture was shredded and the walls suddenly were massively pockmarked by 5.56 caliber rounds on full auto-fire.

Four bullets slapped Jack's body armor and smashed him back against the wall. Jack felt like someone had hit him with a sledgehammer but his body armor saved his life. Mark responded by unloading his full magazine into the Lexan shield of the man that shot Jack. Bulletproof or not, the Lexan crazed and then collapsed. The last six rounds punched the Lister shooter to the floor.

Each one of the raiders got hit at least once or twice. Their saving grace was that the thirteen Lister shooters weren't actual military and made several major mistakes. Most of them ran through their ammo and had to reload. During that activity five of them were killed and two wounded. A second mistake was not force vectoring their fire. No one was directing the effort and too many would concentrate on one of the raiders and get taken out by others who were free to fire back. The cordite smoke filled the room and there was nothing in the room that didn't have bullet holes in it.

As the energy weapon shooter was lining up for another shot, Jack heard Major Wolfman say, "Fear this, sucker" and two orbs flew into the enclosed car. Jack ducked his head and opened his mouth to equalize the pressure to come.

The grenades exploded behind the black man. This settled the question of how to get around his Lexan shield. The shrapnel killed the black man instantly and the blast knocked out the two remaining Lister men. Jack and Mark disarmed the remaining men, dragged them to the end of the room, and put riot cuffs on their arms and legs. Mark tried to examine the strange energy gun but it had suffered a great deal of damage from the grenade blasts.

One of the captured men startled them by yelling, "I didn't want to have anything to do with the doctors. I was just a guard that they conscripted to protect this place."

Mark went over to the man, "What is it you didn't want to have anything to do with?"

The man was terrified and looked at the other captured guards. "Over the last three years the full time security force has culled off kids they took a liking to and kept them down here without Lister ever knowing about it. Some of the girls have even had kids of their own! The security forces eliminate uncooperative people by giving them over to the doctors. I just found out why there never is a trace of them seen again. I thought they just took them away and put them back on the street." The man was shaking his head side to side. "The docs down there get rid of anybody they don't like in an acid bath. Guards, that don't do as they're told, anyone. The doctors are going to eliminate all the kids they've kept on the side for the last three years in an acid bath so that there's no evidence that Lister can find!"

Jack and Mark called the others over to their position. Mark was the expert in these things so Jack let him run the show. "Alright, we have to do what we can to save the children downstairs. How do we handle it?"

The time to make up their minds suddenly ran out. The elevator doors started to close. Everyone jumped, hopped, or leaped into the car. As the elevator began to move downward, Roger remarked that the walls of the elevator showed no damage from the explosion of the grenades. Mark looked closely at the wall nearest to where the little bombs had gone off. Not a scratch or blemish. "This is armor plate, guys." The elevator came to a halt and the doors started to open again.

Since there was no place to hide in the elevator, Jack and the two Sergeants went prone on the floor with their rifles at the ready while Mark, Roger, and the Major crouched above them and also trained their rifles on whatever would appear outside the elevator.

The doors opened onto a corridor about twenty feet wide and ten feet high with another eight armed guards waiting for the elevator. When they saw the raiders they grabbed their weapons and started to fire at the opening elevator. The six men inside were tired of being smashed by bullets and eliminated the eight men in the corridor in less than fifteen seconds.

Major Wolfman eased up to the side of the car and looked out into the corridor. "Clear!" He was limping from a slight leg wound and had blood running down his neck from a bullet that creased his ear. Everyone moved carefully around the bodies in the corridor so they wouldn't slip in the blood that had spilled there.

Jack was feeling the pain and aches from the battering but wasn't going to let that stop him. He and Major Wolfman raced down the hall and slid to a halt next to a window of really thick bulletproof Lexan and a massive steel door which was closed and sealed tight. Behind the shield of Lexan Jack saw a woman in a doctor's smock preparing controls on a panel while a man with a gun, also dressed in a doctor's smock, was forcing children into a small room that must contain the acid bath. Some of the children saw Jack and held their hands out for salvation. The last of the children was crammed into the small room and the door was locked shut.

Jack knew that there was no way that he or any of their team could get to the doctors before they turned on the acid. The piteous look on the children's faces as they were herded into the "shower room", so cried out to Jack's spirit that he dropped to his knees and beseeched Jesus just as Mark ran up to them. "God, you sent us to rescue these children. You knew we couldn't do it without your help. Be merciful Lord, spare these innocent little children." Jack raised his arms in supplication to a merciful God.

As Jack watched the woman reach for the controls to start pumping the acid into the room, something happened. He wasn't quite sure what it was he saw. It could have been an aberration of the lights shining off of the thick bullet-proof plastic, but he could have sworn he suddenly saw a faint image of a tall, powerful warrior in brightly glowing white armor standing directly behind the two doctors. In the warrior's hands it looked like he held a sword with a burning blade held at high guard position above his right shoulder. The sword was swung with amazing speed and sliced through the woman from her right shoulder at the neck, completely through her body and out the other side at the hip. In a blur the swordsman spun to his left and swung the flaming sword in an upward arc that hit the man below the ribs and flashed out the top of his head. Both of the doctors became limp and collapsed lifelessly to the floor.

There were no visible wounds and it all happened so fast that Jack wasn't sure he saw it or was it possible he imagined it? The image of the warrior had been faintly visible only for the time needed to swing the sword. But the results were the same. The children hadn't been killed.

Jack stayed on his knees and thanked the Lord from the bottom of his heart for saving the children. He realized he was full of exuberant joy. God as a warrior was awesome. Yes! Jack grinned and jumped to his feet. He looked at the Major. The Major's face was quite a sight.

Major Wolfman's eyes were wide open, almost as much as his mouth. He snapped his mouth closed and turned to Jack, "Did you see what..., that sword..., Oh, forget it. It couldn't have been what I thought it was."

Jack thought for a second and in his mind asked the Holy Spirit to give him the right words to say to the Major. "Look, John, I think we just saw the hand of God in action. And, while I don't know what happened in there, I know that all the credit should go to God for rescuing these kids. Now, why don't we find a way in and get them out of there."

As the others joined them at the glass, Mark smiled a knowing smile at Jack while Sergeant Morris looked to his equally perplexed officer for answers. They decided to put off discussing it until they could find a way to get the children out of there. There was no way through the glass and the door was heavy metal and electronically locked. Mark was inspecting the area around the door in the belief that there must be controls on this side also. He eventually found a small panel hidden in the wall. The switches inside quickly unlocked the door and allowed the team to move into the rooms on the other side. The frigid air in the room tasted of chemicals and fear.

Jack and Roger Tasker quickly opened the doors to the "shower" and helped the frightened children out into the control room. There were fifteen children and children of children in the group. Three of them were just babes-in-arms. There were a lot of hugs and thank you's.

Mark had been examining the two doctors and walked over to Jack. In his hand he showed Jack a 9mm Glock pistol. The automatic had been cut completely in two and the cut was smooth and even. The two men just looked at each other. Mark put the gun in his pack.

Sergeant Morris found the jamming transmitter in a radio room and was about to shut it off when bullets smacked into the equipment destroying it completely. Three guards that were still functioning had secured themselves behind an armored car in a parking area in the basement and were shooting at the raiders.

The bullets bounced off of the Lexan. Jack, Mark, and the Major ran to the door and started firing back at the shooters. There was a "crump" sound and the armored car flipped up into the air and slammed to the floor. The three guards were not to be seen after that. Roger Tasker came walking toward the team with the smoke still curling from the 40mm grenade launcher under his rifle barrel. "I've always wanted to use this thing." he said as he reached the Major and the others.

Communications were frantic for a few minutes, but calm was restored when Jack let Laura know that they were all right and that they had a bunch of children to bring out.

Jack looked at Mark, "Where are all the rest of the troops?" He looked around again, "And, where are the rest of the children?"

Mark shook his head. "I don't know that there ever were too many of them here and most seem to have left. The last two groups we've met, upstairs and down here, were probably the last of the defenders. I'll bet the doctors were supposed to destroy at least this portion of the ranch after they completed their tasks."

One of the rooms was a control room and they found the vehicle exit. At the surface, this entrance was a distance away from the building and well hidden. They opened it and that allowed several teams from the task force to join them in minutes.

Jack reconvened the strike team and thanked all of them. The medics examined the wounds and bruises of the six-man team and declared them all fit enough to walk out of there. Jack looked at the fist-sized bruises on his chest and abdomen where the bullets had impacted the body armor. He knew that the body armor's trauma plates were great, but the only reason he wasn't dead was the hand of the Father. Every one of the men was bleeding from a myriad of small wounds, and cuts but hadn't noticed it during the battle.

As a matter of expediency the six-man team that had witnessed the simultaneous demise of the two doctors decided to call it 'an unexplainable Act of God'. After all, there were no marks on the bodies and the children were not able to tell the investigators anything.

After Jack, Laura, and Mark were rejoined by Sarah they returned their weapons and armor and after filing the necessary paperwork explaining the attack in detail, they headed back to their original hotel on Highway 59. Jack and Mark filled in the women on details of the raid that not everyone got to hear. Laura listened to Jack's account of the faintly-seen warrior and laughed. When both Jack and Mark shot her questioning looks, she explained, "I wasn't laughing at what you thought you saw. In fact, my guess is, that is was exactly what you did see. What I was laughing about was the timing of your comments and the retro song that's playing on the radio right now. As she turned the volume up they heard:

"You are a mighty warrior, Dressed in armor of light! Crushing the deeds of darkness, Lead us on in our fight! Through the blood of Jesus, Victorious we stand! We place you in the highest place, Above all else in this land!

Thinking back Jack had to admit that what he saw matched that description very well. He looked at Sarah and knew she was upset. "What is it Sarah?"

She looked at Jack for a few seconds. "I was too young to know anything about the horror camps the Germans had during the Second World War, but I have talked to many survivors and what happened here, in America, sounds a lot like what was done to the Jews in Germany.

Jack asked God for help with this answer also. After waiting a few seconds he started to answer her but knew the words weren't his own. "Sarah, you know that the Jewish people have been persecuted since God chose them as his people. Satan has an equal hate for Christians ever since God grafted the Gentiles into the faith. The evil one will use whatever means he can to destroy our faith, in God, in others, or in ourselves. The American people no more endorse what was done here than you endorse the Israeli who shot up the Mosque in Jerusalem. Don't let one evil spawn another in your heart. You are needed in the fight against the evil that entraps people to do things like this to other people."

Sarah stared at Jack for a few seconds and then looked away, out the window for a while. When she turned back to Jack she nodded.

Mark had fallen silent during this time. He spoke up as they neared the hotel, "Let's stay on our toes guys, we haven't cut the head off of this snake yet. He is still out there and other kids are probably at risk."

CHAPTER TWENTY-TWO

Max Lister sat at his desk in a remote hideaway in Northern Mexico. His stony countenance creased by a heavy frown. He looked at the photos of Jack, Laura, Sarah, and Mark with hatred. His plans for a minority uprising in Houston had been effectively canceled by this group's interference. Ike Morris, his main terror activist had disappeared without a trace after a meeting between the fourth man and himself. The shipment of children to Libya had been stolen and his ship was sitting on the bottom of the Houston ship channel. The crew of the ship had identified all four of these people, before they had been taken out and shot for incompetence.

If that were not enough, word had reached him that the authorities, which authorities he did not know, had seized his Children's Ranch and he was being hunted by both the military and law enforcement arms of the U.S. government, the government of Israel and Interpol. There was also a rumor that a federal grand jury had returned several indictments against him for numerous crimes.

Not that any of that mattered at the moment. The embarrassment and burning anger at the situation was a minor nuisance compared to the mental anguish and physical agony he was feeling at the moment.

He felt great fear and dread at Matrice Mujahid's probable response for such great failures. He could understand and appreciate those punishments because they were exactly what he would do, and had already done many times, to anyone working for him who had failed him in this manner.

Screaming in irritation more than desperation as he rose from his chair he demanded, "Why is everything suddenly going to hell? How can these people beat me at every turn?"

Lister heard an evil chuckle in his mind and saw an image of a box with the word "Talisman" emblazed on it. Shaken into crafty awareness, Lister intoned, "Who are these people and what is this talisman?" An image formed in his mind of the four people of the Crossfire Team which matched the pictures on his desk. In Jack's right hand was the crucifixion nail. How Max knew the names of these people or that one of them was holding one of the three nails with which Christ was crucified never even bothered him. He asked one last question of the thin air. "What can I do to torment these people?"

Max was not stupid. He casually noticed that his pain and aggravation were lessened as he sat down again. He called in his new number one man. He showed the pictures to him and identified the people in them. Poking his figure at Jack's image he said, "What can I do to hurt this man?"

Karl Botrow studied the report on Jack Malone. Then he looked at Max with a small grin on his face. "This Malone is a Christian, someone who loves everyone, even his enemies. Obviously he wanted to save the children.

Karl pointed at the report. "According to his file he is in control of an important Christian artifact that is in great demand. How could you make him give it to you and humiliate him at the same time?"

Max thought for a few minutes. "Well, he has something I need and I have something he needs. I can't travel back into the United States and I can't depend on others to get this talisman for me." A plan slowly formed in his mind. He thought about it, embellished it, and agreed with it. He grinned at Karl and picked up the telephone to set the plan in motion. Max thought with satisfaction that even if he couldn't work in America, his money could.

At the hotel that evening, after resting, Jack, Laura, Mark, and Sarah were recounting the ranch raid when there was a knock at the door. Exchanging glances, the team spread out through the suite just in case. Mark answered the door and saw a dark shape looming outside. It turned out to be one of the managers of the hotel with a DVD for Jack.

Somewhat chagrined for being so jumpy, Mark settled down. The manager explained that the DVD had been dropped off at the front desk with a note for it to be delivered to Jack Malone. After the manager left, Mark popped the disc into the DVD player connected to the television in the sitting room of the suite. With no preamble, Max Lister's face was on the TV. No one said a word. Laura looked at Jack and nodded. Jack knew from her frown that this was the man she had seen in her dreams.

On the screen, Max smiled an evil smile. Seeming quite relaxed he looked out at them and spoke. "The four of you have given me a great deal of trouble over the last few days. You have callously destroyed several years of my painstaking effort. You will pay for that, but there is one operation that you did not find. Let me show you."

An indoor scene of an enormous room with dozens of children in various activities such as playing, running, and eating replaced the picture of Lister. Max Lister's voice overplayed the audio section of the active scene and pointed out the happy children. On cue, the camera zoomed in on one little girl of about eleven who was playing with several other little girls. She was blonde and was wearing very adult clothing. As the camera closed in on her face it was obvious that she had gone through a professional hair and makeup session. Everyone in the room immediately noticed the similarity to the face of the President of the United States.

Laura cried, "Good Lord, He's the one that kidnapped Tracy!" The camera view pulled quickly back from the girl and panned upward to the two-story tall roof of the room. Hanging there was an ominous-looking red and white sphere.

Another view showed children playing, and a red and white sphere floating above them. The older ones were taking care of many of the younger kids. Everything seemed self-contained even though it looked darker than when they first saw it. The camera again zoomed into a close-up of the red and white sphere.

As the sphere faded out, Lister's face returned to the screen. He looked almost gleeful. He pounded his fist on the desk in front of him. "I'll wager a sizable sum right now that you're wondering what is in that awesome red and white canister hanging over the kid's heads. Well now, let me show you!"

Another scene appeared on the screen. A young man was pacing the floor in a small room. Lister's voice continued to dominate the tape. "The man you see is an agent for Interpol. He infiltrated my organization recently and was caught with the goods, as you Americans say. His name is Philippe Gaston, he is normally based in Paris, he is not married but does have a child by a mistress and he has a mother in Nice. He has unknowingly volunteered to demonstrate the effects of the canister's contents for you. Here's what one drop of the liquid will do."

A hand reached into the scene on this side of a glass window and rotated a knob. The camera zoomed onto a curette inside the room that expelled one drop of liquid. The results were horribly gruesome. In the next two minutes the man died a terrible death with tremendous suffering.

Reflected dimly in the glass was the image of the two killers that were carrying out the operation for Max Lister. As seen in the reflections of the glass in the video camera, both of these men blanched and looked scared at the sight of the agent's death.

Jack and Laura prayed that God would comfort the soul of the young man.

Lister commented on the quick reaction to the particular brand of nerve gas being used. Like the man himself, his comments were totally callous as to the taking of a human life.

Jack felt physically ill after seeing the execution but was even more staggered by the next comments that Lister made. "Now listen carefully. You have a certain relic from the first century." Lister screamed "I want it!"

He seemed to have suddenly calmed down. "The four of you are going to bring it to me. If you do, I will give you the information so that you can rescue those children. If you don't, a full quart of that same nerve gas is going to be sprayed into the air of the room with the children in it. I can cause it to happen or, it will happen automatically by a timer in less than twenty-four hours. Every one of those children will die just like that agent did, including our star pupil, Tracy."

The absolute coldness of his voice continued to plague them, "Anything happens to me and you will never find them before time runs out and they will all watch each other die. Oh yes. I forgot. How delicious! I have also arranged for them to watch this video one-hour before the gas is released. Just so that they can prepare themselves"

Lister reclined in his chair on the tape and stared out at them. It seemed as if he could read their emotions. "Thanks to your meddling interference, I have been forced to leave the United States and move to a friendlier environment. You will meet me at the airport in Athens, Greece in eighteen hours with the relic or you can prepare one hundred small closed caskets. You certainly wouldn't want the relatives to see them after they die like that, would you?"

The picture ended with a close up of the dead agent's face and the ulcers and horror intermingled there.

Laura came over and curled up into Jack's arms. Sarah just stared at the now-blank TV screen and replayed scenes from the tape in her mind, searching for anything that they could use to derail Lister's plans. She systematically contemplated what resources the Mossad could use to help rescue these children, but she could not conceive of any thing they could do in the time left.

Sarah had not been surprised by the evil use of innocent children. The enemies of the Israelis had practiced these types of efforts since time began. They worshiped the evil god Molec, the destroyer of children. The only thing that rather surprised her was the fact that Lister hadn't used one of the children as the example of how the gas worked. That would have been more up his alley. Of course, she could see why he didn't. He wanted the maximum emotional potential of the threat to the children, not the viciousness of killing them so that he could get what he wanted. Which was what? What 'talisman' was he so interested in?

Mark picked up the telephone and punched in a twenty-three-digit number. When the call was answered he talked rapidly for three minutes. He hung up and made a second call. When he put the phone down he explained to the others what he was starting. He got up and paced the room as he talked. "First I got the NSA to agree to analyze this DVD for clues as to the whereabouts of the children. Second, I got the FBI to start checking all the paperwork we got from the raid on the ranch and their raid on his headquarters. This should . . ." Mark stopped and stared into space for a few seconds. Then he grabbed the telephone and made another call. While he waited for the connection to complete he explained, "I forgot about the notebook I got from 'Ike Morris' at Lister's headquarters." After the call he sat down and stared at the phone for a few seconds before picking it up. "Now comes the hard one."

Jack nodded, "The President, right?"

Mark also nodded and placed the call. When he was finished with that one he looked grim. "The President has made the complete resources of the government available to us and those working with us to find and rescue the children. But, he wants us," he looked at each person, one at a time, "to go to Athens just in case they aren't found."

Everyone agreed to go but, Sarah quietly advised Mark, "You know Lister won't keep his word, don't you? Even if we give him this 'talisman' he wants, he'll still kill those children and us too, if he can."

Laura added, "You know he's under the control of Satan. That's the only reason he could know about or want the treasure. You also know he is pure evil like a demon. That's the only reason he arranged for those innocent children to see that horrible tape just before he kills them, to terrorize them. That is what demons do. They delight in terrorizing children, just like Lister."

Mark smiled a viscous smile, "Yeah, I know all that, but it might give us a chance to catch him. I also wondered about him not using a child in the video. It was probably an older image he had to use because he couldn't get back into the country to use one of the kids."

It was decided that they would do what they could to help in the search for the children and then travel to Greece to meet with Lister. An hour later they had a dozen different agencies and groups involved in the search for the children. The NSA analysis of the DVD indicated that the room was actually two rooms and both of them were underground. A guesstimate was that both rooms were somewhere near Houston and less than twenty minutes apart.

They watched a copy of the DVD several more times while getting back reports of no progress by the teams involved. Jack was certain there was something that they had missed in the tape that would give them a shot at finding the kids, but, what?

Jack and Laura prayed for wisdom and help in finding the children but did not come out with anything that would be of help. They decided to brainstorm the problem. Mark was in the third round saying, "All right, if Max Lister had additional facilities for holding children, then he didn't put it on any of the records we have access to. If their computer files had been captured it would of been a great help, I think."

That comment gave Jack a clue. "Wait a minute. You say that there is no record of other children holding areas in any of his records?" He thought he was on the edge of losing the thread of his idea when he got a solid hold on it. "Okay, I think I know where the kids are."

Mark looked at his watch and said, "I hope you are right. We have less than ten hours to be in Greece and less than two hours before the President gets here himself. We would be helping a lot more if we had any solid leads."

Jack's face was grimly animated. "Sarah." The Mossad agent turned her head in his direction with a glimmer of hope in her eyes. Jack continued, "When Lister was telling us that he had an operation we haven't found, did he say, haven't or didn't?"

Sarah thought for a few seconds and replayed that part of the DVD in her mind. Her profession had greatly amplified her ability to remember trivial or insignificant details. "He said, *"There is one operation that you did not find."* Why?"

Jack smiled, "Because Max Lister is very precise in his use of the language. Due probably to his limited education, he is very careful about the words he uses, a habit that he is probably not even aware of anymore. So, when he said 'did not' rather than 'have not', I think that means we were wherever the kids are and 'did not' find them. Rather than not having been where they are when we would 'have not' of found them. See what I mean? I'm betting the kids are at the ranch and we missed them somehow."

Laura was nodding her head while Sarah jumped to her feet and Mark grabbed for the telephone again. Twenty-five minutes later they were back at the elevator in the administration building on the ranch.

There were seismic crews from NSA and NASA along with the FBI and Major Wolfman. Mark's eyebrows rose at the sight of the Major. "Don't you ever sleep or take a break?"

The Major smiled at seeing all four of them again. "Don't get paid for sleeping or resting. Actually, I did catch twenty winks in the comm. trailer. Listen, I understand your concept of another room but, I'm not sure where to look for it after what we already found, any suggestions?"

Mark looked at Jack. Jack waved his hand and made a guess. "I would think that it had to be off of that tunnel we found at the bottom floor of the big freight elevator. Why? Because it is underground and there are few underground facilities anywhere near Houston. And, because it had to be near where the children were without the outside being able to see the transfers." The whole crew left the building and toured outside to the major ramp entrance in the field away from the buildings. Walking down the ramp with the Major and the seismic crews, the team felt their hopes building for finding the children. The seismic crews started at the tunnel end of the administration area near the ramp. It took less than fifteen minutes to locate the room hidden at the other end of the tunnel past the freight elevator.

Jack, Mark, Sarah, and Sergeant Bowers held a quick conference. Sarah pointed in the direction of the hidden room. "I would not charge in there. If I were Lister, I'd make sure that the gas would be released as soon as anyone forced their way through any entrance." The Sergeant nodded his agreement. "That would definitely be his style based on what we've seen so far."

Mark checked the time and shook his head. He turned to the Major and requested a mini-cam with a fiber-optics head for observation of the interior. Once he had the equipment, Mark went back down the hall several feet and used a small drill to bore a quarter-inch hole through both dry-wall segments making up the wall. Inserting the fiber-optic head on its cable he studied the layout inside the room. He could see some of the children and the red and white sphere that were in Lister's tape. Studying the layout of the wall on the inside of the room he then pulled the head of the lens back inside the wall between the drywall panels. Switching on the miniature light next to the lens he was able to observe the space between the studs in the wall.

Pulling the fiber-optic cable out of the wall he used a piece of putty-like material to plug up the hole in the wall. Sarah asked him why he did that. Mark's years of training and counter-terrorism work had given him a wealth of experience that only a handful of people in the world could equal. He gestured at the room, "Due to the construction of the room, the air flow through the small hole I made, and from what I can see, I'm pretty sure that Lister has the control to the gas also linked to a positive-air-pressure switch. If we were to open up a large panel in the wall, like the door, then the air-pressure in the room would drop and trigger the gas. At least that is what most of the cunning terrorists would do."

Jack said, "Okay, how do you propose we get in there quickly without setting off the gas?"

Mark thought for a few minutes. "We don't have time to requisition or build an air-lock to hold the pressure while we cycle the children through. But, we do have a way to measure the difference in air pressure and see if we can't bring this hall up to the same pressure as in the room with the children. It is a pretty large room compared to this small hall. We should be able to equalize the pressures and make a large enough opening so we can evacuate the kids into the hall, then close-off the opening we've made, and get everyone outside to safety."

Getting the equipment to do that took less than twenty minutes. Two large evacuation fans were available in the Environmental Hazard Emergency Response Team truck parked on the site just outside the major access.

The pressures were quickly equalized and an opening six feet tall by eight feet wide was cut. Laura held her breath as the entire wall section was removed as one piece. This allowed several teams to access the room and the children. The red and white sphere didn't spray deadly gas. Quickly rounding up the kids, everyone evacuated the area except the HazMat Team and military bomb squad who began the delicate task of disarming the red and white sphere.

When all the imprisoned children were outside in the beautiful Texas afternoon air, Jack and Laura found Tracy and talked to her. She had scrubbed all the makeup off and fixed her own hair back into a ponytail that she liked. It seemed much more appropriate for her age. The young girl looked at the two people who had again dressed in their body armor and side arms in the slight possibility that there could be other surprises. She pulled on Laura's hand. Laura squatted down to her level and asked her, "What is it, honey?" She smiled a bright smile and said, "I knew you'd come and get me. I saw you when I was sleeping." Then she gave Laura a big hug, "Thank you." Laura just grinned and hugged her back.

Jack saw the limousine in a security convoy with the President arrive and pointed it out to Laura. Laura took Tracy by the hand and led the little girl over to her anxious uncle. Jack had an irreverent thought that Andrew Bollen was Tracy's Uncle Sam.

As they escorted her out of the crowd and over the mediam toward the entrance of the ranch, the Secret Service cadre protecting the President surrounded them. As they crossed the grassy knoll Tracy stumbled somewhat and Jack caught her other hand and kept her upright.

In his executive limousine the President looked at the three of them coming across the grass and recognized, in every detail, the vision he had gotten from God. The tears in his eyes weren't just for Tracy, but for thanks to a loving God that cared enough to save a little girl and honor his prayers. He got out of the car and, going to one knee, he hugged her tightly. "I am very happy you're coming home."

Tracy smiled and hugged her favorite uncle. "I missed you" was all she said. The smile she was wearing was payment enough for everyone involved. The President stood up and shook Jack's hand and then Laura's. He looked at both of them and said, "I owe you more than I can ever repay. If you need anything, now or in the future, please call me." It was very obvious that he was speaking as Andrew Bollen as well as the President of the United States in his sincerity.

There was a bustle and movement in the people surrounding the President and then one of the rescue team came through the ring of Secret Service people and talked quietly to Mark. Mark indicated that Jack and Laura join him to one side. "It seems we still have a problem." At their questioning looks, he said, "There were only forty-eight children here. That means that Lister has fifty kids in another room somewhere else and we don't have time to search for it. I told them to keep looking while we try to meet with and deal with Lister in Greece."

Mark pointed out that they were running out of time if they hoped to meet Lister in Athens. Sarah walked up, looked at her watch and asked Mark, "Okay, this worked out very well so far, but now, how are we going to make it to Greece in just over five hours?"

Mark smiled and pointed at the sky. "The good old U.S. Air Force has agreed to get us there in time. But, we will have to report back to Ellington Air Force Base in the next fifty minutes and your friendly air taxi is waiting."

Jack spent the next half-hour, during the helicopter ride, in prayer with Laura. He was confident that Mark would get them there in time. His confidence was based on the fact that he knew they were working on God's time and God is never in a rush, but he is never, ever late.

As they headed to the air base Mark noticed that Jack was carrying the case he had gotten out of the hotel safe with the crucifixion nail in it. "You're not thinking of taking the real one to this character are you?"

A peaceful calm settled over Jack as he looked at his friend. "That seems to be what the Lord wants me to do, again." Mark looked knowingly at the man that had become one of his best friends and realized his reference was to the way the nail was used in Denver to help destroy Don Miland. Jack smiled and continued, "Don't you think the forces of darkness will know and tell him if I'm not bringing the real thing?"

Mark did not overlook things normally, but he was still an infant in spiritual warfare matters and he knew it. Nodding he smiled, "Yeah, I guess they would."

Mark hoped that God was sending His judgment against Max Lister using them, as the Crossfire Team raced to the air base in southeast Houston.

CHAPTER TWENTY-THREE

The Colonel reread the order from the President of the United States. The order was absolutely clear and unambiguous. The Air Force was to get the four people presenting themselves to the base commander at Ellington Air Force Base from Houston to the home of the 31st Fighter Wing at Aviano Air Base in Aviano, Italy. He had less than six hours to accomplish his mission. The order left it up to the Commander to determine just how to do that with the aid of one Major Mike White. Colonel Harry Trent was up to the challenge. He was a career officer in the Air Force and had achieved his position by earning it.

He personally cut the orders and assigned the pilots. When the two men and two women arrived at the base by helicopter, he met them himself. Introductions were brief.

The Colonel strode into the room where the Malones, Mark, and Sarah had been taken, a small ready room where pilots were briefed on their operations, before a flight. Jack noticed that Harry Trent looked like a trim version of John Wayne and he had similar characteristics. He cut a dashing figure of a command officer.

He asked them to sit down for a minute. He didn't ask for anything more than their first names. He then outlined the President's order and his solution.

"I received this presidential order less than twenty five minutes ago. It requires me to have all four of you in Aviano, Italy in approximately five hours. Since the shortest route my planes can take from here to there is 6,345 miles, it works out to 1,600 miles per hour." He stopped and looked at his audience. There was no panic and no smiles either. "Good" he thought, "They understand the situation." He continued, "An alternate form of transportation will be waiting at Aviano to take you to Athens."

He paced the front of the room. "I don't know what training you people have and I don't want to know. I also don't know if you have had any time in a jet fighter. But you're about to have both the training and the experience at the same time. To achieve the goal the President has placed before us I need to put each one of you into the back seat of an F35C Advanced Tactical Fighter and we don't have time for politeness. So, if each of you will skin down to your underwear and come over to this scanner, we will get started." He led them into a large room and turned to a door and called out, "Specialists."

Four men and four women answered that summons by rushing into the room. As the team quickly took off their outer clothing the air force specialists formed two-person teams, men to men and women to women, and moved each member of the team into a high-resolution, 3-D, whole-body scanner. The Colonel explained what was going on. "The scanner maps two million reference points on each one of your individual body shapes. The scanning takes only 15 seconds. We then match the design criteria against available G-Suits. We have a large selection which is computer logged and we should be able to provide you with a suit that is very close to what you require."

A few minutes later the airman teams began quickly suiting up each of the Crossfire team with a flight-suit. All four of them required only small alterations in the suits to make them fit reasonably well. While this was going on, the commander continued his lecture. "These suits will have to do. We normally have suits custom made for each pilot and we take several days to do it. You should have no problem as long as your planes don't get into action or you have to eject. Both cases are very remote and I wouldn't allow you to take the chance if I thought anything like that could happen. Also, as far as anyone else is concerned this version of this aircraft does not exist yet, except possibly as an experimental model. You will forget everything you see, hear, or experience on this flight."

The commander walked over to Sarah. She faced him squarely and returned his gaze. He realized she was not only not worried but very confident. He nodded, "Miss, we both know what service you work for and your honor-bound requirements to that service in regards to our new hardware. Since you have been ordered to travel with this group by our President I am not going to stop you. But, I cannot allow you to observe these particular versions of this aircraft until they are announced to our allies, of which your country is one. Therefore, I can offer one of two options, which one is your call. I can have you sedated before leaving this building for the duration of the flight, or I can blindfold you and keep you isolated until you get to Italy. Which do you want?

Sarah smiled, "Colonel, we not only have the latest specifications for the F35C in all three configurations, but videos of the combat flight characteristics. One of our pilots has already flown a beta test model. The top speed of the aircraft with a new coat of wax is 2,800 km/h or 1740 mph, or over 1500 knots per hour. The power plants are two 255.68 KN Pratt & Whitney F119-100 augmented turbofans. The actual service ceiling is over 70,000 feet, and the armament includes 20mm Cannon, internal bays for two AIM-9 and four AIM-120A or six AIM-120C air-to-air missiles, or two AIM-9 and two AIM-120, and two air-to-surface missiles. External hard points are available for four more AIM-120s or other ordnance. The radar is an APG-77C, which is a joint venture of your Westinghouse and Raytheon companies. The avionics package is capable of 82 channels of simultaneous data presentation in the current mode. But there is a modification to the system that is on the order of a magnitude of improvement in the display of the forward-looking FLIR system and Doppler radar information. And, unless you have moved ahead of that design I would really prefer to stay awake and alert during the trip. Now, as you Americans are fond of saying, the ball is in your court."

Mark winked at Jack and Laura. None of them were at all surprised by the extent of the knowledge that Sarah possessed about the secret American aircraft. Both Sarah and the Mossad had proven to be on the leading edge when it came to the intelligence business. The commander stood still and stared at her for about five seconds while he digested the classified information the Mossad agent had given him. In characteristic style he did not let the change in Sarah's status due to her knowledge throw him. "When will the modifications be available to us?"

Sarah frowned and tipped her head to the side. "Your process flow says in two weeks. The Russians, who are having a really bad time getting microchips for their MIG-35, think that it may be several months. My people feel it will be more like three weeks due to the approval hang-up of the new DRAM chips by your DOD auditors and the review by DARPA."

The commander nodded and thought for a second. Then he grinned and told her, "Okay, you have just briefed yourself. You are now qualified to fly while awake." Then he looked at his watch. "Snap it up ladies and gentlemen. We've got exactly ten minutes to get these people to their aircraft." He then addressed the team again. "Do exactly what your pilot tells you to do. Do nothing else." He stared at Sarah, "Even if you know everything about the aircraft. For your own safety, do not touch any controls. This is important. The positions you will be in are fighting positions and these planes need to be fully armed considering where they are going. We don't have time to deactivate the systems where you will be. Again, do exactly what your pilot tells you to do and nothing else, Clear?" Everyone nodded, even the Air Force specialists helping prepare the team.

The four of them were fitted for helmets and Laura agreed with the others that these were really good fits. The commander wished them God's speed, and gave them the thumbs up sign as they were rushed out onto the airfield to the waiting fighter aircraft. As Mark was leaving he shook the Commander's hand and thanked him for his help. The team then boarded an open shuttle vehicle to race to the planes.

Up to this point, Laura had been in a slight state of shock. Dancing around in your underwear with your husband, with six other men and five other women watching was somewhat stressful. Being trussed-up like a Thanksgiving turkey was even more stressful, not to mention heavy and constricting, and the dreary colors. But the most stressful was yet to come. Seeing the formidable-looking airplanes they were being ferried out to, brought back to her full functionality, like a bucket of cold water. "Jack!" She said rather forcefully, "I can't just jump into a supersonic jet fighter and blast off into the air." Looking at the small smile on his face she punched him in the ribs and added, "I wasn't brought up to do things like this."

Jack reached over and hugged her as best he could with all the gear they each had on. "I would spare you the trip if I had anything to say about it, you know that. But Max Lister has made it clear that if we don't meet him in Greece by tomorrow he will kill as many of those kids as he can. You volunteered to go, and if the truth be known, I need and want you there."

Laura knew that, and she knew she was going to get on that plane and go to the Mediterranean even though her stomach had just voted for hiding in her throat. It was a good thing they hadn't eaten for a while. As they neared the aircraft, she had third thoughts about it. The two-seater warplane was huge! Since it had been through preflight, already fired up, and running, it not only looked sinister but radiated a sub-audible rumble that jellied her nerves. Waves of heat boiling off the high-bypass jet engines and the smelly exhaust buffeted her. Before she knew it, she had been separated from Jack and the others and led to a ladder on the side of the plane.

The noise was tremendous and she was glad she was wearing the liner and the pilot's helmet. The specialists with her urged her to climb the ladder, which she did, on shaky knees. One of them came up right behind her and helped her climb into the seat without hitting any of the controls that ringed the seat. The airman was wearing sound mufflers on his ears and was quickly buckling her into the harness. She looked to her right and saw the same thing being done on the other three aircraft. The specialist gently pushed her helmet back against the headrest and snapped a small tension cord to her helmet.

The Airman started plugging the hoses and cables from her suit and helmet into places in the cockpit. Suddenly there was a clear mid-western voice right in her ears. She realized it was the pilot talking to her over the intercom. "Like the Colonel said Ma'am, just sit back and let me do the driving." Laura asked him his name but there was no answer. Then the Airman went down the ladder and someone else came up. Laura was surprised to see a very pretty woman in BDUs and Captain's bars on her collar. She also had a headset on and reached down somewhere and plugged in a cable. Suddenly, she and Laura could talk.

"Hi" the brunette said with a big smile that lit up the scene, "I'm Captain Sanderson. I'm one of the pilots assigned to this outfit. I know you guys are in a real rush but I thought I had better let you in on a few things before you take off." She winked at Laura.

Three minutes later Laura knew how to operate the intercom, 'use the facilities', how to sleep without firing off a missile. She also learned what to expect on what Gayle Sanderson called a 'rocket-propelled roller-coaster' ride for the next five hours. Laura grabbed her hand and smiled. The

Captain squeezed her hand and smiled to let her know it would be all right. Laura released her hand and the Captain let go of the top of the ladder and, putting her feet on the outside of the ladder, she quickly slid to the ground. The ladder was removed and the plane began to taxi immediately, even while the canopy was still closing. Laura craned her neck to force her helmet and its little cord around so that she could see the other three planes in line behind her plane.

The plane did not ride softly across the tarmac to the flight line but then comfort wasn't a design criterion in a warplane. Laura switched the "comm" switch the Captain had shown her and she could hear the pilot talking to the tower. She didn't understand much of what they said, but knew when they got clearance to 'roll'. She braced herself and wondered if she was really ready for this. She didn't have long to wait. The pilot shoved the jet into full military thrust and afterburner at one time. Laura felt like a house had slammed into her back.

After a seemingly short run, the plane leapt from the ground and angled sharply up into the air. Laura couldn't get her breath and she almost blacked out. The force of the forward acceleration was almost too much for her not to mention that her G-suit was squeezing the juice out of her legs and torso. Just as she felt herself actually start to black out, the acceleration eased up somewhat as they begin to gain altitude. After a few seconds the pilot shut off the afterburner and the ride, while still rough, got almost reasonable. The pilot keyed the intercom and said, "I hope that you don't have too rough a ride Laura, but we are on a real tight string and can't take it too slowly. Okay?

Laura felt like she had just lost a three round fight with a Mack truck but managed to key the intercom and tell the pilot, "I think I just completed my aerobics classes for the next three months. I will probably be black and blue for a week after this flight. Anyway, you've got me at a disadvantage. They obviously told you my name but I don't know yours."

He came back with, "Well, my name is Mike White but everyone here calls me the 'Mechanic'." Laura did not realize that Mike was the same pilot that had saved them at the hotel a short time before the ranch raid, and flew Mark in the battle at the armory.

Laura wondered about the nickname, "Why Mechanic?"

"Well, it seems that everyone knows I used to work on cars when I was younger and I'm real interested in how these birds work mechanically. When I was about to graduate from advanced fighter school, an incident involving me caused them to dub me with this handle."

Laura thought for a few seconds. "Okay, I'll bite, what was the 'incident' that got you your 'handle'?"

The entire time they were talking Mike led the flight up to 60,000 feet altitude and headed east-northeast. After liftoff, the plane had angled its wings back to the high-speed position and there had been only a slight shudder as the plane went supersonic and entered super cruise mode. Laura looked at the airspeed indicator and saw that they were just over Mach 3, which was like 1600 miles per hour. Looking out the Plexiglas canopy she looked at the curvature of the earth and the thousands of miles she could see from the edge of space where they were traveling. It was so beautiful. The sky had lost all its color and was a uniform grayish black. Part of the Earth was an achingly deep, bright blue-green and she didn't seen connected to it at all.

The plane she was in seemed to be everything and the rest of the world was remotely distant. She didn't know it but she was sharing a feeling that all pilots have, that she was totally isolated and in the neighborhood of the Lord. The slightly rubbery smell or taste of the oxygen mask and the hiss of the oxygen became background issues, but the feeling of mastery of the sky and earth was very heady. She thought, "I feel like I am right up here with God." It seemed like a dream to travel so fast and so high. She sensed the presence of the Holy Spirit and knew that she was in God's hands. It gave her such a feeling of peace and contentment.

Even though a great deal of the work was being done by computers, Mike was quite busy with flying the aircraft and making sure the other planes were matching his flight profile and matching the mission requirements. After things became routine, he had time to tell Laura about the training incident.

"It seems that I had an aircraft that wasn't as quick as the ones that the instructors used, so they had a real big edge during combat simulations. I was flying an older model F-16 and they were pretty smug about how they could out fly me. Well now. It wasn't me they were out flying, it was my air-plane. So, we were coming up to final flight-testing and I was dreading it. So much so, that I didn't ask for a weekend pass to town before the test on Monday."

"Everybody else took off and it was pretty much my airbase over the weekend. I didn't have anything to do so I walked down to the flight line and watched the aircrews maintaining the planes. While I was watching I saw one of the small red, inspection flags fly away from a missile bay door on one of the aircraft this master sergeant had just checked over. I was going to mention it to him when this Major shows up and starts checking the plane over. By now the flag had blown into the grass at the edge of the concrete."

"Well, now. The Major finds a flag missing and called the sergeant over and begins to rag on him. The sergeant assures the Major that the flag had been there and looks around to find it, which he can't do. This is going to be big trouble and I don't want to see an honest man get docked pay for something that wasn't his fault. So I walk over to the grass and pick up the flag and take it over to the sergeant and tell him I saw it blow off the airplane. Well, the Major is mollified and the sergeant is happy. Eventually the Major flies off into the wild blue yonder and the sergeant and I get to discussing aircraft and maintenance. During the conversation I mention that old number 094, my F-16 is a real dog in flight performance. He nodded and says he'll look at her and see what he can do. We shake hands and he thanks me for saving his bacon. I told him I expected he'd do the same thing for me."

"Monday comes and we take off for the trials and I can't believe I've got the same airplane. I mean, it was the same airplane, old 094. But it's like it's got a rocket attached to it. Well now, I blew them all away with the performance on the test and out maneuvered the instructors so badly they conceded the battle and gave me the top grade. All the other pilots wanted to know what I had done, so I told them the truth, 'Nothing." They didn't believe me and somehow they got the story started that I had tricked up the engine of the plane and that's how I became "the mechanic.""

"I looked up that sergeant before I shipped out and bought him dinner. He told me he wanted to test the latest version of the engine that they had just gotten in. I guess it got tested real well."

Laura enjoyed the story and noticed that they were already crossing over the East coast of the country and headed out over the Atlantic Ocean. So she asked Mike how he liked this plane compared to old 094. He didn't even hesitate. "Ma'am, you have got to understand something about jet fighter pilots. We always want the latest and greatest. I liked that old plane, but this honey is so sweet and sophisticated that I fell in love with it the first time I saw it. The F35C is so quick that it does what you want before you know you want to do that. It gives you so much information through the PFD and MFDs that it's like having another person with you that thinks like you do but much, much faster. It is absolutely the neatest plane I've ever even heard of!"

Laura liked his enthusiasm and drive when he talked about the plane. "What's a PFD or a MFD?"

The pilot chuckled, "I always forget that people, real people that is, not jet jockeys, don't talk in acronyms. PFD is military jargon for Primary Flight Display and MFD is for Multifunctional Display. These are the display screens from which I get my information about the plane and everything around it. You've got an echo display of the PFD back there right in front of you."

Laura looked at the screen and all the colored data represented by it. Many of the displayed items were constantly changing and sometimes portions of the display would change. It was all very confusing and she was glad Major Mike was there to drive the bus. The pilot spoke up in the middle of her musings, "Excuse me Ms. Malone, but you've got a call on the flight intercom. I'll switch it over for you."

A second later she heard Jack's voice in her ears. It was a wonderful sound. "Hi honey, how is it going?" She thought about all the things she could say, but just kept it simple. "Great! How about you?"

"Same here, these planes are fascinating but I think I'm going to see if I can catch a little sleep and try to get ready for our meeting tomorrow, or I think it will be tomorrow. As fast as we're going, it might be yesterday."

A funny thought struck her and she struggled to keep her voice flat as she told him, "Well, don't think about the meeting too much. We don't want you to get 'Maxed' out, now do we?"

She heard a long low chuckle at that. He told her good night and switched off. She was as happy as she could be locked in a G-Suit going three times the speed of sound. She talked to the pilot and watched the other aircraft for a while and then noticed that the speed was dropping. She heard the pilot talking over the radio and then he came on the intercom and informed her that they had to refuel. Laura wondered where they were going to land since they were out over the Atlantic Ocean. Then suddenly she felt the plane jerk around a bit and a big thump. Looking around the pilot's helmet she saw the bottom of another aircraft and a long cable with a little mushroom attached to the end and it was locked onto an arm that jutted out of the plane they were in. Then she realized he meant in-flight refueling. She'd read about that a while back. She looked over and she could see the other three planes being refueled at the same time. Jack's plane was also hooked to the tanker her plane was connected to while the other two were hooked onto another tanker. It only took a few minutes and then they were free and rocketing back up to speed again.   After that she was surprised to find that she not only could sleep, but that she missed three-fourths of the overwater journey, including five more gas breaks. They were coming into a guarded air base in Italy before she was even aware that they had reached their destination.

CHAPTER TWENTY-FOUR

Laura thought that Italy is a beautiful country to visit, warm, inviting, and friendly. If you did more than just climb out of one plane and into another and take off again immediately. Their total time on Italian soil was less than twenty minutes.

As the CIA aircraft flew out over the Mediterranean Sea in a southern direction, Laura thought back to the last half hour of their flight in the fighter jets. Word had come that Lister's plane had been denied landing privileges at Athens' airport because Interpol now listed him as an international terrorist. Lister's plane flew toward the Libyan coast from Athens. The pilot took the most economical speed and altitude to stretch his reserves.

As the F35Cs raced into the Mediterranean area on the approach to Aviano, a radio call had been forwarded to Jack. Cramped and tired after the majority of the flight, Jack listened to Lister's demand that they pursue a course that would allow them to meet with him on friendlier ground, friendlier to him, of course. But the latest word was that the children still had two hours to go and had not been found as yet. So Jack relayed the requirement to his pilot who passed it on to the flight commander. The message eventually got back to the White House. The response was ten minutes in return, practically the speed of light where legislators are concerned. Major White informed all four passengers at the same time. "Folks, the head shed understand your needs and the requirement to follow this character into Libya. Now, understand that there is absolutely no way, these aircraft can be risked on the new mission. An alternative means of transportation has been identified and will be ready at the Aviano Air Base upon our arrival. With the latest data from our satellites, your man Lister is taking a real slow route. The brains in Langley think that he has to do that to conserve fuel. So, there will plenty of time to catch up with him. Sit back and relax. We will be landing in about twenty minutes."

Jack punched up the intercom and talked to Major White. "Who did they stick with the job of flying us into Libya?"

The pilot just chuckled, "Some poor sucker, you can count on that."

Their arrival was fast and the landing rough. But once down, the planes were taxied directly into a military hangar and the doors were shut to keep the F-35Cs out of sight. Climbing out of the aircraft was not as difficult as getting in had been. Laura felt like she had come to have a special relationship with both the plane and the pilot and she thanked him for his courtesy and friendliness while she patted the side of the big, silver-gray bullet that had just carried her between continents. They were allowed a quick shower and given a chance to change back into their regular clothes before they were hustled into a plush interior and taxied back out to the flight line and into the air again.

This aircraft was as different from the F-35C as a limousine was from a Lamborghini. The four of them were riding in soft, luxurious seats that reclined and had lumbar adjustments, a built-in TV in the arm of the seat, and a padded footrest that felt great after the fighter plane's cramped interior.

Mark was checking out the cockpit and the instrumentation. He had never seen some of it. It reeked of leading-edge avionics and he moved to the seat to the right of the pilot and asked him about the plane. The pilot looked over at Mark and laughed, "Small world isn't it?" Mark stared at Major Mike White.

The pilot explained. "The President said to use this plane for you people. The CIA pilot, his boss and his boss all flatly refused to reveal the existence of this aircraft to anyone who wasn't in the CIA, so all three of them are now on their way to their new jobs. One went to Bosnia, one to Baghdad and the other to the South Pole. The newly promoted bosses at the CIA decided that the President could do whatever he wanted with the aircraft. So, since you had need of a pilot immediately, the President asked me politely, to drive you guys. I just happen to have had a crash course in this plane last month, strange coincidence, Huh?" The Major started off with the easy points. "Well, it is based on a commercial design but actually is a completely different aircraft with a much stronger frame and skin structure built from the ground up in the Skunk works."

He checked his readouts and HUD and continued with his comments. "This beauty was designed to fool people, professional people if you know what I mean. It looks like a typical corporate business jet, but it has advanced military engines and avionics. It isn't armored nor is it armed. It would be obvious to the most casual observer if it were. But it can fly with a lot of the military jets in the world. So far, I'm the only non-CIA type who has been given an opportunity to fly it, and where we are headed, I might be the only one who ever does. I've been given permission by the Chief of Staff of the U.S. Armed Forces to fly you into Tripoli if necessary. Heck! I've already flown two of the hottest platforms available, this will be the third, shot up half of Houston, broke the transatlantic speed record for military jets and I'm still not qualified to know what you guys are doing! But that's okay, I like the job."

Mark looked at his friend. "You must be tired. You just flew half-way across the world. Now you tell me that you'd fly this thing into Tripoli and make it a present to the Brotherhood?"

The pilot ruefully smiled. "Yes. And no, I'd fly you into Tripoli but I'll push the self-destruct button as we leave the plane. There won't be enough left to sift for clues."

Mark looked grimly at his friend. "Yeah, but you have all that knowledge in your head. They are experts at prying it out of people. Have you thought about that?"

Mike mulled that over for a few seconds. "Hum... yeah, that could be a problem." Then he brightened, "Hey, don't worry about them torturing me. I doubt that any of us will arrive alive on the mad man's soil anyway."

Mark nodded, thinking that is the way the world worked. "Okay, the mission is this. The man in the plane we are to meet with is named Max Lister. He is a rich terrorist with a penchant for little children and . . ." The pilot held up his right hand to stop Mark. "I do know about Max. But, why don't you just shoot the silly goose out of the air instead of following him all over the globe?"

Mark went on to explain about the children under the threat of the Sarin nerve gas that Max had set up as a threat to lure them to him. At that point Mike got very quiet and grim. He was also very aware of the effects of Sarin nerve gas. The conversation petered out and Mark started checking the communications to see if any progress had been made in locating the children back in the States. Nothing yet, but they had some good leads. Great, the remaining kids have less than one hour and are probably watching that evil DVD.

The pilot called Mark's attention to the radar a few minutes later. "Look, he's not making for Tripoli. He seems to be heading for the eastern side of Libya. Why do you think he would do that?" Mark shook his head.

The Major thought about it for a few minutes and then started running fuel estimates on the computer. He looked up at Mark. "I have a really good guess where he is heading and why." When Mark just stared at him, he continued. "He doesn't have enough go-juice to make it to Tripoli, but he does have enough to reach this point." He pointed at a mountainous region of the eastern end of Libya. Mark looked at his map but could find no real cities or airports in that area. "Why? Is he just going to land on the sand?"

The pilot grinned because he knew something his passengers didn't. "No, he doesn't have to ditch. There's a secret base there in the flat area of the mountains at 2500 feet. There's a runway on it long enough to land that plane."

Mark sat back, "If it's a secret base, then how do you know about it?"

The Major looked hurt. "It's my business to know things like that. Anyway, the Libyans aren't real good about keeping secrets. Especially when they let General Mujahid, build one out in the hills directly under the paths of two of our spy satellites. But, I don't think that we want to follow him there. The CIA says that they are really sensitive about keeping their precious secrets. Also, they are armed to the teeth with tanks, anti-aircraft guns, and a brand new surface-to-air missile battery according to the latest NSA update. No, I really don't think we want to go there."

Mark looked at the man. "Mike, if that's where the louse goes then that's where we have to go. The invitation is probably bogus but right now it's the only hope for those kids." The discussion was over at that point.

Forty minutes later they were almost to the Libyan coastline when the pilot informed them that Lister's plane was definitely headed directly for the mountain base. It had started to descend to a landing and was only sixty miles ahead of them. A tell-tale started rapidly blinking on the pilot's console which tightened up the Major's gut. At the same time a message came in for Mark from Houston. Mark put on a headset and keyed the microphone. "This is Connelly." Major Wolfman came back at him. "We've found the kids! We'll have them out in ten minutes. Get out of there and let him go! Either the Mossad will get him before long or General Mujahid will kill him for his failure to destabilize the U.S." Mark grinned, "Thanks, out."

He turned to the Major, "Okay Mike my friend. They've found the kids and we don't have to be here anymore. Take us back to Greece." He stared at the Air Force pilot who wasn't sharing his joy at the relief of the tension. "What's the matter? Aren't you glad that we don't have to visit Mujahid's base?"

The pilot flicked a switch and Mark could see a magnified picture from a camera mounted on the underside of the plane looking backward. He saw six or more jet fighters. Looking closer he could see that they were MiG-25s. He didn't have to see the Libyan markings on the hulls to tell him that they weren't friendly. The pilot shook his head. "They aren't going to let us out of the net. I don't have enough speed to outrun those buckets. I think we are going to visit the General after all."

CHAPTER TWENTY-FIVE

As Lister's plane touched down on the desert airfield, he finally felt safe from the pursuing enemy, although he had botched up the very costly American plan. He knew General Mujahid was going to be volcanic but, he thought that he could realign the General's thinking as soon as he offered to repay Libya for the cost of the failure. As the plane taxied into a protected revetment, he actually laughed out loud. He noticed that this startled several of his men who had never heard him laugh before.

Deplaning took only a few minutes and he was met on the ground by General Mujahid himself. As one of terrorism's top military experts, the General was somewhat of a rebel. He understood the correct use of explosives, heavy weapons and how to successfully use strategy to win in a combat situation. The mere fact that he was in command of his own top secret base in the middle of nowhere near the coast of Libya and the border of Egypt was proof enough that he could do as he wished.

His job was to protect Libya's most valuable secret. No one was to suppose to even remotely know that this base existed. Now he was suddenly saddled with this traitor who had failed him completely even though he, General Matrice Mujahid, had personally given him over three hundred million U.S. dollars to make certain things happen.

The General was painfully aware of Max Lister's failures and his flight from the now-incensed west. Every agency including Interpol was chasing him. The General thought that he really should have denied him landing rights. "How did I get involved with this imbecile?" thought the General. He thought back and remembered that he had bid, successfully, on one of the children that Lister's efforts had secured for the Middle East. "But, still, he should not be here." the General thought. "Mahout Mohammad" will be furious if he finds out."

The General's frown increased with his next thought. "Of course, the fact that as the commander of the secret base Mujahid was secretly held in high esteem by the new ruler of Libya. That fact did not prevent that self-same ruler from reminding Mujahid that he was only allowed to stay on Libyan soil because he hadn't become an embarrassment to the

Libyan government. Mohammad publicly denied any association with Mujahid but knew allowing him a base enhanced his own reputation with the terrorists of the world. General Mujahid knew the Libyan commander-in-chief probably wouldn't want his country identified with the presence of an international criminal staying boldly at a secret base in Libya."

General Mujahid was aware of the political situation in the Middle East. While many of the Arab nations were boldly announcing their anti-terrorist policies to the world, most still supported the clandestine organizations.

General Mujahid was pleased that an un-named sponsor had given him an armor force of sixteen tanks and two Russian ZSU-23 4 anti-aircraft batteries. Suddenly, yesterday, that same un-named sponsor had replaced fully half of his tank force with brand-new trainees on a two hours notice. In addition, three days ago, He was given a surface-to-air missile battery. This really irritated him. He was an ex-tank commander himself. He didn't understand, nor care for, the mobile, yet fixed, anti-aircraft missile battery. He had his tanks in revetments so that they were protected from air strikes, yet their heavily armored turrets could rotate and fire in all directions. These vulnerable missiles were just standing there on top of the ground like sitting ducks.

The General was far more pleased with the ZSUs. He knew the narrow-slot radar gave their four 23mm guns an excellent kill ratio against low flying aircraft. This protected his tanks. He thought about the mobile anti-aircraft guns and was reminded about their capabilities. He was proud of the fact that he knew the Russian words for ZSU, which stood for Zenitnaya Samokhodnaya Ustanovka. His "Shilka" ZSU-23-4 anti-aircraft, self-propelled guns were capable of acquiring, tracking and engaging low-flying aircraft while either in place or on the move. The General employed the two he had, 200 meters apart, 400 meters behind his tanks. Their armament consisted of four 23mm cannons with a maximum slant range of 3,000 meters.

On the other hand, the General had been livid about the new crews he was assigned for his empty tanks. True, these new troops had been trained on the tanks he had, but at least half of them had never been off-base with their tanks, let alone fought in them.

But, for the moment, the General was stuck with Max Lister and his problem because the Western powers were following him. For the General to kill him or send him away would compromise the security of this base and possibly, reveal his involvement in the Houston riot adventure. Mujahid determined Lister could live and stay as long as he did not attempt to interfere with the on-going military operations.

General Mujahid was a diplomat as well as a good soldier. That is why he knew that he still survived after being in the terrorist world for fifteen years. But his great contribution to the war against Israel could not be endangered. These Americans following Lister's plane could not be allowed to let the world know more about this base. Therefore, the General would eliminate the threat to his base, at the same time saving Max Lister's hide. Who knows, maybe Lister would give him a couple of free American children to do anything he wanted with them.

Max Lister shook the General's hand and asked if he knew the situation involving the pursuit. The General shook his head and had Lister follow him into the quiet command trailer. The powerful air conditioning was like a wall of ice water after the heat of the desert. Leading the industrialist over to the plot board, the General explained what was taking place. The pursuit was by a lone American aircraft, which was not even a military warplane. The plane was less than ten minutes out from the coast and closing at approximately six hundred kilometers per hour. He then pointed to a large radar screen above the plot table.

"You see the eight blips farther out than the blip representing the American aircraft?" After Lister's nod he continued. "Each of those eight blips represents a Russian-made MiG-25 supersonic fighter that I have "borrowed" from Libya. Each one has four missiles which the Americans call "fire and forget" which will continue to track and destroy the target while the fighter goes on to other targets. Each one also carries four infra-red heat seeking missiles designed to home in on engine heat and destroy the target."

Turning to the plot again the General pointed out the four hundred ground troops which were on high alert and the sixteen main battle tanks that were already receiving ground radar information on the target aircraft. He then indicated the ZSUs and the ground-to-air missile battery which would have lock-on in just one or two minutes. "So you see Mr. Lister, even if they realize the forces they are up against on the ground and turn tail and run, they won't get away. I will eliminate these dangerous people you have led to my base and protect my future. They will not survive the next few minutes. I guarantee it!"

Lister suddenly broke out into a sweat despite the air conditioning. He had been told in a dream to acquire the talisman for the Prince of Darkness. Lister knew who his boss really was, and to destroy what Satan wanted, just when it was within their grasp would be very, very bad. "General, I must insist that you force that plane to land and capture the Americans in it. It is in your best interest because of what one of them is carrying. You can't destroy the plane because it would destroy the talisman."

The General raised an eyebrow and stared at Lister. "Just what is this talisman that is so important that I should jeopardize my base, not to mention my career and my life?"

Max Lister knew that he had to convince the General, so in his urgency he did something that was totally abnormal for him, he told the truth, and he wasn't very good at presenting it. "It is an item from the crucifixion of Jesus Christ. It is extremely valuable and very powerful and we need to acquire it at all costs."

The General eyed Lister with distaste as he thought. "How dare this idiot traitor come onto my base, against my orders, and tell me what to do. And, all about some Christian fairy tale about a prophet who was rightfully killed two thousand years ago." It was with great effort that he was able to maintain a flat voice when he spoke. "Sergeant, if this man opens his mouth again, Shoot him. Do you understand me?" The Sergeant nodded and took his pistol out of his holster and held it pointed directly at Max Lister. The General was not a man to disobey.

Max Lister knew to talk would be his death sentence. But if they destroyed the crucifixion nail, they would die anyway. He realized that he had no way out and he collapsed into a chair and buried his head in his hands as he waited for the horrible doom that was sweeping over him.

The General picked up a small microphone and addressed the troops. "There will be no quarter given. Destroy the American Infidels on my command only. Anyone who disobeys me will not live to regret it." Switching to the aircraft frequency he addressed the fighter aircraft, "Stay close enough to ensure that the American aircraft cannot escape. We will destroy it from the ground." As an ex-Army commander, General Mujahid knew he had command of the aircraft and knew their arsenal, but he had little or no knowledge about their tactics or vulnerabilities.

Receiving confirmations of his orders the General reviewed the situation and determined that it was overkill and overwhelming odds against the Americans. "Good." he thought "I will achieve a great victory with little effort and the terrorist community will honor me again." He was quite sure that nothing could go wrong this time. He felt the power that he had command of and knew he was in control.

On the CIA aircraft, Mike White looked at Mark Connelly and said, "Uh oh." He was looking at a MIL7886 heads-up display that was so new it hadn't even been provided to the USAF yet. The data output it displayed was staggering. He could see at least twenty ground-based radars, all of them searching for him and several already locked onto his aircraft. The advanced display also relentlessly displayed the attack aircraft behind them and the battle radars they had locked on to his aircraft. The highest priority flashing displays were the surface-to-air missile battery which indicated a multiple missile capability of ten SAM missiles and the two ZSU-23-4s.

Mike shook his head and said, "We're toast no matter what we do. I hope your friend back there has got an ace up his sleeve because we are going to need it in about thirty seconds. They aren't going to let us get down on the ground except as ashes."

At that exact moment, Jack was seeking the conviction and assurance he had when he directed the aircraft toward the shoreline where Max Lister's plane had landed. Jack was concerned he had missed God's plan and put all of them in mortal danger. He earnestly prayed to the Lord for guidance.

Jack closed his eyes and saw a flaming sword. Jack opened his eyes and was startled. He saw the same warrior he thought he'd seen underneath Lister's ranch. The imposing figure was still wearing the armor that looked like pure light it was so bright. Jack then noticed that the warrior was drawing the sword of fire. Just as the vision was beginning to fade, the warrior, who had been looking forward through the front of the aircraft, lifted his flaming sword, the helmeted head briefly turned toward Jack, and the warrior winked at Jack. He looked to the front again and began to walk forward through the front of the aircraft as he faded completely out of sight.

Then, Jack knew that God was about to smite General Mujahid and Max Lister. It didn't matter what happened to them. He knew they were in God's hands.

Jack looked at the others in the cabin. Mark was up front with the pilot and Laura was deep in prayer. When he looked at Sarah he knew that she too had seen the angel. She had a most intense look on her face. Sarah looked at Jack and nodded, "Yes, I saw him too. Praise Yahveh, God is with us."

Mark knew the odds against them and as he listened to Jack and Sarah talk about someone he hadn't seen he recalled the time that he had been with Jack when God had delivered them from Satan's grasp in Colorado. He now saw the same look on Jack's face as he had in Don Miland's basement. But he had to make sure. "Jack, are you sure?" Jack looked back at his friend with sorrow that Mark hadn't been blessed to see what he and Sarah had seen and with happiness because of the absolute assurance that God had given him. "Mark, God is with us, right now, right here. He is using us to bring His judgment on Max Lister." This was delivered with such rock solid confidence that Mark was completely reassured. He turned back to Mike and smiled. "Keep your present heading, speed and altitude. We'll be okay."

Major White knew that the odds ranged against his aircraft were more than a hundred times the amount required to destroy them. But that didn't matter because he couldn't do anything else anyway. So he nodded and kept his heading directly toward General Mujahid's base. For the first time since grade school he prayed, really, really hard that God would keep his soul.

As the aircraft, flying at 200 feet altitude, entered into the trap, the General allowed them to continue to approach even though the missile battery crew was urgently requesting permission to fire. "Those upstarts can just wait." he thought. "He was Army after all. His tanks had as much right to kill Americans as those missiles." When the aircraft was a mere eight kilometers from the base the General commanded all units to "FIRE!"

The crew of the Russian-made missile battery was still untried in combat. In fact, they had never fired a missile before. Oh, they knew the drill, they had to do it over and over again with dummy missiles because real missiles were too costly to train with and could not be risked. Therefore, the missile battery commander elected to fire all five missiles in the top rack at the American aircraft when the General finally gave the order. At the same time all twelve tanks fired their main battle cannons in a pre-computed parabolic arc so as to arrive at the position the aircraft would be at in four seconds. The ZSUs held their fire in reserve as needed.

The closing speed between the aircraft and the missiles was approximately 3000 meters per second. The aircraft would cover approximately one thousand meters before reaching the impact point. The missiles would cover the remaining 2000 meters in less than one and one-half seconds.

When the heads-up display indicated that SAMs had been launched, Mike followed established procedures for acute angle, head-on missile attacks, He ejected chaff to confuse any lasing or radar beams, emitted a jamming signal to break any possible radar lock-on, and slammed the throttles of the engines into the afterburner position in a calculated attempt to make the missiles miss. Since the missiles were coming at such an extreme angle, just below head-on, the jamming and chaff would cause the missiles to maintain their present heading. Then, by accelerating suddenly the plane would move ahead of the pre-computed position. In theory, this should make the missiles pass behind the aircraft. This was basic combat training for all flight crews. Mike knew that the American aircraft hid unexpectedly powerful engines with afterburners. A fact had not been taken into account by the shooters on the ground. He saw two of the trailing MiG-25s go into afterburner to match them.

Mike's HUD showed him that the ZSUs got into the action at this point but had to rotate to acquire the American plane which had already over flown their position. The eight 23mm cannons opened up with huge gouts of flame as they threw as many cannon shells as they could at the fleeing plane. Two of their rounds hit the aircraft but only slightly damaged the right wing and the body at the rear. The Major noted that none of the MIGs were behind them but one of the ground launched missiles had reversed its course and was rapidly approaching them.

Mike assessed the damage while he was flying at treetop level to avoid the last missile. The missile drove toward the plane, homing in on the heat of their exhaust. Suddenly Mike saw a brighter source of heat to his right. This attracted the simple tracking computer of the missile and it turned toward the new source and away from the plane. It flew beyond its preset limits and detonated.

Racing furiously westward at well over the speed of sound to escape an expected second missile launch, the American aircraft had stayed in nap-of-the-earth avoidance procedures. This dropped the aircraft to within fifty feet of the ground, which would make it extremely hard for a surface-to-air missile to lock on.

One minute of westward travel at 400 miles per hour included climbing over and descending behind a range of low mountains. Therefore, the nap-of-the-earth procedure had the interestingly helpful side-effect of placing almost ten miles of desert rock and sand between the American aircraft and the base. Suddenly Mike detected a nuclear explosion from behind them. The small mountain range's ground effectively shielded them from the light, heat, and blast effects of the detonation. But it didn't keep them from being affected by the nuclear explosion.

CHAPTER TWENTY-SIX

As they flew West, Mike knew that the electromagnetic pulse generated by the explosion radiated outward from ground zero at the speed of light. When it passed through the American aircraft it effectively shut down all electrical activity on the aircraft for several seconds. Several seconds in a jet aircraft flying fifty feet off of the ground at supersonic speeds is usually quite fatal.

When he saw the flash from behind them, Mike knew what to expect. As the power died, he eased back on the controls to attempt to gain some altitude before they smashed into the earth. This provided some extra time to give the advanced military electronics, specifically hardened to survive a nuclear EMP, time to surge back into service.

By a strange coincidence, the aircraft glided out over a desert valley at this precise time. This added sixteen hundred more feet of air space between the bottom of the aircraft and the ground. As the air speed bled off, the plane nosed over toward the ground and gathered speed. Mike was then able to ram-start his engines and pull power before becoming a permanent fixture in the Libyan Desert landscape, although it was a near thing.

As they circled widely to the south to avoid the radioactive mushroom cloud Jack could see the area where the secret base had been. The utter destruction in the area previously occupied by the military base was incredible. All around the area there were avalanches and earthquakes. Gases poured up through huge vents ripped in the earth. The sun was turned to a blood red color by the debris thrown into the air by the nuclear blast.

Jack thought that the scene was a vivid picture of God's anger, a literal hell on earth and a well-deserved end for Max Lister. Jack remembered Genesis 19:24 about the destruction of Sodom and Gomorrah for gross sexual perversion similar to that of Lister's, *"Then the Lord rained down burning sulfur on Sodom and Gomorrah - from the Lord out of the heavens."* Jack thought that the area around the military base must look like Sodom and Gomorrah had to Abraham when he came to gaze upon the destruction of the cities the next morning.

No one said a word until they were several miles off the coast of Libya and the effects of the ZSU's anti-aircraft damage were becoming noticeable. The handling was becoming sluggish due to the wing damage. But worse were the rapidly falling fuel stores. One of the anti-aircraft rounds must have punctured a fuel line. Mike knew they weren't going to make it back to Greece and he doubted that they would be popular back in Libya.

An American voice came through his headphones and suddenly they were being vectored to an American aircraft carrier less than twenty miles away.

At 80,000 feet altitude, the SR-71 Blackbird spy plane called in the nuclear event to his control.

On the CIA aircraft, as it circled to approach the aircraft carrier, everyone on board was reflecting on the events of the last hour and in a communal sense of gratitude, each said thanks to the Lord in their own fashion. Mark looked up at Mike White and said quietly, "Man, don't ever, ever get God mad at you!"

Mike glanced out of the corner of his eyes at Mark and Jack. He wasn't even going to get these guys mad at him, let alone God.

Sarah sat looking out the window, smiling. Not only had that madman Max Lister met a horrific end, quite probably so had General Matrice Mujahid. Tel Aviv would be delighted. She knew that she could now set in motion a plan to divert this team of people to Israel to unravel a threat that could easily plunge the entire world into a gruesome holocaust.

She thought about everything that had happened since she had met the Malones above the Children's Ranch. It was funny in a way. All of her life she had obeyed the laws of God and was a devoted Jewish woman, within the reality of her employment. And yet, she had never felt the real power of God, and she had never before actually seen God's presence like she had in the company of these Christians over the last week or so. She stared at the box sitting next to Jack and considered what she had been taught all her life against what she had seen and experienced lately.

Although this was only the seventh carrier landing Mike had made, the weather was fair, the light good, and the seas calm. He made an acceptable approach and caught the third wire. All in all, an excellent landing considering that he had a damaged bird.

Mike disappeared into the radio room and the team ended up in a debriefing flight room while the Navy worked to quickly fix the plane. After they had been debriefed they were allowed to relax and roam around. Each of them had an opportunity to use the communications room to contact their previous lives and let everyone know that they were still alive and well.

An aircraft carrier is a small city on the water. As an ex-Navy SEAL, Mark was very familiar with the layout and was able to guide Sarah and the Malones through the ship to various destinations and interesting points. Right after eight bells of the fourth watch they were invited to dine with the Captain. The meal was excellent and the Captain very polite and interested in their views of the events of the day. Twenty minutes later a message was delivered to the Captain and he requested the team to join him in his ready room for a teleconference with the President.

President Bollen looked pleased and congratulated them on their success on wrapping up Max Lister. Although he thought using a nuclear bomb was a bit extreme. He was effusive in his praise and brought them up to date on current events. He smiled as he told them, "Libya filed a protest with the United Nations stating that your plane dropped an atom bomb on defenseless peasants in the mountains of Libya and they want a full apology and reparations in the hundreds of millions of dollars."

He looked away and back to the camera. "Unfortunately for them, their secret base was pretty much common knowledge throughout the intelligence community and therefore the political community as well. The fact that the bomb's nuclear signature identified the nuclear material as being Russian in origin didn't back up their claim. The real clincher was the fact that the Russians are claiming that the nuclear material and devices had been stolen from their arsenal five months ago and are demanding Libya pay for the stolen stuff. Libya is denying all involvement with General Mujahid or his toy."

Mark interrupted the President's speech. "Mr. President, aren't the Libyans going to claim the United States stole the bomb and dropped it on Mujahid's base to create a division between Tripoli and Moscow?"

The President shook his head and smiled at Mark. "Always on top of the angles aren't you, Mark? Yes, that's pretty much what we thought that they would do too. But they lost the battle about twenty minutes ago when the Israelis produced one Anatole Korpov." Everyone looked at Sarah as she put her right hand into the air, made a fist, and pulled it down quickly saying, "Yes!"

Jack looked at her for a second and asked her, "Been in the States for a while, huh?" Everyone including the President laughed at that. Sarah just kept smiling.

Mark asked the President, "What did Korpov give the Israelis?"

The President looked at his notes and then back at the camera. "Just about everything it looks like. The Israeli Intelligence group said that he had been 'very cooperative' and was 'eager' to unburden himself of years of terrorist activities. One of the things he explained was how the nuclear material had been stolen. Since he was the one that stole it he should know. He knew details that confirmed the theft and the delivery of the weapons-grade nuclear material to General Mujahid's base. He also provided a great deal of inside information on Max Lister's activities. He said he had a list of the children that had been sold overseas, who the buyers were, and what the dates were. Unfortunately he lost the information before he was captured. He..."

Mark interrupted again. "Mr. President. We have that list. I mean the FBI has that list. Call Agent Gary Rhodes of the Denver office and he can get you Korpov's notebook that I "relieved" him of before he fled the country."

The President slammed his hand down on the table and said, "If his information is correct, then there is a chance we can get some of those kids back." He turned away from the camera and dictated the FBI Agent's name to someone off screen and told them what to do.

Mark spoke up, "Mr. President, I would like to help in retrieving those children we can identify from Korpov's notes."

Looking back at the team again he leaned back in his seat and studied them for a minute. Making his mind up about his decisions he started talking again. "I would very much appreciate your company at a state function that will be held here at the White House next month. I mean, I am inviting all four of you to be my guests at a little celebration."

The four people looked at each other and nodded. Mark spoke for the group, "We'd be delighted to attend your "celebration" Mr. President."

After farewells, the President signed off and the four team members thanked the Captain and left for their temporary quarters. They would be leaving in an hour for Rome and a commercial flight home, compliments of the United States government.

Jack and Laura sat quietly talking in their small quarters which normally was inhabited by one of the Captain's officers. It had been graciously donated to them during their short stay. Jack asked Laura, "What is your impression of everything we've gone through since we got back from our "vacation"?"

Laura had been thinking about that during the entire time they were shuttled to Greece, to Libya, and to the carrier. "At first, I didn't think I could do it. You know, keep up with the demands and dangers, and the secret agent stuff. But as things went along, I kept praying that God would give me the ability to handle it when I couldn't. He always did. Then I realized that we were doing God's work. Since then, I have done my best and realized that all he wanted was my cooperation and commitment to Him and His plans. If He wants me to take over the world, and tells me to do it with Him by my side, then say hello to the next world ruler. Or, if he tells me to set up a stand in Denver by the railroad station and wash people's feet for free, bring on the towels." She stopped for a second while she gathered her thoughts.

She smiled at Jack and continued. "What was my impression of everything we've gone through since our vacation? I'd say it was the next step in my learning to be a Christian. When we were in the mess in Denver with Don Miland, I learned to lean on the Lord and accept Him as my Savior. Since our vacation I have learned that we have a God-given mission that he passionately wants for us to accept. I have learned to accept His will.

Jack had followed his wife's reasoning and was amazed at the similarity to what he had been thinking. He nodded. "You've been reading my mind again." he smiled as he said it. She looked at him and said quietly, "Not me my love, it's not me who's reading your mind."

Mark called the couple back to the briefing room for a wrap-up of their "mission" which had been analyzed by the NSA using a lot of inputs.

Tom Bradden was the analyst that described what NSA knew or surmised happened during their brief flight over Libya.

"I want you to understand that a lot of this is supposition and conjecture. But on the good side, the people that put this together are rarely wrong."

He looked at his computer. "I picked up your vacation trip to the sands of Libya right after the ground-to-air missiles were fired at you."

"The sudden acceleration of your aircraft effectively placed it out of the radar view of the majority of the missiles. After reaching two seconds and arming themselves the only targets four of the missiles could acquire were six of the eight MiG-25 aircraft.

"A review of the films being made from an altitude of 80,000 feet by a SR-71 Blackbird of the event showed that the anti-radar tactics and the unexpected acceleration did cause the missiles to track behind your aircraft. We feel that General Mujahid was unaware of the fact that the surface-to-air-missiles had to wait two seconds before they armed themselves and therefore they did not detonate as they passed behind the aircraft at one and one-half seconds. We know that the missile crew could not have actually forgotten that fact. But from the record of the base communications they had expected to fire their missiles long before the plane got into tank cannon range. When the General commanded them to fire, they did so, probably knowing full well that the only way the missiles would knock you down was if the missiles actually ran into the plane. Even though they were only on the base three days we feel that they knew the General's only response to soldiers who disobeyed his direct orders. Apparently they didn't care if the $200,000 missiles couldn't function properly. They were doing what they were told to do."

Changing screens he continued. "As far as the MIGs were concerned we watched their reaction to the sudden, unexpected missile attack. Two used afterburners to chase your aircraft. The remaining six aircraft attempted to evade and distribute chaff to confuse the missiles. It looked like each man was rapidly turning to avoid the oncoming missiles, three aircraft collided and exploded. Three of the missiles impacted on three more of the MIGs, reducing them to airborne scrap metal. The other missile had detected the exhaust heat of the two MIG fighters that were following you. It had reversed course in a tail chase. It was closing on the fighters rapidly."

"These last two fighters which had followed your plane and accelerated were within your jamming signal and had been ignored by the other missiles. We watched the lead MIG-25 fighter explode into a ball of flame. This was caused by one of the tank cannon shells, which were now on a downward arc and impacted on the aircraft. The second aircraft veered to the right to avoid the explosion of the first fighter and ran into another of the descending cannon shells. This one lost a wing and the pilot ejected. That eliminated all of the trailing fighters. The remaining missile must have malfunctioned because it turned away from your aircraft and detonated over the desert."

Tom smiled as he read the next information. "We monitored the base communications from the command trailer on Mujahid's base. Apparently there was total unbelief that your aircraft could have avoided the missiles and the cannon fire. The General was yelling over the radio at the missile battery, the ZSUs, and the tanks to immediately continue to track and fire at your aircraft. We assume that he could not allow you to get away with the knowledge of his base. He was screaming insane threats at the troops which showed that he lost his control. After reviewing all the actions after that, we think his troops made two bad decisions."

"The first bad decision apparently involved Mujahid's tanks. These are used Russian military hardware and their turrets have relatively slow aim and fire capabilities. Especially when trying to down a jet aircraft passing them. These troops were green and untried. They had just been posted to Mujahid's base in the last few weeks. Apparently one of the new officers, whose tank was pointed to the south, pulled his tank out of its revetment and rotated the entire tank in an attempt to lock onto your high-speed west-bound aircraft. Our military tank commander thinks that in his haste to be the first to destroy the enemy the new tank commander ordered the tank gunner to take a snap shot at you while the tank was still rotating. Apparently the gunner saw your aircraft in his sight and pulled the trigger on the main battle cannon. What we saw was that at that precise time, the tank driver stomped on the brakes to lock the tank down. This braking caused the barrel of the cannon to depress below the horizon as it fired.

The 90mm explosive cannon shell traveled two hundred meters, penetrated the wall of the command trailer and detonated. We feel that General Mujahid, Max Lister, and any troops in there were instantly reduced to fragments and never knew that it was their own troops that had killed them."

Switching screens again the analyst continued the reconstructed history of the last minutes of Mujahid's base. "The second mistake the now-dead General's troops made was the haste of the new crew on the missile battery."

"Our analysis of the pivotal action of this battle is that during the initial setup, the missile technicians had decided they only needed the first rack of five missiles. They probably did not remove the mechanical locks on any of the second rack of five missiles. While the crew was spinning the launcher around to fire again at your plane they forgot to rectify this mistake, even though we're pretty sure the launcher was flashing a warning on its panel. It's not unusual for Libyan technicians to remove the fail-safe that would have prevented a launch because they didn't think it was needed."

"We saw the second he fired the second rack of five missiles. The missile engines ignited, but the missiles couldn't leave the launcher. So, the engines tried to leave without the missile bodies. The resultant explosion simultaneously destroyed the missile battery and detonated the nearby ammunition dump. If you'll look closely in this photo the mistake happened because a curious battery technician had opened the ammo dump blast door to watch the destruction of your plane. The expanding fireball from the exploding missiles disintegrated that guy and rushed into the wide open ammo dump exploding everything in an escalating blast of pure energy. It is obvious that as the ammo dump went up, General Mujahid's secret, which he had been zealously protecting, got into the act."

Tom explained some history for the team. "Over the last two years the General has been able to purchase enough Russian nuclear technology to produce a large nuclear weapon without any fissionable material. Recently Mujahid acquired a stolen Russian nuclear warhead they mated to the missile. We feel the Libyans didn't want to import eager, and easily available, Russian technicians even though they had executed the earlier Russians to prevent them from revealing the presence of their nuclear efforts.

The Libyans simply emulated the Russian technology. According to an unnamed source that was privy to the effort, the electrical detonation circuit and firing mechanism were a Russian design, but the construction was pure terrorist interpretation. Our nuclear scientists believe that the combined force of the exploding missile battery and ammo dump succeeded in overloading their primitive fail-safe circuit, which detonated the five-megaton device.

CHAPTER TWENTY-SEVEN

As they headed across the flight deck of the aircraft carrier to the newly patched-up CIA plane they had come in on, a member of the flight deck crew intercepted them and told them that the Captain had asked them to return to the ready room.

In the ready room, as they were waiting, Jack was explaining the 'LifeCape' project and the progress to Mark and Sarah. Since he and Laura had left Denver for Chicago they had made a working model. "They've got the first batch of test models completed and are ready to field test them. It works, at least in the lab, it works. Hopefully, they'll get good test results and we can refine the first production models to an acceptable state."

Sarah was very interested in the project and told Jack that there were a great number of uses for such a humanitarian aid in the near east. She was about to expand on her comments when the Captain came into the ready room. The Captain said "At ease!" out of habit before remembering that everyone here was a civilian and already at ease around officers. He motioned everyone to gather around him and sat down at the end of the conference table.

He had a communication flimsy in his hand and he referred to it before he started talking. Exhaling in a sigh he looked at Mark, Jack, and Laura. "I have been instructed by the President to "ask" the three of you to put off your return home for a little while."

The Captain continued. "It seems that one of our allies, Israel in this case, has requested, at the highest level, that the three of you travel to Tel Aviv to assist them in resolving a terrorist situation. The President sends his regrets for leaving you in the game. He says that this is very important to the United States and also to him personally, and he hopes that you will agree to aid him in this matter. Also, he's sorry he couldn't ask you himself, but he is handling another crisis at the moment." The Captain looked at the four civilians and waited for their response. Jack watched as Sarah nodded as expected. Mark was equally agreeable. That left them. He recalled that they had been tending to nothing more demanding than their new marriage and unruly front bushes until two months ago.

Jack asked if they could have a few minutes alone. When everybody else had left, Jack looked at Laura and took her hands. "We'd better see what the Lord wants us to do. They bowed their heads and prayed.

A few minutes later Jack looked at his wife and raised his eyebrows. "What do you think of that?"

"I'm really not sure but, I would guess He wants us to move along in our walk with Him and the next step involves our relationship as His children to His chosen race, the Israelis. That's what I think my convictions mean." She looked to him to confirm that course. Jack thought about that and nodded.

Jack was glad that both he and Laura were at peace with the President's request. When they called the others in, Jack told them that they would need to make some more transatlantic phone calls and then they would be available for whatever was needed.

While Mike filed the new flight information, they waited in the ready room. Mark stared at Sarah, "Okay lady spy, what have you got us into?" Sarah looked at him coolly but answered, "I asked the Institute to push our leadership to request that the four of us be redirected to Israel. I did this because a unique problem requires Americans with no connection to the intelligence community. Watching you three at work is rather awe-inspiring and I thought that your President would agree with me. I really appreciate his decision to have you help us." She looked at the other three people with satisfaction.

Mark evaluated her for a few minutes and then grinned. "Something you are not aware of could have messed up your plans." At her raised eyebrow he continued. "In the United States citizens are not required to serve as the President wants them to. Also, our religious orders and our government branches are separated by law, unlike your country, where the political parties are the religious parties. Jack and Laura did not have to accept this assignment, and for that fact, neither did I."

Sarah thought that over for a little bit and said, "You're right. This is a concept I did not take into account. I had forgotten completely that none of you is actually in the employ of your government. I wasn't trying to trick you into helping and I truly thank you all for agreeing to help on your own initiative. I applaud your courage."

Jack and Laura looked at each other and Laura answered her. "Thank you for being that considerate. You really could have asked us yourself and we would have probably helped you anyway. Regardless, we feel that the Lord wants us to take part in this operation and if he asks us, we do it."

Amazed again, Sarah just shook her head and smiled. Mike poked his head into the ready room, "I'm ready." he said waving a handful of papers.

A few minutes later, the team was being slammed back into their seats by the catapult and flung into the air on screaming jets.

In Israel, a quiet man with intense eyes read a FAX at an American-run software company in Tel Aviv. The message was routine but had special significance for his people. The two line FAX from Turkey said. "Requested packages on the way, beware of faulty inspectors. Urgent! New defense line being shipped immediately by air. Destroy them at first opportunity."

The Crossfire Team will return in *"**Israeli Crossfire.**"*

---

* Kirk Dearman - 1988 Integrity's Hosanna! Music/ASCAP

If this story has awakened your spirit or moved you to seek the love of Christ and His power for your life, whether you've never accepted Jesus as your savior or you've fallen away, repeat the following prayer and begin a most wonderful journey into eternal life with Him today.

Father God in heaven, As You said in Your Holy Word, (Romans 10:9) that if we confess the Lord our God and believe in our hearts that God raised Jesus from the dead, we shall be saved.

(The prayer on the next page is a sample prayer when asking Jesus into your heart as your Savior. You can also pray this in your own words.)

Salvation Prayer

Dear God in heaven, I come to you in the name of Jesus. I confess to You that I am a sinner, and I am sorry for my sins and the life that I have lived; I need your forgiveness. I believe that your only begotten Son Jesus Christ shed His precious blood on the cross at Calvary and died for my sins, and I am now willing to turn from my sin.

Right now I confess Jesus as the Lord of my life and my soul. With all my heart, I truly believe that your Holy Spirit raised Jesus from the dead. Today I accept Jesus Christ as my personal Savior and according to Your Word, right now I am saved.

I thank you Jesus, for your unlimited grace which has saved me from my sins. I thank you Jesus that your grace that never leads to license, but rather it always leads to repentance. Therefore Lord Jesus, transform my life so that I may bring glory and honor to you alone and not to myself.

I thank you Lord Jesus, for dying for me at Calvary and giving me eternal life.

Amen.

If you just said this prayer and you meant it with all your heart, believe that you are now saved and have been born again.

You may ask, "Now that I am saved, what do I do next?" First of all you need to get into a spirit-filled, bible-based church that teaches the Scriptures, and you need to study God's Word.

Once you have found a church home, you will want to become water-baptized. By accepting Christ you are baptized in the spirit, but it is through water-baptism that you publically announce your obedience to the Lord Jesus. Water baptism is a symbol of your salvation from the dead. You were dead but now you live, for Jesus Christ has redeemed you for a price! The price was His atoning death on the cross. May God Bless You!

Books by Stephen L. Thompson

The Crossfire Series

Colorado Crossfire
International Crossfire
Israeli Crossfire
Believer's Crossfire
Spirit Crossfire
Faith Crossfire
Chinese Crossfire
Texas Crossfire
Dark Crossfire
Island Crossfire
Jagged Crossfire
Violent Crossfire
Russian Crossfire
Nuclear Crossfire
End Times Crossfire
Revelation Crossfire
Gates of Hell Crossfire
Assassin's Crossfire
Albatross Crossfire
Global Crossfire
Far East Crossfire

The SFO Series
Station Force One - Onset

www.ingramcontent.com/pod-product-compliance
Lightning Source LLC
Chambersburg PA
CBHW071332250626
47159CB00004B/1575